FLIGHT

JoLyn Duffy-Shields

Copyright © 2020

JoLyn Duffy-Shields

& WM Partners LLC, Publisher

All rights reserved.

ISBN: **979-8-6940-4932-0**

DEDICATION

I would like to thank the following characters and the authors who brought them to life. They inspired me:

Hillary Green, created by Faith Martin

Beatrice Stubbs, created by JJ Marsh

Winifred Page, created by Mildred Abbott

Julia South, created by Agatha Frost

Patricia Fisher, created by Steve Higgs

I would also like to thank my partner in life, who has always been my rock, and my muse. Without your constant support, guidance, and encouragement, this would not have been possible.

I love you.

INTRODUCTION

From
JoLyn Duffy-Shields

Hello! Welcome to The Outer Banks Cozy Mystery Series! If this is a return visit to the OBX, welcome back, if this is your first visit, welcome! Since this is the first book in the series with overlapping subplots, you've started at the right spot. The thriller in this story can be enjoyed as a standalone, and I won't leave you hanging.

Please enjoy! And when you are finished, don't forget to leave a review on Amazon. They really help a lot.

ONE

"Damn it! What the hell is going on?" Will shouts to no one in particular as she slams down the phone. "Angela, are you here? Can you come into my office please?"

"I'll be right there. Just let me finish up this client note." Angela calls out from the outer office.

Peering around the door frame sheepishly, Angela asks "What can I do you for, Old Sport?"

Momentarily stunned by the literary reference, a game they often played in the office to relieve the stress and anxiety of managing a multi-million-dollar insurance agency in one of the prime hurricane locations in the country, Will responded "Good lord, are you reading Gatsby again! Look, I just got off the phone with Avalon Pier. They're cancelling their insurance. Said our price is too high. Can you call and talk them off the ledge? I can't seem to ..." Will's voice trailed off as she saw a news bulletin pop up on the computer.

The Outer Banks Bank & Trust. Robbery & hostage standoff in progress. Live report now on WAVY News 11 was in a box at the bottom. The rest of the screen showed a picture of the bank with police vehicles littered all across the 5-lane road in front. Nothing was moving on the bypass now.

"What is it boss?" Angela asked nervously as she moved around the desk to look over Will's shoulder. "Holy crap!" rolled out of her mouth when she saw the screen. "That's... that's...."

"Yes, that's our bank!" exclaimed Will.

TWO

"Paperwork! Jeez, that's all I seem to do anymore!" complained Jack Strong. "I used to be a valuable Sheriff's Deputy, an investigator, a real policeman, but now I'm just a glorified paper pusher!"

"Jack! Let's roll" The call came from Sheriff Betty Thompson.

"Yes, ma'am, I'm on your six." Jack shot back, and he was out the door. "Where to Sheriff?"

"I need company for lunch. I'm tired of all the ass kissers and politicians around here. Let's get something quick and easy and talk, OK?" responded Betty. "I need a break."

"Me too," Jack replied. "I need to get away from all the budget reports, requisitions, and general stuff pilling up on my desk. I've never been much for bureaucracy." He replied as they strode out of the County Building toward their marked patrol cars.

"Let's take two cars. I have some meetings with local businesses this afternoon." The Sheriff ordered.

"Whatever you say, boss." Jack responded as he clicked his key fob and started his blue Ford Explorer with orange *Dare County Sheriff* stenciled on the sides. "Frank's?" he called across the roof before hopping in.

"Roger that" came the reply from Betty as she slid into her sleek midnight blue Dodge Charger with the same orange *Dare County Sheriff* stenciled on the sides. Her engine roared to life as she sped down the road away from their office.

It was early spring, so the road from Manteo to Kitty Hawk was clear and they both cruised along at speed under a brilliant sun. They crossed the causeway connecting the two islands, past the old Oasis Restaurant and cruised through the curve at Whalebone Junction to head north. The ocean was on their right, past the endless rows of cottages, most boarded up waiting for the rental season to begin in a few weeks. Nags Head had many of the oldest cottages, with their dark cedar weathered shingles and long wrap around porches. The farther north you went the more modern the cottages became, although modern in the materials used and their relative age, but not the style. All the homes had character. The ones on the beach were usually bigger to take advantage of their views and the lucrative rental season, but they almost all had porches, and were raised on pilings to protect from storm damage. You could see that some owners had purchased multiple lots and built identical homes, just painting them different shades of the popular pastel colors found in many beach communities.

Jockey's Ridge sat on their left as they cruised through Nags Head, the massive sand dune looming over the landscape as it had for hundreds of years. The tallest sand dune in the eastern US has constantly changed shape like a living thing, blown by the never-ending winds that whipped the Banks. No one knows how it was formed, or how long it will last.

Local businesses lined the road, everything from mom and pop shops to fast food chains, banks, clothing outlets, drug stores, and family amusements. Many of them were open for "winter hours" and showed some activity, but by and large, the beach was quiet. The whirl of the wind generator at the Outer Banks Brewing Station signaled entry into Kill Devil Hills, and The Wright Brothers Monument stands testament to the enormous human achievement of controlled powered flight on December 17, 1903.

The Explorer and the Charger pulled into Capt'n Frank's gravel parking lot just after 12 noon and the Sheriff and Deputy strolled into the comfortable restaurant. Pictures of the famous and infamous who ate there, as well as snaps of the area over the past forty-five years lined the oak panel walls. Booths were against the north wall. Tables in the middle and a counter gave you a ring side seat to the kitchen, which ran along the south wall. Some of the locals sitting at the counter turned and noticed the two law enforcement officers as they peeled their tactical sunglasses and adjusted to the indoor lighting. Frank called out from behind the counter "Sit anywhere you like, we're not very busy yet." Jack waved back and went to slide into a booth against the wall. Betty went to say hello to the owner.

"Ready for the season, Frank?" Betty asked confidently.

"Yep. Started hiring the summer help last weekend when the colleges had spring break. Looks like a nice crop of kids this year. Hopefully, they won't cause you any trouble." Frank replied.

"Good. I hope so." The Sheriff always knew that bringing loads of summer help on to the island was necessary, but it usually came with its share of headaches. Sometimes she wondered if the islands didn't turn into one huge frat party from Memorial Day to Labor Day. "We're gonna chat for a bit, but I know I'll have the usual and I think Jack will too." The sheriff said as she walked back to where Jack was seated. A few seconds later, their order was clipped to an overhead line and flung down the counter to the grill, where the cook pulled the ticket and began fixing their order. It was a familiar scene for the locals who took no notice.

It wasn't that long ago that a black woman couldn't get a seat in most restaurants in the South, let alone become Sheriff. Betty wasn't old enough to remember any of that, but she still felt the occasional critical glances and wondered if it was because she was a woman or black, or both. She'd heard stories from her parents and grandparents, and she was thankful that those times were long gone.

Her grandfather, her mom's dad, was one of the first black police officers hired on the Washington DC force. He served with distinction for thirty-two years, retiring as a detective. He still lives in the DC area but doesn't get away from the assisted living home very much anymore. His wife of fifty years passed a few years back, and Alzheimer's is slowly robbing him of his memories, and his life. Betty would like to see him more, and she makes the four-hour drive back to the home of her youth as often as she can, but, well, work, life.... There's never enough time.

Tim Thompson, her dad joined the Washington DC police force the year before she was born, and he's still working cases forty years later, although now as the owner of a private security firm. He retired from the force after his twenty and got to work making real money from the entitled elite that populates DC. Security is BIG MONEY in Washington, and Tim has the connections and know how to tap into them. He and his wife of forty-one years, Lizzy, are doing well enough that she was able to indulge her passion for food and open a sandwich shop and catering company, using Tim's contacts to double dip in the entitlement trough. They laugh about that all the way to the bank! Betty doesn't have to travel up to DC to see her folks. They have a vacation home in Southern Shores and come to her most weekends.

"So, how you doing boss?" Jack asked with his matter of fact, take no prisoners stare with his piercing blue eyes.

"Funny, that's exactly what I was going to ask you!" said the Sheriff in reply. "I know you've been buried in paperwork, and you're too good a cop to be stranded behind a desk pushing paper."

"Thanks boss, but somebody's got to do it."

"Yes, yes, they do, but it shouldn't be my most talented investigator, my best soldier. I knew when I hired you, no Navy Seal should be anywhere but in the field. I appreciate you taking on the thankless administration job after Bob left, but it's time I make some adjustments."

"Yes ma'am." Jack said matter-of-factly. After a distinguished six-year stint in the Navy, with two tours in Afghanistan, a purple heart, and a medal for valor, he knew how to obey orders, but secretly inside he was shouting for joy! 'Praise Jesus, somebody has heard my prayers' was echoing in his head. As he adjusted himself in the booth, he asked "Is this a demotion boss?"

"Hell NO, Jack! You are and always will be my #2, err, ah, what I mean, my right hand, my second in command" she said as her face blushed. They both had a chuckle over the double entendre. "You're Operations, Jack, not Administration. That's where you belong and that's where I need you. I'm reallocating my assets. You're taking over the new Criminal Investigations Unit. Tateway is moving over to take Admin. She's better suited to that with her accounting and business degree, and frankly, she was a concern in the field. I'm not sure if she had the balls for it." They both chuckled again at her choice of words.

"Thank you. I appreciate your confidence in me." Jack said as he saw the waitress bringing their food.

"Ah, perfect timing" said the Sheriff as four hotdogs and a large fries and large onion rings were put in front of them. Frank brought over her unsweet tea and his water.

"Betty, how do you drink tea like that?" Frank asked incredulously. "God made it with sugar, girl!"

"Frank, I got all the sweetness in me anybody can handle" she responded playfully.

Jack sat quietly and admired the banter. Betty was a damn fine-looking woman, and if he didn't work for her, he'd ask her out in a heartbeat, for sure. She was an average height, five six or five seven, but it was her figure, and the way she just popped in her uniform, that caught most men's attention. She had a gorgeous figure, but for Jack, it was her mocha skin and her beautiful face that made him dizzy. She had beautiful big brown eyes, a pert little button nose, full lips and a smile that would melt, well, anything. She had a natural beauty that didn't require much fuss. She was light on make-up and kept her hair straight and pulled back in a tight ponytail. Her personal grooming was impeccable, nails manicured weekly, kept short but beautiful with just a light neutral color, and she always has just a hint of perfume, so others wouldn't forget she was a lady. What was remarkable about her, Jack thought, was that she was stunning without being flashy. But, in the few years he'd worked for her, he'd never heard her talk about dating anyone. He admired her ability to shift gears on the fly, talk shop with a businessman, inspire the troops, haggle like a politician with the County Commissioners, be firm and polite or friendly and playful as the situation required. In short, from where he sat, she was a pro, and he loved having her as his boss.

As they began to enjoy their lunch a call came across the radio. Well, so much for a relaxing meal.

Within seconds they were both out the door and headed to their cars. Frank called out from behind the counter as they left "Don't worry, it's on the house. Stay safe guys." He knew that when they moved that quickly, they were running headlong into danger.

FLIGHT

THREE

"Shots fired! Shots fired!" came screaming over the police radio.

"I'm two minutes out" came the reply from Jack as gravel kicked up from Capt'n Frank's lot when the Explorer peeled out and surged down the roadway.

"I'm right behind him" called Sheriff Thompson. "Contact SWAT and have them roll out. Get the mobile command center over here. Get EMS on site. Go! Go! Go!" Betty knew they trained for these situations, and her people would do their best to support the FBI once they showed up, but that could be hours and the people in the bank didn't have that luxury of time. She kept her foot on the floor and stayed right behind Deputy Strong. "Thirty seconds and we'll be on site" she called over the radio. "I can see the responding officers up ahead."

Two local patrol vehicles were blocking the road on either side of the bank and Deputy Strong rolled in to add additional support on the south end of the road. Betty took her Charger and put it on the north side of the bank. The Outer Banks Bank & Trust building was a one-story white stucco stand alone with parking surrounding the branch. It was essentially a nondescript structure built 30 years ago when function was more important than style. It was a bank. All traffic was stopped on the main artery and cars were detouring off on the side streets and heading to the beach road to get away from the scene. The local cops were with the Town of Kitty Hawk, but Sheriff Thompson was the ranking officer and took charge. There was a playbook for these situations, and she knew it by heart, but the criminals usually didn't, and she was worried they might panic now that their plan was in the crapper. She was pretty sure they already had, since shots were fired inside the bank. Betty just hoped to God that they were warning shots and not an execution.

As more patrol cars rolled up, Sheriff Thompson instructed them to quickly move to the back of the bank and hold their positions. She got on the police radio to communicate to the troops. "Everybody stay alert and be vigilant. We want the hostages safe and we want the robbers taken alive. DO NOT SHOOT UNLESS YOU ARE BEING FIRED UPON!" Then she switched to the loudspeaker in the Charger. "YOU HAVE BEEN SURROUNDED. YOU CANNOT ESCAPE. COME OUT WITH YOUR HANDS UP."

Silence.

She repeated her commands.

Silence.

Her radio squawked. "The swat team is 10 minutes out. EMS is 2 minutes away. Additional back up is 30 seconds out" called the 911 operator. Before Betty could respond the operator came back "The robbers have called us! I can patch them through."

"Do It!" Betty barked, "but just to me. No open frequency, got it?"

"Roger that" the operator chirped back. A second later a voice came over the radio that shocked Sheriff Thompson. She was talking to a child, a teenager at best.

"You gotta clear out. Get away from here so we can leave! We don't wanna hurt nobody, but we will if you make us." The young voice said with a good amount of fear as he spoke.

"Ok" said Sheriff Thompson, "How many people are inside the bank?"

"Who is this? I don't wanna talk to no secretary! Get me a real cop!" the young voice blurted out.

"Right. This is Sheriff Betty Thompson with the Dare County Sheriff's Department. I'm the top cop you can talk to here, at least until the FBI shows up." Betty replied. "If you want to walk away alive from this you need to do as I'm instructing you and put your weapons down and your hands up and come outside and kneel down."

"FBI? Why's the FBI coming?" the young robber asked frantically.

"You're robbing a bank! That's a Federal offense. The FBI handles all Federal crimes." Betty responded calmly, but she mumbled "*dumbass kids*" under her breath. She took a second to assess her force readiness and saw that she had been joined by at least a dozen deputies and local police officers as well as her SWAT team.

The SWAT team leader was putting a diagram of the bank layout on the side of their mobile command center and holding a debrief with his unit while they donned their tactical gear. She switched the radio to LEO ONLY and communicated with the team around her. "I said it before, DO NOT SHOOT UNLESS YOU ARE BEING FIRED UPON. We want the hostages safe and we want the robbers taken alive. Nobody gets trigger happy here. We have a lot of firepower surrounding this bank. Let's use our intel resources to get the best outcome possible. Deputy Strong, I need you here with me. Copy?"

Strong responded immediately "Roger that" and moved up the road to her position. "What's up boss?" he said with a slight smile. She turned and pressed her key fob to pop the trunk. "Get my sniper rifle and scope. I want you to have eyes on that bank and give me intel pronto. I know you were a sniper in the Marines. I need someone I can count on. The guys in SWAT are good, but you're better." Betty wasn't throwing complements, just stating the facts.

The SWAT commander, Captain Tony Antonelli, came over and gave Sheriff Thompson a sitrep. He was deploying their robot to gather intel and placing his sharp shooters on roofs across the street from the bank.

He also had an assault team ready to go if she ordered a breach. She told him to deploy but hold firm until more intel has been gathered. "We need to know how many hostages they have, and how many bad guys we're dealing with before we do anything" she said looking square into the Commander's eyes. "Copy that?"

"Yes ma'am" Captain Antonelli responded without missing a beat. He turned and returned to his command vehicle. The robot, which looked like a small Mars Land Rover, slowly crossed the street, and made its way to the front of the bank. It was streaming video back to the command vehicle where Sheriff Thompson and the SWAT commander watched. The view from the front doors of the interior of the bank showed them nothing.

"Can we get a better look?" the Sheriff asked to no one in particular. "I can't see a damn thing with this view! From that angle, it's an empty bank!" Before anyone responded, the phone rang again. "Hello? Sheriff Thompson here" she said confidently.

"Ok, what is that thing doing outside? Move it now or hostages die!" came the young voice on the other end of the line.

"Calm down. It's just giving us a safe look into the bank. We need to see that the hostages are all right before we can agree to anything with you." Betty said calmly, knowing she was pushing the envelope a bit, but guessing the young man on the end of the line didn't have a lot of experience negotiating.

"I've got movement inside" whispered Deputy Strong.

"Ok Jack. Can you identify anyone?" asked Betty patiently. "We're still basically blind here and I can't make decisions without more intel" she said to anyone who was listening. "Commander, any thoughts?"

The SWAT commander was talking on his comm to his team when he caught Betty's question and stiffened "Other than a straight breach and taking our chances, I think we have to play the waiting game."

"Ok, Commander, do we have the technology to listen at the windows of that building?" The Sheriff asked a bit frustrated since she hated having to think for her men.

"Oh, err, yes ma'am. We have sonic devices we can mount on the glass to eave drop."

"Great. Do it! I need to know what's happening inside that building!!!" Betty barked, her patience wearing thin. "Jack, see anything else through your scope?"

"It's still pretty quiet. I can see a few shadows moving around but I can't identify anyone." Jack said as he kept the scope up to his eye and the gun trained on the door. A couple of SWAT team members advanced along the side of the bank and placed small devices on the windows.

The crackle came over the radio "We've acquired the signal and we can hear inside. Sounds like a couple of kids goofing around. No other sounds."

Just then the 911 operator called out "Sheriff, I have one of the bank employees on the line. They say the Branch Manager suddenly closed the branch earlier today and sent everyone home out of the blue. She saw the news report and thought y'all would like to know. The bank has been empty since just before noon."

THE OUTER BANKS COZY MYSTERY SERIES – BOOK 1

FOUR

Ralph Midgett was wealthy. Not comfortable wealthy, he was obscenely wealthy, and he wasn't shy about making sure everyone knew it. He obviously never read "The Millionaire Next Door" because his over the top opulent lifestyle would make Donald Trump blush.

Ralph came to the Outer Banks when he was 28, tasked with opening a new bank branch for a Virginia bank that wanted to expand and take advantage of the growing interest in the beach communities of North Carolina. He was ambitious and wanted to climb the corporate ladder. He wasn't interested in the political uprising and social change happening everywhere. He wasn't sad when MLK was gunned down, or Bobby, and he proudly voted for Nixon in 1968, his first election as a new resident of Kitty Hawk. All he cared about was opportunity, and there was plenty of that in this sleepy southern beachfront community.

The young banker worked tirelessly to make contacts with developers, contractors, politicians, and other important local businessmen. He joined the brand-new Duck Woods Country Club as a founding member to entertain and impress. He grew his small branch quickly, and people noticed.

The bank decided to open additional branches and made Ralph Midgett the Regional Vice President. Nags Head was next, followed by Buxton, and a satellite office was opened in Duck. After 15 years, of hard work, Ralph Midgett had built an empire, for someone else. He was pissed. Sure, he made a good living. Sure, he was important and influential, but he still worked for other people. He wanted to build an empire for himself.

About that same time, 1982, he realized that having a wife might be an asset. Someone who was frilly and girlie and took the rough edges off his "take no prisoners" personality. He was born and raised southern in the great State of Virginia, but his family did not move in the social circles he needed. Sanitation workers like his dad didn't.

One afternoon, relaxing at the Club with some friends, he noticed a young woman coming off the 18th green. She was tall and very pretty. He liked what he saw, and he wasn't put off by the wedding ring on her hand.

Six months later, after a quick divorce and a whirlwind courtship, Carol Lawrence was the first Mrs. Ralph Midgett. She was attracted to his money and ambition, and she tolerated his personality and looks. Ralph was not handsome. Average height, thinning hair, bookish glasses, and a paunchy belly were not the things that made Ralph noticeable. It was his money, and his brash ambition, and Carol loved those in spades.

She was perfect for what he needed. Heads turned everywhere they went, and he made sure she dressed to kill. She liked to show off her sexy body and wore tight clothes and heels everywhere. She became the talk of the town. Hell, she became the talk of all the towns on the OBX. She raced all over the islands in her red convertible Mercedes with the vanity license plate – FLY 69 – a reference to the year she was born, but the overt sexual meaning worked too. Parties at their house were a regular occurrence with caterers coming and going constantly. Ralph loved to stand on his deck overlooking his pool and the Atlantic beyond and watch his bikini clad wife flit about with all his guests. Her perky breasts, flat stomach and long legs put on quite a show. He was a KING.

When the Virginia bank was swallowed up in a hostile takeover, Ralph saw his opportunity. He cashed out his stock options, leveraged his contacts and bought the OBX branches and started his own bank – The

Outer Banks Bank & Trust. The national bank was going to close them anyway, so he seized the opportunity to get them for a song. He was now making money for himself, and boy, was he ever.

After a slight dip in the early 80's, the economy took off and growth on the islands was astronomical. People flooded in from Washington DC and points north to take in the family friendly beaches and quiet atmosphere. Developers and contractors could not keep up with the demand. Beach houses, stores and commercial developments were built at a breathtaking pace, and money flowed. Ralph's timing couldn't have been better. Over the next ten years, all Ralph Midgett had to do was count his money.

By the mid 90's, The Outer Banks Bank & Trust had branches from Corolla to Ocracoke. Ralph and Carol built a fabulous new house in Southern Shores, on the ocean, of course. They had a son and a daughter, a nanny and a cook and two housekeepers, and everyone thought, the perfect life. Everyone but Ralph.

King Ralph had grown tired of seeing his wife only between her constant trips to New York, Milan, and Paris. And when she was home, she wasn't. Off to the Club for lunches with girlfriends or meetings with causes she embraced. The days of bikini clad parties had faded, and Ralph Midgett did not like that at all.

One of Ralph's best friends was a lawyer in Manteo, Lester Finch. Carol didn't know what hit her, and six months later, the second Mrs. Midgett arrived.

Kelly Anne Fuco had all the same attributes that made the former Mrs. Midgett so attractive. Young, maybe not as tall, but shapely with a naughty, sexy twinkle in her mischievous eyes and willingness to play whenever, wherever, and most importantly, however Ralph wanted. They met when Ralph stopped into The Hurricane Bar to meet with the owner, who was behind on his loan. Usually Ralph had other people make collection calls for him, but Ralph needed to unwind and liked the free booze and eye candy. Kelly was a cocktail waitress and she caught Ralph's eye immediately. They married in the Dare County Courthouse, with two paid witnesses attending. It, like Kelly, was quick and dirty.

Ralph loved having children, just not around him. He put his son and daughter into exclusive boarding schools and only brought them home for special occasions, like his birthday, Father's Day, and Christmas Day. Everyone looked fabulous together in the family portrait in the front hall and the custom printed Christmas cards each year, but the children hated their new step-monster, and loathed their father for abandoning them and ruining their family.

Now, as the century was ready to turn over, Ralph had one ex-wife, another on the way, two children, a host of businesspeople and a few girlfriends who hated him. Ralph was turning 60 and living his dream!

FIVE

With the phone cradled to her ear and her fingers flying across her keyboard, Will Moore was the picture of a modern-day insurance agent, franticly trying to make everyone happy at the same time!

"Ok, can I get back to you on that?" Will asked breathlessly. "Great, I'll call you as soon as I know anything." As she hung up the phone and spun around in her chair, she called out "Angela, are you out there?" That was a common refrain around the office. Angela Peterson was Will's everywoman and was always there when she needed her.

"Let me finish this client file and I'll be right in" she called out from the outer office. "Ok, done. What can I do you for, boss?"

"I'm trying to get Tommy Mills, the Kitty Hawk Outer Banks Bank branch manager on the phone. I was hoping to get some info about this robbery, but he's not picking up or returning my calls. The insurance company is frantic for details. They want me to run point on the claim!" said Will with a small level of joy in her voice.

Will had built a nice business over the last few years. She came to the Outer Banks after college and began working in insurance because it paid the bills and it gave her a chance at independence one day. Eight years ago, out of the blue, that day came.

Her boss, a friendly cherub of a man who took Will under his wing, died of a heart attack. He was fifty-two. She'd only been working for him for six years, but she was now thrust into the corner office. She did not realize that the owner of the OBX Insurance Agency had a life insurance policy with her as the beneficiary! They had talked about continuing the business if something ever happened to him, but now she had the money to pay his family and own the company outright.

His wife knew that was his plan, and she wanted no part of owning an insurance agency, so she gladly agreed to the transfer. The personal life insurance he had, plus the sale of the business meant she had all the money she'd ever need.

Oh, how Will's life had changed.

She was raised by her father after her mother bailed when Will Moore was too young to remember. She grew up bouncing from station to station while dad chased his FBI career. Everyone called her Will, except her father, who called her Wilma, or sometimes Ruth, unless he was mad at her, and then she got the full name treatment – WILMA RUTH MOORE! After college at East Carolina University, she wanted to set down roots, which she never had as a child, so she moved to the Outer Banks, not far from where her dad retired in Edenton NC. She was close enough so the two could visit regularly, but far enough so she could be her own person. She became a well-known and respected member of the business community on the islands.

Her five-foot eleven-inch frame and athletic figure and long blond ponytail makes her easy to spot, even without her trademark heels, and she plays tennis and golf regularly. She always turns heads with her stunning features, flawless tan, sharp wit, warm laugh and charm, lots of good ol' southern charm. At thirty-five, she is single and in no rush to settle down with just one person. She's not married to her job, but she's not ready to settle down either.

Under Will's stewardship, The OBX Insurance Agency has flourished. She was able to add two claims investigators other than herself to the new Claims Investigations Department, one personal lines CSR making a total of six in the office handling auto, home and all the toys that go with them, and three new commercial account reps other than herself, which gave the Commercial Department a total of nine employees. Accountability and transparency were big in the office, and honesty was unwaveringly essential. If you lost trust, you lost everything in the business.

Angela Peterson is the office manager, and the glue that holds everything together. A native of Dare County who taught herself how to be indispensable to her employer, she can handle any assignment and is a wiz at the computer. She got lucky when a position opened in Will Moore's office five years ago, and she proved herself to be an invaluable asset. She is married, but many aren't sure if it's to her husband or the job.

Angela is twenty-nine, not very tall, and "Rubenesque," which is to say, she carries her weight sensually with a nice bust, less than thin waist, and bigger than average hips. No one confuses her for a runway model, but she is pretty, and everyone likes her because of her sincerity and desire to help. Her friends and acquaintances all think Angela is 'F'ing Delightful' because of her easy manner and quick, sharp wit. She is an avid reader. Loves the classics but is addicted to crime thrillers and romance novels. She also has a soft spot for strays, and she mothers over several, including the office cats, an orange tabby, Orville, and a silky jet-black cat with white whiskers and paws, Wilber. With her husband traveling for work constantly, and no kids cluttering up the house, her insatiable lust often has her picking up other "strays" as well.

"Boss, I got Ralph Midgett on line one for you. He might be able to help you locate Tommy" Angela called out.

"Hello, Ralph?" Will said calmly. "Can you help me locate Tom Mills? I know you haven't been a part of the bank for a few years, but I'm guessing you still know where most of your former employees like to hide."

"You're right on both counts, Will" Ralph replied. "Tommy has a little hideaway in Corolla he likes to disappear to from time to time. I have his number there, and his other cell number too. Want them?"

Other cell number? What's he hiding? thought Will, and then replied "Sure. Thank you very much."

"Ok, I'll text them to you now. Got 'em?" Ralph asked.

"Yep. Yes, I do. Thanks. I'll let you know when I track him down. I need his help on this bank claim after the botched robbery attempt. You've been a huge help Ralph. Thanks again" and she hung up the phone and leaned back in her chair. "What is he hiding..." she mumbled to herself.

SIX

"Ok, where were we?" Ralph asked, standing shirtless in trouser and loafers at the end of his king-sized bed.

"You've been a good boy getting off the phone so quickly. Now come get some sugar, sugar..." cooed his ex-wife, Kelly, as she unzipped his pants. She wore low rider cut off jean shorts with the top button undone and a cutoff football jersey that showed her aging belly but provided easy access to her ample chest. She was trying her best to hang on to her sexy youth, but Father Time was winning that battle. Her face showed the scares of too much sun and too little protection, and way too much booze and coke, the drug, not the drink.

Ralph had not seen her since the divorce six years ago, until she knocked on the door earlier today. He was surprised, but he liked a roll in the hay as much as the next guy, and she still looked damn good at forty, especially since, at his age not many women were throwing themselves at him anymore. What the heck. Mrs. Midgett number three was off shopping on the continent and wouldn't be home for a few days, and he was tired of playing golf.

SEVEN

"What are you doing here?" Sheriff Thompson asked seriously.

"I'm trying to find Tommy Mills" said Will, as these two strong willed women stood eye to eye on the front porch of *Tommy's Hideaway*. Will towered over Betty, but Betty was used to having to deal with that from most men, so she stood her ground. "Aren't you a little out of your jurisdiction Sheriff? I passed the Dare County line five miles ago."

"Currituck asked us to come up and help out. They have a scene on the mainland they're working. Interagency assistance. Teamwork, for laymen. But you're too late anyway, Will" Jack Strong interjected as he walked out of the house and between the two women, separating them a bit. "He's dead in the living room."

"What?" blurted Will. "How did he die?" She asked, but she already knew the answer. She's heard her dad say it a thousand times when he was with the FBI.

"Ongoing investigation" Betty shot back before Deputy Strong could react.

"Got it. Thanks", Will replied as she turned to leave.

"Wait a second there, Ms. Moore. We have some questions for you" Sheriff Thompson said as Deputy Strong stepped in to block Will's path. "This is a murder investigation, and you show up out of the blue? How did you know to come here?"

"Fair question" Will responded. "When I couldn't find Tommy with the phone numbers I had, I contacted Ralph Midgett. He hired Tommy at the bank and knew him pretty well, so I was guessing he'd have some idea where he'd hide if he was trying to get away from all the aggravation from the botched bank robbery. I needed him to answer some questions for the insurance claim we're investigating." She paused for a second, and then said "But seriously, who names their hideaway cottage *Tommy's Hideaway*? Subtle much?"

"Tommy, I guess" Jack deadpanned. Everyone gave a little chuckle and stepped to the side as the coroner wheeled the body out.

"Sheriff Thompson?" the radio crackled. "We've got another dead body. You need to get to the Midgett place pronto."

"Roger. Christ, I gotta go. Strong, you work this scene. Wait for the crime tech guys to get here and then join me at Midgett's" the Sheriff ordered.

"Hey, I just talked to the guy yesterday. I'm coming too" said Will.

"The hell you are. This isn't a Nancy Drew novel, Ms. Moore. You know the rules better than most. Stay out of the way or you'll be looking at an obstruction charge." Betty was forceful and authoritative, and Will froze. She hated to be told what to do, but she knew the Sheriff was right.

"Right... you're right. Sorry." Will offered apologetically. 'I'll just stay here with Deputy Strong and see what I can get from him', she thought.

Betty hopped in her Charger and took off down the street. Jack Strong came back to the front porch to stand guard over the scene and wait for the crime techs. "Can't go inside Will, you know that, right?"

"I know Jack. Can't I just hang out with you while you wait?" Will asked sheepishly. "A bank robbery and two murders…. Maybe I need a big strong Sheriff's Deputy to protect lil' ol' me!"

Jack let out a full belly laugh. "Really! You! Playin' the damsel in distress! Stop! You're killin' me!"

"Poor choice of words, Jack, given the scene, don'tcha think?" Will said with a smile.

Jack laughed some more but nodded in agreement. What he was thinking, he couldn't say out loud, but he liked Will's company and she looked amazing. Short tight skirt, white blouse stretched tight across her chest, four-inch heels making her almost as tall as he was. 'Damn'....

Will could sense the effect she was having on Jack, so she thought she should press the advantage with some probing questions. "Any clue how long Tommy was dead, Jack? I know I hadn't been able to reach him for at least a couple of days, and the folks at the bank didn't have any clue where he'd gotten off to." She stepped down off the porch just one step so she was below him, and he could look down on her. All of her.

Jack swallowed hard before following the standard line "Open investigation, can't comment on it." Betty pouted just a bit, and Jack caved. "He's been dead for a few hours, best we can tell, but exactly, we have to wait for the coroner."

"Gosh, I hope he didn't suffer" Will offered just a bit more breathlessly than before. "You sure it was murder and not a heart attack, Jack?"

"I'm sure" Jack chuckled. "Never saw anyone lose half their skull from a heart attack."

"Oh my!" Will feigned shock and turned away quickly, causing Jack to offer her his shoulder for comfort. "It must be awful inside that house!"

"It is, Will. Blood and brains everywhere. A lot of its dried and stuck to the walls and furniture. Tech guys are gonna have a field day, but I'm guessing dinner will be hard to swallow after working this scene." Jack offered, surprising Will in how much he shared. "It's not the first time

I've seen something like that, but you never really get used to it. One of my buddies over in Afghanistan had his head blown clear off by a 50-caliber bullet. I threw up right there next to him. That was tough. The SEAL training gets your ready for combat, makes you a warrior, but you're never prepared for the carnage. Never."

Everything went very quiet after that. Will was genuinely shaken. Jack was just lost in his thoughts. The crime tech van rolled up and two techs got our and grabbed their gear. "Inside guys, in the living room. Can't miss it" Jack called out as they walked past. He headed down the driveway to his Explorer. "You coming Will? I can't leave you hear. Get in your car and follow me to the Midgett Estate, now." He said the last word with a great deal of force and authority, and she obeyed.

They pulled out of the driveway of *Tommy's Hideaway* and cruised down the road out of Corolla, past the big brownish red lighthouse to their right, some of the wild horses grazing on an open patch of parkland in the shade of a majestic old Live Oak, passed the massive beach houses with their fifteen plus bedrooms and even more bathrooms. They sped down the road to Duck, past Coastal Cravings restaurant, where the gang liked to congregate on Friday nights, listen to live music and toast the end of another week, and then Southern Shores, where the Midget Estate stood out from all the other newer homes simply because of its size. It made the Corolla properties look like, well, like cottages.

EIGHT

"What can I do you for Boss?" Angela asked when Will came back into the office. She spoke before looking up. When she did, Will's face was drained of color and she was unsteady. Angela immediately got her into her corner office and sat her down. "Will, what happened?" Several of the other employees of the agency gathered outside her door, shocked to see their "Fearless Leader" shaken so badly. Even the office cats that Angela rescued several years ago, Orville and Wilbur, took time from their busy nap schedule to wander through the crowd and rub affectionately on Will's legs.

"I don't know where to start." Will said as she reached out to accept a bottled water from one of her concerned employees. Wilbur, a big black American shorthair with white whiskers and paws jumped up into Will's lap, and she began stroking him.

"What did Tommy Mills say that has you so upset?" Angela asked reluctantly.

"Nothing. He was dead!" Will said blankly, looking off into the distance at nothing in particular. "Deputy Strong told me Tommy had his head…" she choked up and needed a sip of water. "He was shot" she finished after collecting herself. "Then Deputy Strong gets called to the Midgett Estate, so I follow him and there are two bodies and a bloody machete!" The police and Sheriff's department won't discuss the case, but I saw one deputy walk out with a machete in an evidence bag. I can't imagine what the scene inside looked like."

There was a general rumble of shock and upset over this news rippling through the office as the crowd began to disperse. "If one of the dead was Ralph Midgett, it'll be interesting to see who comes filing the claims for those life policies" one employee said to another as they walked back to their desks.

Will and Angela sat together, neither talking, both in shock. After a few minutes Angela asked "Why did Tommy have a Hideaway in Corolla? He lived on the beach here! What was he hiding?" They looked at each other, and Will said, "I thought the same thing."

NINE

Betty stood in the enormous master bedroom of Ralph Midgett staring down at the bodies. She had no words for the carnage before her. The torsos of a man and a woman lay at the foot of the bed, the hands and feet were scattered around the room. The heads were propped up on the bed near the pillows laying facing each other, eyes still open in a shocked expression, mouths agape. Blood was everywhere. Pools of the sticky red liquid had soaked into the carpet where the torsos lay. Streams of blood followed the body parts, as if they were thrown helter-skelter after they were hacked off. The center of the bed was covered in a pool of blood. The machete, which Sheriff Thompson assumed was the murder weapon, was coated in blood and discarded near the French doors that led out to the Italian marble porch and the beach beyond.

"Any idea on a motive? Any suspects Sheriff?" Jack asked when he walked up to Betty Thompson. She spun around and looked hard at him. "We need to ID the bodies first. I'm pretty sure one is the homeowner, Ralph Midgett, but who the woman is...." Her voice trailed off as she turned away, watching the coroner's men roll the bodies out of the room.

"Right" Jack shot back. "I think I can help there. The face looks familiar. Could have been his ex-wife. Have to double check but her name was Karen, Carol, ...no, Kelly. She hasn't aged badly" he blurted out without thinking.

"She's dead! I'd say that pretty much sums up *aging badly*, don't you

Deputy?" Betty shot back, with a look of bewilderment on her face. "Sometimes, Jack…" she shook her head and walked away.

Police personnel worked around her taking pictures and notes, and police tape and barricades kept anyone without credentials back off the property. A forensic team had just arrived and began their work of collecting as much evidence as they could find. One of them tagged the machete and bagged it in an evidence bag and then handed it to an officer to take to the forensic van. The patrol officers doing crowd control out front all turned when the crowd that had gathered gasped at the bloody knife as it was carried to the vehicle. Will Moore was one of those shocked bystanders.

She'd followed Deputy Strong down from Corolla and parked across the street when he turned into the estate. She knew she wouldn't be able to see much, but she had to stay. What she was most concerned about was the fifty-million-dollar life insurance policy he had taken out a few years ago. She wanted to know if Ralph was the victim or the criminal. The patrol officers were understandably reserved. "They were not at liberty to discuss an ongoing investigation" was the party line uttered repeatedly to questioning onlookers. Michelle Wagner, a reporter with the Coastal Times newspaper pushed her way to the front of the crowd and was barking questions in the hopes that someone would answer. A hush fell over the crowd as two body bags were brought from the mansion and loaded into the back of the coroner's hearse.

"Do you have an ID on those bodies?" Michelle begged one of the patrolmen for details. His radio squawked and he listened intently and then repeated the message to anyone who wanted to know "The Dare Sheriff's Office will hold a press conference regarding this criminal investigation at 5pm today at this location. Further details will be forthcoming at that time."

Will Moore had seen enough. She returned to her car and made the quick drive back to her office. She knew she'd get the details soon enough.

FLIGHT

TEN

Angela's fingers started to dance across her keyboard. She had an idea. "Boss, what if the bank robbery, Tommy Mills' death and the Midgett massacre are somehow all related?"

Before Will could answer the Five O'clock News came on with the lead story – *Murder in Southern Shores.* "We are taking you live to a press conference with Sheriff Betty Thompson of Dare County at the Estate of Ralph Midgett, the Southern Shores resident and banking tycoon who was savagely murdered inside his home" the newscaster crooned before switching to the shot of media microphones haphazardly assembled at the driveway entrance to the estate, and Sheriff Betty Thompson walking toward them.

"I have a prepared statement, and then I will take some questions" Betty said calmly. "Today, two bodies were discovered in the bedroom of the Midgett Estate. They have been tentatively identified as Ralph Midgett, age seventy-eight, of Kitty Hawk, NC and Kelly Ann Fuco, age forty, of Raleigh NC. Ms. Fuco was Mr. Midgett's second wife and they have been divorced for the past six years."

"Was this a murder suicide?" one reporter shouted. Another called out "How were they killed?" A third reporter asked, "Who found the bodies?"

"One at a time, folks. I'll try and answer your questions, but let's go one at a time" Betty tried to quickly quell the barrage of questions and regain control of the press conference. "Now, this was not a murder suicide. I can say that with a degree of certainty given the nature of their deaths, but I cannot go into any more details about that at this time. As to how the two victims were killed, I can confirm that a machete appears to be the murder weapon, and it was recovered in the room and is back at the crime lab undergoing analysis. The third question was....?"

"Who found the body?" the reporter repeated.

"Right" said the Sheriff. "The bodies were discovered by one of the housekeeping staff. She came to the room to perform routine cleaning. She immediately called 911, and our investigation began. Ok, you..." as she pointed to another reporter.

"Do you have any suspects?" he asked quickly "And do you anticipate an arrest soon?"

"We're not going to comment on those parts of the investigation. We are in the process of working this scene, gathering clues, and interviewing all related parties. When we make an arrest, all of you in the media will be informed. Ok, yes, you in the green dress..."

"Yes, does this scene have anything to do with the murder discovered in Corolla this morning? Tommy Mills was the bank manager at the bank Ralph Midgett used to own" Michelle Wagner asked confidently, as a murmur in the surrounding crowd grew. 'She's good' thought Angela as she watched the office TV. 'I need to pick her brain over coffee soon.'

"We are not prepared to link these two incidents. The death of Mr. Mills has not been officially ruled by the coroner. At this point we are considering them suspicious coincidences." Betty tried her best to deflect the question, but she knew there could be more to this. A lot more.

"A follow up, Sheriff?" asked Michelle Wagner. "Can you tell us where the current Mrs. Midgett is right now?"

"The housekeeping staff confirmed that Tatiana Milanovich Midgett was traveling in Europe. We have contacted her, and she is cutting her trip short to come home." Sheriff Betty Thompson continued to field questions but was tiring. She wished she had an information officer to deal with all this, but events like this were just so rare on the OBX.

Angela tuned out the TV as the press conference continued to drone on in the background while she worked on researching Ralph Midgett. "Will, you should look at this." She called over her shoulder to her boss in the other office. It was after five and most of the employees had left for the day. Angela never left until after seven, even when her husband was home from his latest road trip for work.

Will popped around the corner and asked "Whatcha got, Angie?" Angela has been called Angie by family and friends since she was a baby.

"Remember when Ralph sold the Bank?" Angela asked without looking from her computer screen. "Did you think that was kinda strange? I mean the bank was making Ralph a ton of money, and he ups and jumps off that wave? Didn't seem like the kind of move he'd make. I get that he was no spring chicken, and he was getting wife #3, so maybe he wanted to just sail off into the sunset, but it just seems off."

"Hey, maybe the buyer *made him an offer he couldn't refuse*?" Will said with her best New York accent, as a smile slowly worked its way across her face.

"You Godfather'd me!!!" Angela exclaimed. "Wow, and all these dead bodies makes that movie seem appropriate." Angela turned back to her computer. "What if he was forced to sell? Maybe the bank was doing something shady, and he decided to get out before it blew up on him. Six years ago, he was getting divorced, but he didn't need to sell for that. He had a pre-nup. And six years ago, the economy was starting to turn around and banking was heating up. Why get out then?"

"That's interesting, but what does it have to do with his insurance? I'm not seeing a connection" Will asked while looking over Angela's shoulder. She loved that Angela would grab an idea like a dog with a bone, but she worried that it would pull her away from more productive office matters.

"Well, when he took out that huge life policy, he made some statements about his health and finances, that, if false, would invalidate the policy. Think we should explore that? I think we have fifty million reasons to, don't you?" Will's eyes grew wide with Angela's unassailable statement, as she nodded in agreement. That would be very productive use of her time.

"Let me know what I can do to help?" Will said as she walked back to her office. Angela was lost in another google search and didn't acknowledge her boss. She was on a mission now, and nothing would stop her from putting this puzzle together. She started opening new windows on her screen, typing in search information about the bank, about Ralph Midgett, and cross referenced his family.

Carol Lawrence, wife #1, had moved back down south after the divorce. She remarried and appeared to be leading a quiet upper middle-class life just outside Atlanta, Georgia in the affluent suburb of Roswell. She had received a generous divorce settlement and monthly child support checks that would keep most people comfortable, so Carol was not suffering in her new life. Her husband did well in business as a consultant and she was involved with local charities, played tennis at a local club, and traveled with her husband regularly. She had not seen Ralph Midgett since the day she was led out of their house and sent packing.

The two children Carol had with Ralph, Steve and Jennifer Midgett, were in their 20's now. Both had graduated from UVA, courtesy of their father, and moved with work. Steve was in commercial real estate in Norfolk, and Jennifer was in pharmaceutical sales in Richmond. Both of them had changed their names to Lawrence after turning 18. Angela chuckled to herself. 'Steve Lawrence and Jennifer Lawrence... subtle. They must really resent their father to change their names' she thought.

Keeping the Midgett name would certainly make life easier, at least when they walked into a bank or business meeting. There was nothing about their lives that jumped out for Angela. They both seemed normal, 20 somethings dealing with the struggles of becoming adults and living on their own. Neither had any criminal records. No financial calamities. Both registered to vote. Steve owned a townhome. Jennifer rented a condo in town. Neither seemed to be in a long-term relationship, at least not according to their Facebook pages. Social media showed that they were very close to their mother, but never interacted with their father. The closest they came to dear old dad was spending their allowance he deposited into their checking accounts on the first of each month.

Kelly Anne Fuco, wife number two, had moved to Raleigh NC after her divorce and lived in a modest upscale neighborhood with her beau du jour. To say she was playing the field was a gross understatement. She was well known to the neighbors and the police for her loud lifestyle and dramatic break ups. There were men all over Raleigh who hated her for the way she treated them, but she seemed to think she was untouchable because she was once a Mrs. Midgett.

The new Mrs. Midgett, Tatiana Milanovich was a bit of an enigma since she came from Eastern Europe, and records were sketchy at best. She apparently came to the US after living in Poland, although she was not born there. Records indicated she was born in the former Czechoslovakia, but her family fled when the empire collapsed, and civil war erupted. Except for her foreign ancestry, she was the prototypical Mrs. Midgett. Taller than number two, but not as tall as number one, she had an exceptional figure and beautiful face, full lips and flowing long dark hair. At twenty-eight, she was fifty years younger than her husband, so the phrase most locals used was "gold-digger" or "mail-order bride" but Ralph Midgett seemed genuinely smitten with her. He was thrilled to have the bikini parties again and loved watching the faces of his friends and business associates as she pranced around, flirting, and fawning over them, but always worshipping him. Like the women before her, she was at his beck and call to perform whatever spousal services he required, and she lustily obliged.

Angela was also pulling information from their office system about the in-force life insurance. Several policies on Ralph, of course, but also policies on each wife and the two children. Carol had a two-million-dollar cash value policy that was still in force and premiums were up to date. Kelly and Tatiana each had a one-million-dollar cash value policy. The kids had five hundred thousand dollars each in cash value. All life insurance policies had Ralph as the owner and "the Estate of..." as the beneficiary. There was a long paper trail, and that was just for the policies they had written. Ralph was careful to insure what he owned, and protect those he loved, even after he stopped living with them.

She also looked into Tommy Mills, and boy, did he have a past. Never married, but women and child support that would cripple most men, but he seemed to thrive - a nice house in Kitty Hawk, two late model luxury cars, a newer fishing boat, and a "hideaway" on the beach in Corolla that most people would have gladly called home. He had all the trappings of a man who came by money easily. How'd he pull that off? He made a good salary at the bank, but nothing close to what would be needed to support the lifestyle he used to enjoy. New details and information only made Angela more curious and her fingers flew across the keyboard.

Something on the TV caught her eye and she turned quickly to look. A sheriff's deputy was walking out of the mansion with a large white dog, which was partially covered in blood. The beautiful great pyrenes owned by the late Ralph Midgett may be the only witness to the murder, and it appears he stayed faithfully by his owner even after he died. Angela was taken by the image. She was a sucker for a pretty face, and the deputy and the dog both had one. She made a mental note to see about "rescuing" both of them, as a mischievous smile curled up in the corners of her mouth

"Focus, Angela! Focus" she muttered to herself, as her mind pulled back from the fantasy, she was creating with herself and that deputy.

ELEVEN

"Ok, what have we got?" shouted Betty Thompson forcefully to the members of her team assembled in the conference room. "We need answers fast. It's been twenty-four hours since the bodies were discovered, and I've got Chairman Taylor and DA Anderson getting on my last nerve. When one of our most prominent citizens is butchered in his own home, they see a PR nightmare coming into tourist season. Fill me in on what we've discovered so far."

Bill Anderson slipped into the back of the room and surveyed the scene. The Dare County District Attorney was close to retirement age but hadn't lost his love of the law and the chance to prosecute criminals. Most around the courthouse figured he'd never retire. After moving to the outer banks as a teenager, he'd made it his home for 50 years. He loved the laid back, casual lifestyle, and the good ol' southern charm the barrier islands provided. He was portly, with his stomach protruding over the belt of his khaki slacks, average height, and had a round cherub face with thinning blond hair. He rarely wore a tie, except when in court and he tried to avoid that as much as possible, and never wore socks. His reputation as a deal maker with defense attorneys earned him the affectionate nickname "The Barefoot Trader". The DA had a close relationship with the County Chairman, Barney Taylor, and everyone in the room knew that he'd be reporting back any information about these homicides. High profile cases like this didn't come along very often in this tourist mecca, and everyone wanted the press to head home as quickly as possible.

"We've gotten the coroner's report!" one of the deputies called out. "Nothing there we couldn't already see. Decapitation and massive blood loss were the cause of death. Some cocaine and alcohol in their system, and Viagra in Mr. Midgett's, and semen in her stomach and vagina." With that revelation came a chorus of chuckles, and one anonymous "Agona, you have made a man of me!" which caused a huge outburst of laughter from everyone, except the coroner, who had slid into the room and stood beside the DA.

Cora Mae Basnight, the longtime funeral director, respected member of the business community and County Coroner had also acted in the local outdoor historical drama "The Lost Colony" for more years than anyone can remember. She played the Indian girl, Agona, who falls in love with the drunken English settler "Old Tom". Her part consisted of her running around the stage chasing after the man, and giggling! She had no lines, but in one quiet, tender moment right before the climax of the show, a sober Old Tom delivers his memorable line. She was always teased by the locals for her "celebrity."

"All right! All right! There's enough of that. Let's show some respect for our guests." Sheriff Thompson ordered, as all heads whipped around and looked at the Coroner and DA. "Sorry about that, Cora. And thank you for expediting your report." Betty offered.

"Glad I could lighten the mood" came the quiet response from the Coroner. "Now, how about we show some respect for the dead, and a little professionalism too!" she scolded. "Thank you, Sheriff. The Coroner's Office recognized the high-profile nature of this case and we worked 'round the clock to get our results."

"What else have y'all gathered over the past twenty-four hours?" Bill Anderson chimed in. "You know lots of people are watching this case, here and around the state. Hell, we got reporters here from AP, USA Today, even the Washington Post! A whole lotta folks from DC come here, spend their money, and want to relax. Murders aren't good for that. This county needs your best!"

Like deer in headlights, the assembled group of deputies all turned back to Sheriff Thompson. "Right, Got it. No pressure. Now, let's go around the room..." she said calmly and in complete control. "We got anything on the murder weapon?"

"Nothing" came the response from one of the deputies. "No prints, and all the blood was the victims. The machete was a stock model purchased at any hardware or home improvement store. We're running that down with the manufacturer to see if we can come up with a point of sale, and maybe get lucky with a buyer. Longshot, but we'll work it."

"Good. Keep me posted. Now about the scene. Any clues there?" inquired the Sheriff.

"The scene was completely dusted for prints, and cross matched against the household staff. The only prints in the room were of the two victims. There was a shoe print on the carpet where someone walked in the blood, but that ends at the balcony. We've taken impressions and are trying to match it to known footwear, but it's a stretch since the impressions are not strong and smeared. Looks like the killer wore cover booties like so many tradesmen do today." reported another deputy.

"Looks like whoever did this wore protective cover ups to mask their identity. Obviously pre-meditated" offered Jack Strong, standing to the side of the room, as he looked at Betty and then back to Bill Anderson. "Seems we need to look at motive if we're gonna solve this one. Doesn't appear the physical evidence is gonna catch our man."

"About that," a voice called from the middle of the room. "I've been looking at both victims in Southern Shores and Mr. Mills in Corolla. Their online presence and all relevant public records for each" said the bookish youthful looking deputy, "and all of the victims had lots of enemies! LOTS." The young deputy said with a groan, which was echoed by most in attendance. Everyone knew what that meant. Grunt work. Good old-fashioned grunt work.

"Ok" Betty said calmly. "Can you print out the names and addresses and motives you've identified so far? Let's start running them down, one by one. Deputy Jennette, you keep after the research and keep feeding us names. Deputy Strong, you're in charge of the field work. Pick a good team and make it count. Jennifer, are all the names local?"

"No ma'am" the young deputy answered crisply. "The female victim lived in Raleigh and most of the names associated with her come from that area. The first Mrs. Midgett lives in Roswell, Georgia, and her two kids from her marriage to Mr. Midgett live in Virginia Beach and Richmond."

"All right," Sheriff Thompson acknowledged. "Jack, coordinate with those local police departments and ask them to do the interviews. If anything pops, we can send a team over to look further. I'm going to talk to the widow. While I'm doing that, we need to figure out why Ms. Fuco came to visit Mr. Midgett. Can you look into that Deputy?" Betty asked, looking at Deputy Jennifer Jennette, who nodded in the affirmative. "And we need to figure out if that bank robbery and murder in Corolla are related to the murders in Southern Shores. We've got to connect the dots, people."

A general rumble began over the group, everyone recognizing that the formal meeting was breaking up, so side discussions were starting to erupt. "Wait a minute, everyone, wait!" shouted the voice of Bill Anderson from the back of the room. "I wanted to tell you that you have the full support of the DA's office and the County Commission. I don't need to tell you that Ralph Midgett was a very influential man. He had friends, and he had enemies, but most of all, he had far reaching influence. Let's catch the son of a gun who did this and bring them to justice. And let's do it quickly."

"Sheriff, Jack, a word please?" asked DA Anderson. "If y'all need anything, search warrants, subpoenas, anything, you call me night or day. I'll get 'em for you. I'm good with Judge Griffin, and he'll agree to just about anything I ask for, short of waterboarding."

"Ok, Bill. Understood. We'll keep you posted." Betty offered with a wink and a nod, as she turned to go back to her office.

"No waterboarding! Damn, Bill, why'd I leave the Navy!" Jack chuckled as he slapped the back of the DA. "Don't worry, we'll get this son of a gun."

TWELVE

Sheriff Thompson rang the bell and stepped back from the impressive entrance to the Midgett mansion. The house looked more suited for the Italian riviera than the outer banks of North Carolina. It was marble columns and marble floors and marble staircases. Tapestries and artwork were everywhere, sculptures and paintings from the masters, pre-Columbian, Chinese, Indian and even some African art revealed the breath of Ralph's travels. The wind was up and whipping squall lines of rain sideways. On the drive over on the causeway from Manteo to Nags Head, she saw white caps on Roanoke Sound, and now, looking to the ocean, she could see the storm that was building off the Georgia coast might just deliver the gut punch the weather forecasters have predicted. Betty had called before she made the drive, knowing that Mrs. Midgett may not have been taking company so soon after the death of her husband, but was surprised to see a very composed woman open the door with a welcoming smile.

"Hello! You must be Sheriff Thompson." Tatiana Midgett said with a slight Eastern European accent. "Please come in. Apologies for the condition of the house, but we have not been allowed to clean since…. since Ralph died. I've been staying in the guest house, but I thought you'd like to talk here. Is that OK?" she asked very sheepishly.

"Yes. Yes, of course. Really, wherever you're most comfortable. I appreciate you taking the time to meet with us. This is Deputy Cudworth." Betty said. "If you'd rather go to the guest house, I completely understand."

"No. Thank you. The rain is coming, and we can be comfortable here. Would either of you like something to drink? Coffee, tea?"

"Yes, thanks. Coffee black for me" Betty answered. Tim Cudworth just shook his head. "I'm sorry we have to meet under these circumstances. We're very sorry for your loss."

"Thank you, Sheriff" Tatiana said bravely as she straightened herself and braced for the wave of emotion that washed over her. "Ralph was a good man, a fine husband, and a wonderful member of the community. He will be missed."

Sheriff Thompson shot a quick glance to Deputy Cudworth, wondering if he thought that speech was a bit rehearsed. Sounded like a press release to her, but Tatiana was a grieving widow, and English was not her native tongue. Although Betty noticed she didn't say he was loved. "Well, if we can ask just a few questions, we won't take up any more time than we need."

Tatiana shook her head and smiled. "However, I can help."

Getting right to the heart of the matter, Betty asked "Mrs. Midgett, Tatiana, can you think of anyone who would have wanted to kill your husband?"

"No! Well, Ralph was a powerful man. He had worked very hard to build a legacy. I'm sure somewhere along the way he made enemies, he bruised feelings, he ... well, he hurt people. Business, banking, can be like that. 'Nothing personal. Just business' ... you've heard that before, yes?" Tatiana implored. "I know Ralph was bold, and brash, and aggressive. Successful men, successful people usually are." She went on "but he hasn't worked for the bank since we got married 6 years ago. He's been retired, and I haven't seen him happier and more relaxed. He loved our life."

"I appreciate your forthright answer." Betty offered with a slight smile. "Now, just to dot the I's and cross the T's, we know you were traveling in Europe, Tatiana. Can you provide us with your itinerary so that we can verify your whereabouts?"

"Of course! I was visiting family in Poland and I traveled to London, Paris, and Milan for shopping. I can provide you my hotel and airline information. Can I email it to you?" Tatiana answered obligingly.

"Yes, of course. Deputy Cudworth will provide you his card. He will follow up with you. He's my card. If you have any questions, or anything comes to mind that you think would be helpful, please don't hesitate to contact me." Sheriff Thompson said while standing to leave. "One more question Tatiana, if I may?"

"Of course," Mrs. Midgett responded politely.

"Do you know why Kelly Anne Fuco came to visit your husband?" Betty had to ask, but it was a question she didn't enjoy.

"I... I... have no idea. When the police told me what happened, how Ralph was found... I..." and then she dissolved into tears, sobbing hysterically. Her brave front cracked completely, and she melted back into her chair.

"Thank you, Mrs. Midgett. We can show ourselves out." Sheriff Thompson and Deputy Cudworth left quietly. "That was no fun," Betty mumbled as she walked outside and was slapped by the wind and the rain. As she got into her Charger to make the drive back to the office, her radio squawked. "Sheriff Thompson here, over"

"Sheriff, a Will Moore with OBX Insurance has asked you to call her. She has some information you might find useful regarding the Midgett case." The operator droned.

"Great, I'll call when I get back to the office." Betty responded.

"Well, she asked if you'd meet her at Coastal Cravings in Duck. She said she's buying you lunch." The operator said quickly, knowing the Sheriff was about to cut the call short.

"Oh, hell, all right. I guess meeting with local business owners is part of the job, and I gotta eat, and I love the food there. I'll call her now. Sheriff out." She turned to Deputy Cudworth, "Tim, I'll catch up with you back at the office." Betty picked up her cell phone and dialed Will Moore.

THIRTEEN

"Hey Sheriff, over here!" Will called from a booth by the windows. The interior of the restaurant was small, tucked behind a BP gas station, and had mostly booths. There was outside seating as well when the weather accommodated. The ambiance was pleasant, but you came for the food. That was the star of this show.

" Hi Will, good to see you again. Mind if we sit back here. I always like to sit against a wall. Old policeman's habit." Betty suggested.

"No problem. I should have thought of that. My dad's the same way" Will offered while she picked up her iced tea and moved to the back booth. "Thanks for meeting me on such short notice. When I heard you were at the Midgett Estate I figured I'd save us both a trip."

" Ok. Was your dad a cop?" Betty asked with real interest. She'd known Will Moore for a few years, met socially at Chamber functions and various charity events, but never really had the chance to talk more than just polite chit chat. Betty was always taken by Will's easy manner and beauty. She seemed to glide around a room, and she was always impeccably dressed, spotless minimal make up, and hair kept in a tight ponytail so that her beautiful face was unobstructed. Betty knew that she could hold her own with Ms. Moore in almost every way, but the five inches she gave up in height made all the difference when it came to turning heads.

"Yeah, well, no, he was FBI. He's retired now after 30 some odd years with them." Will answered, looking straight at Betty's beautiful face, strong cheekbones and jaw, creamy mocha skin, and big brown doe eyes. Will could see the steely determination to succeed in Betty's face, but her soft full inviting lips gave her a very feminine allure. "He's just up the road in Edenton. He loves livin' the small-town life and boy has he relaxed since he retired. Anyway, what do you want for lunch? My treat." The waitress came over and took drink and food orders and then disappeared back behind the counter. "I know you're gonna think I'm crazy, but our office, specifically my office manager, has been doing a lot of follow up on the Ralph Midgett murder. There are several claims in the works, and for really big money, and the insurance company has asked us to take a look. Anyway, she's a wiz on the computer and has uncovered some information that raises more questions than answers, and we thought you and your people might be interested."

"Hummm. Well, we appreciate public involvement, but..." Sheriff Thompson began in her official voice, trying not to sound too condescending or disrespectful.

"No. I get it. Stay in our lane and all that. We've got our investigation and you've got yours. Understood. Different strategies. Different outcomes. We don't, I don't want to interfere in any way. We just would like to pass on what we've uncovered. No two-way street. No quid pro quo." Will quickly jumped in. "I don't want to step on anyone's toes."

"Thanks. I appreciate you understanding." Betty said as the food arrived.

"Lobster Roll for you" the waitress glanced at Betty while sliding the plate in front of her, "and Crab Cake Sandwich for you, sweetie" she smiled at Will. "More tea?" she asked.

"I'm good." Will and Betty said simultaneously, and then grinned at the coincidence. The waitress left them alone to enjoy their meal and continue their conversation.

"The food here is always so good, breakfast, lunch or dinner!" Betty cooed as she slid the lobster roll into her mouth. "Yumm!!!"

"I come here as often as I can" Will said while chewing a bite of her crab sandwich. "Weekends outside with live music is fun too. I'm guessing your deputies stay busy here."

"Not too often" Betty offered. "Scott Foster runs a good shop here, and he makes sure the crowds stay safe and have fun. He gets it that this is a family beach." They sat in silence for a few minutes while they ate their food.

"Ok," Betty said, breaking the silence after they both finished their meal, "have your girl contact me and I'll set up a meeting with our team so she can review over what she's found. After the lecture I got earlier from DA Anderson and Chairman Taylor I can use all the help I can get."

"Crème Brule muffin for dessert?" the waitress cheerily offered.

The two women looked at each other with a devilish grin, and then said in harmony "Let's save that for next time."

"Ok, then. I'll bring the check." The waitress turned and walked away, leaving Will and Betty to sip their tea.

"Will, thanks for lunch. I enjoyed the company, but I've got to run." Sheriff Betty Thompson said as she got up to leave. "There's a break in the rain, and I need to get back in the office."

"I understand. I enjoyed it too. Hope we can do it again soon. I'll tell Angela to get in touch with you to coordinate a meeting, and, Betty, don't sweat Bill or Barney. I've been doing business with them for a few years, and they are both pussycats. Tigers like us can eat them for …. Lunch!" Will laughed as she patted her stomach. She sat back and gave Betty a sideways look as she watched her walk out of the restaurant and get into her Charger. Hummm, that would be fun, she thought to herself, as a devilish curl to her lips emerged.

"See something you like there Will?" asked Scott Foster as he came out of the kitchen and approached the table.

"Matter of fact, I do!" exclaimed Will happily. "How you been, Scott? And why the heck haven't we talked insurance yet? How about we set a date and get 'er done, bud? I really want your business." she said with a sly look and all the down home sweet southern charm she could muster.

"Let's do it! I'd love to give you the business!" Scott responded with a grin. "But first you need to pay the check!" He smiled, gave her a wink, and slid the paper across the table to her. Walking away, he thought to himself "every man on this island wants to give her the business."

FOURTEEN

"Jack, this is Angela Peterson from OBX Insurance." Sheriff Betty Thompson was making introductions in the hallway just outside the main conference room. "Angela, this is Deputy Jack Strong. Angela, Jack is my point person on this investigation. You can talk to him like you are talking to me."

Angela had a bit of the 'deer in headlights' look on her face as she stared at Jack Strong. "Nice to meet you" came out reflexively as she took his extended hand and shook it. This was the deputy she saw walking out of the mansion with that beautiful Great Pyrenes dog during the TV news report. 'Lord, he was better looking in person' she thought to herself as her mind began to wander. 'I could get lost in those dimples' she thought.

"And this is Deputy Jennifer Jennette who handles most of our computer research." Betty continued. "I thought you two should meet so you can coordinate your information." Angela hadn't noticed the young, pretty deputy with the dark brown ponytail and glasses framing her blue eyes standing next to Jack Strong. Angela stammered for a second and then shook Jennifer's hand. "Good to meet you" Angela smiled, but barely stopped looking at Jack.

Sheriff Thompson looked at Jack with confidence and said. "Jack, I'll leave you three to get after it. You're in good hands, Angela." With that, she spun around and retreated to her office.

"Well, Angela, thank you for coming out in this storm. It's raining cats and dogs out there today. Why don't we come in here and get to work?" Jack motioned to the open conference room and let Angela and Jennifer enter. "Would you like something to drink? Coffee? Water?" Jack offered. Angela agreed to some coffee, and Deputy Jennette was dispatched to pick it up. "I'm guessing you need power for your laptop and want to connect to our projection system so we can all see what you've brought us." Jack suggested, as he motioned to the podium at the front of the room. "All the hook ups are there. You probably know how to do all that better than I do" he said with a chuckle.

"Since we have a second alone, can I ask you something?" Angela asked shyly. Jack nodded agreement but was now second guessing his decision to be alone with her. "Whatever happened to that beautiful dog from the Midgett place?" she blurted out. A wave of relief and a broad smile came over Jack's face.

"I adopted him!" he exclaimed. "Mrs. Midgett didn't want him. She said he was Mr. Midgett's dog and she never really liked him. I've already got Molly, my goofy golden retriever, and the two of them get along like peas and carrots." Angela could sense that Jack and she shared a love for their furry friends, and she smiled inside and out to Jack Strong.

"I'd love to see him sometime" Angela said as Jennifer walked into the room with a tray of coffees, creamers, and sugars.

"Whatcha gonna show her Jack?" Jennifer wisecracked. "Don't tell me you have dirty pics on your phone!" she laughed.

"I wanted to meet Jack's, err, Deputy Strong's dog and the rescue from the Midgett place. I'm a huge animal lover" Angela answered over the chuckle from Deputy Jennette.

Jennifer laughed and sat on the side of the conference room table assembling her coffee, four sugars, two creams. "Don't worry Angela. Jack's one of the good guys. I was just pulling his leg. Now what did I miss?" Angela looked down, a flush of embarrassment filled her cheeks, and finished the computer set up. She had a presentation opened which they all could now see on the screen at the front of the room.

"Ok, I've done some digging in public and not so public databases on several people and found some interesting threads. If you've already uncovered any of this, just stop me and I won't waste any more of your time." Angela paused to look at the two deputies and saw acknowledgement in both their faces, so she continued. "First let's look at some of the key players. Tommy Mills, the OBX Kitty Hawk Branch Bank Manager. He was hired by Mr. Midgett personally and seemed to have a very close working relationship with him. It appears from the paper trail that I've uncovered, Mr. Mills worked off the books as a sort of 'fixer' for Mr. Midgett. He made payoffs to people for influence, or their silence, and handled the dirty work so Midgett would stay clean and have 'plausible deniability' if questioned. For all that, Mills was compensated well above his pay from the bank, and all of it seems to have been 'under the table.'" Angela looked at Jack and Jennifer to gauge their reaction, and seeing them both leaning forward and engaged, she continued. "Ralph Midgett had made a lot of enemies. He had two ex-wives he dumped unceremoniously. He had a slew of bank clients who lost everything when he foreclosed on them, and he had business partners who he muscled out of huge paydays on their deals. He was ruthless."

"Ok, we got most of that, and we know we have a large suspect pool. Currituck County is working the Tom Mills murder, so we don't have much on that." Deputy Jack Strong interjected, "We're focusing on the two murders here in Southern Shores and motive alone does not get us an arrest. We need the big three – motive, means and opportunity. You got all that in your PowerPoint presentation?"

"I think I do, but y'all will have to work with me, because I can't get some information that you can." replied Angela confidently. She looked into their eyes to see if there was any indication of push back. She saw intrigue and resolve, but no hesitation. "Well, all right then! Let's keep going.' I think the murder in Corolla and the murders here are all related, and I think that bank robbery was part of it too! I know the FBI took over that, but have you gotten any word on what those two kids had to say about why the tried to rob the bank?"

Jack and Jennifer shot each other a glance, and Angela could see that they knew something and were just trying to decide if they could discuss it. As the senior officer, Jack took the lead "You know we aren't supposed to discuss information on an ongoing case."

"Yeah, I get that Deputy, so let me tell you what I know. My boss, Will Moore, her dad worked for the FBI his entire career, so she talked with him and he called a few friends. Apparently the two knuckleheads that were arrested were quick to point the finger for their crime at "some guy" who paid them $1,000 each to meet him at the bank. He let them in and gave them the shotgun for the crime. They said he told them to count to 100 and then shoot the gun into the ceiling and then stall the police for as long as it took to have the FBI show up. The guy left out the back and disappeared. The kids did what they were told, and when they were arrested by SWAT, they each had $1,000 in crisp new bills. The shotgun was on the floor right under the hole in the ceiling."

Jack sat dumbfounded by this revelation. "You know as much as we do!" he blurted out. "How in the hell?"

Angela chuckled this time "Pays to have friends, huh?" She looked at both Deputy Strong and Deputy Jennette and saw the same look of admiration, so she continued "Now, here's why I think the crimes are related. Let's look at the timeline. Robbery was on Monday around noon. Midgett and Fuco were killed between 1-4 Monday, according to the reports I've seen, Mills was killed between 3 and 6 Monday. Mills was discovered Tuesday morning and shortly after that the two bodies in Southern Shores were discovered by the maid. How am I doing so far?"

Both deputies shook their heads in agreement and Jennifer gave a slow whistle of acceptance. "You have done a lot of work on this. What's your background again?" she asked with a mixture of amusement and intrigue.

"Oh, I'm the Office Manager at Will Moore's insurance agency. I thought y'all knew that?" Angela responded quizzically.

"We do!" Jack interjected, "but you seem to be quite the investigator."

"I like to do research, and when my curiosity is peaked, you can't pull me away." Angela explained. "Ya gotta admit, the OBX doesn't get a lot of crimes like this too much, so I was interested. And then you throw in that one of the victims is one of the most prominent men here, and one of our biggest clients, well, I was hooked."

"Yes, it seems you are." Sheriff Thompson said from the doorway. She stood leaning against the frame; arms crossed across her chest with an impressed look on her face. "Angela opening any doors for us yet, Deputies?"

Both Jack and Jennifer shot a surprised look at their boss, and Jack responded "I think so, but it's early days yet. We've got a lot more ground to cover."

"Ok, well, I need to steal Angela for just a minute. Can we talk in the hall?" Betty looked at Angela and motioned to her. When they were both outside, she closed the door. "Please tell your boss how much we appreciate her loaning you to us. We're 48 hours into this investigation and, frankly, we need all the help we can get. Obviously, you are a valuable part of her team and time away from your work is productivity lost, so let her know we are grateful." Angela smiled and acknowledged that she would pass on the message. "Also" Betty continued, "will you let her know how much I enjoyed our lunch together the other day, and that I look forward to seeing her again soon." Betty said this with the same pleasant authority she always used in her official capacity, but Angela got the feeling this was more like passing notes in school.

"I sure will" Angela replied while trying to suppress a smile. Angela recalled the glow Will brought back to the office after their lunch and could see that there was more than just professional admiration between these two women. She had not given much thought to her boss's sexuality, but she could definitely see there was an attraction, and apparently, that attraction was mutual. "And thank you for the complement Sheriff. I better get back in. There's a lot to discuss." Angela opened the door and slipped back inside.

"Ok, we were talking while you were out," Jack started, "and we can tell you that the description of the guy who staged the bank robbery doesn't match anyone in our suspect pool."

"Ok, can I get the description so I can work on that?" Angela asked, expecting to be told the usual 'ongoing investigation" bull.

"Sure" Jennifer shot back. I'll email it to you now." She picked up her phone and was typing "What's your email address?" Within seconds a new message popped into Angela's inbox. Angela sat stunned and thought to herself 'now I'm in the inner circle. They trust me' and she beamed contentedly like the Cheshire Cat.

Jack picked up the conversation "So our mystery man is in his 20's, Caucasian with fair skin, about 6' tall, thin and has dark straight hair. He was dressed in dark slacks, dark hoodie, and wore a black knit cap pulled low over his hair, and black leather driving gloves. Interestingly, one of the robbers said he wore really nice polished dress shoes. The two robbers couldn't offer much more than that. Nothing unusual. No visible tattoos. No flashy jewelry. No unusual physical features. I get the feeling that once he flashed the money, these two geniuses didn't notice anything else. There were no finger prints on the gun, other than the one kid who fired it, but the FBI crime lab did find a partial print on some of the shell casings that doesn't match either suspect in the robbery."

"Any ideas why they agreed to this hair brained scheme?" Angela asked with real interest. "Seems like it was a suicide mission."

"Well, the story these kids tell is that they were approached at a food kitchen and asked if they'd like to get some easy street cred and make a $1,000 bucks each. Easy money." Jack said while shaking his head in disbelief. "Stupid kids thought being arrested was a great idea! Free room and board. Free meals. And they come out with recognition! They ate it up since they were basically living on the streets."

"Wow, that's really sad. Don't their parents care?" Angela said, and then quickly looked away. She knew the answer to that question. "Ok, well it seems our mystery man could be just about anybody, but at least we can rule out anyone over forty, which cuts the suspect pool seriously. Most of the businessmen and homeowners Midgett foreclosed on were over forty and Tom Mills was way over forty. So, who's in their twenties that would want Mills, Midgett and Fuco dead?"

"Well, that's assuming the crimes are related." Jennifer shot back quickly. "We need to think that each crime brings its own pool of suspects to the table. Who would want Mills dead? Who would want Fuco dead? Who would want Midgett dead? Clearly, being killed the way they were, Midgett and Fuco was a crime of passion. Personal. Hate filled. The Mills murder was more a crime of opportunity. The bank robbery... well, that was just a diversion is my guess."

"Trying to buy some time while the murders are committed. Seems reasonable." Jack added thoughtfully. Everyone sat in silence for a few minutes, all mulling the information. Jack broke the silence and spoke first "Let's focus on the mystery man. See if we can pin down who he is, then go from there. The FBI has the bank security footage, so we can ask for a peak, but I won't hold my breath, unless your boss can work another miracle?" Looking at Angela with the question.

"Never hurts to ask." Came her reply. "Who's pulled security footage from stores around the bank? Maybe we could get lucky with a clear shot of the person."

"I've got Deputies Tink Taylor and Jefferson Daniels looking into that. Sheriff Thompson went personally to all the local businesses to ask."

Jack confirmed. "We're also reviewing footage from the Midgett mansion and some surrounding properties. Fingers crossed we get a break."

"Jefferson Daniels? I went to Manteo High with him. He was a football stud back then. Lost touch when he went to college. When did he move back here?" Angela asked quizzically. Her interest was piqued by the news. She always thought Daniels was handsome and really fun to be around, but her insecurities back then kept her from letting him know just how much she liked him.

"He joined us about a year ago, just after I came on board. Football ended with injuries, so he took his criminal justice degree and put it to good use. He was a NC State Trooper for two years and then, when his momma got sick, moved back here. We're really happy to have him on the Sheriff's detail. Good cop. Really good man." Jennifer spoke with genuine affection and admiration in her voice, telling Angela to tread lightly.

"Why don't you share information with Jennifer if you locate anything on our suspect, since she's maintaining the murder book for us. Sound good?" Jack looked to each of them and they nodded in agreement. Angela was hoping to work more closely with Jack, really, really closely, but… maybe another day. She'd have to curb her enthusiasm for that hunk of man for the time being, but she couldn't wait forever!

Walking out of the room, Angela turned to Jack and asked "So, when can I come see your beautiful pups?" Jack smiled and walked back toward the bull pen, leaving Angela panting, and he knew it.

FIFTEEN

The outer bands of the storm were lashing the Outer Banks pretty good now even though the center of the storm was still swirling off the Georgia coast. Winds were blowing rain sideways. Streets were starting to flood from too much surface water. The ocean was boiling with foam all the way to the horizon and waves crashed on the shore, gouging out sand as it retreated. The National Weather Service had issued a severe storm warning for all of the barrier islands along the North and South Carolina coasts, with small craft advisories up along all of coastal North Carolina. This storm was growing in strength and looked to be developing into quite the killer. The US Navy was moving the fleet out of Norfolk and the Air Force was sending all their planes inland from their bases in the tidewater area. It would still be days before the full impact of this massive weather system was felt on the OBX.

"Hey Jennifer, it's Mom. How's everything in Richmond? You settling in Ok?" Carol Lawrence asked nervously. She didn't want to be a prying mother, but she was concerned about her baby girl starting her new life in a strange city.

"I'm great Mom. Thanks. And before you ask, No, I haven't met a nice man yet. Met several bad boys, a couple of dirty old men, but no one you'd think was 'nice'." Jennifer Lawrence chuckled. She loved being a smart-ass, especially to her Mom. "How have you been adjusting to life without kids?"

"Well, that's sorta why I called. I've had no luck trying to reach your brother and I was wondering if you'd spoken to Stevie?" Carol said with real concern in her voice. "With this storm brewing, and Norfolk seems to be right in line to get walloped…. I'm just worried he's safe."

"Mom! He's a twenty-eight-year-old man. Pretty damn successful too, so I'm not worried he'll take care of himself. He can handle rain, and wind, and flooding, and the looting and civil unrest that usually follows a natural disaster!"

"Oh stop, Jen. You're torturing me now." Carol and Jennifer laughed, and Jennifer reassured her mother that she would try and reach her older brother, but knowing him, he was probably just off with "friends" living the high life and had his phone turned off. Their conversation meandered to other things, pleasant chit chat about old friends and family, and then Carol got quiet.

"Mom, what's wrong? Don't worry about Steve…"

"It's not that." Carol interrupted. "I need to discuss something with you. I got a call yesterday and you probably will get the same call soon. Your father has been murdered."

"Oh, yeah, I heard on the news a couple of days ago. Did the police call you? They don't think you're involved, do they?" Jennifer Lawrence was laughing with the thought. "I know you wanted to kill the man, but you've moved on from that years ago."

Carol sat quietly. She didn't expect her baby to take the news so easily. Softly, she asked "Are you OK?"

"Mom! Yes, of course I'm Ok. I really hardly knew the man. He shipped us off to boarding school when I was very little, and we hardly saw him. Why do you think we changed our names to Lawrence? We saw you. We loved you. You loved us. We were family, not him. I mean, I heard he was really butchered up something awful, but I also heard he was killed with that skanky ex-wife he left you for, so there is poetic justice. Karma, huh?"

"Ok, well, I don't need to go there. I was told it will be a few days before the medical examiner releases the body and the funeral can be arranged. Did you want to drive down and go to the funeral with me? I could fly into Richmond, or you could pick me up in Norfolk."

"Whoa, let me think about that one for a bit, Ok? I don't know if I feel that comfortable with that, but since you asked, I'll give it some thought."

"Alright. Call me tomorrow, or sooner if you connect with Stevie, Ok?" Jennifer and Carol said their goodbye's and hung up. Carol looked at her phone and hit the speed dial button labeled STEVIE. Straight to voicemail. She didn't leave another message. 'Where was that boy?' she thought to herself. 'I hope he's not in any trouble.'

SIXTEEN

Angela ducked around the corner and looked into Will's office. "Boss, you got a minute?"

"Sure, whatcha need Angie?"

"We just got a claim request on the big life policy for Ralph Midgett. Apparently, the coroner has signed off on the death certificate, and a claim came in yesterday for Tom Mills. Currituck County coroner ruled the death a homicide. I also got some info from Jennifer Jennette at the Sheriff's office" Angela offered coyly.

"Oh... give and take with the Sheriff? Nice work girl!" came the humorous reply from Will. "Spill the dirt. What did you get?"

"Well, they got a partial ID on the mystery man at the bank. Seems he tried hard to avoid the security cameras but got caught on a neighboring business camera that looked across the parking lot. They think it's the same guy caught on security footage from the Midgett mansion. The house across the street also caught the guy coming back to his car, and they got some of the license plate. They are running it down now." Angela was excited to be able to share these details with her boss, showing she was "inside" the Sheriff's office. "If the coroner is releasing the body for burial, the funerals will be soon. Are we going to put in an appearance?

"Of course!" Will shot back without even thinking. "Tom and Ralph were two of our longest, best clients. We have to pay our respects, and that will be a great time to mingle with a possible pool of suspects too!" A wry smile came over both of their faces. They were thinking the same thing. "The policies on Ralph were payable to 'the estate of...', so maybe it's time I have a chat with Lester Finch and see when the Will will be read. Think I'll call him and invite him to lunch. Think I should take him to 1587, or The Outer Banks Brewing Station, or Tortuga's Lie?"

"Well," Angela thought for a second, "take him to 1587 if you want to date him, and Tortuga's Lie if you want a cheap lunch with everyone sitting on top of you listening to your every word. I think OBX Brewing would be perfect. Great food, especially since their previous chef came back, and the seating can afford you some privacy to discuss business. It's also pretty close to his office, so there's that too."

"Ok, I'll call him and set it up." Will turned in her chair to grab the office phone and Angela twirled out of the office and back to her desk.

SEVENTEEN

Will stood at the entrance to the restaurant watching Lester Finch climb out of his beautiful new Porsche Cayenne. Lester wasn't particularly tall, or particularly good looking, or particularly stylish, but he had a quiet confidence of a man comfortable in his own skin, and Will liked that about him. He was a good ol' southern boy who'd gone off to Georgia Tech for his undergrad studies and then went to work for a congressman in Washington DC for a couple of years before attending Duke Law School. He moved out to the Outer Banks after a few stops in law offices in Raleigh and set up his own practice. It wasn't long before he corralled Ralph Midgett as a client, and he quickly became the consigliere to the Godfather of banking in eastern North Carolina. He made a very good living but wasn't flashy or boastful. He liked the quiet, unassuming lifestyle on the OBX and felt the OBX liked him. He'd married and had two kids, and then divorced when his wife went a little batty and needed to be institutionalized. He raised the kids as a single father and didn't date very much. Now in his early fifties he was an empty nester and thinking maybe having company would be nice. That's one reason why he was quick to agree to lunch with the beautiful, and available, Ms. Moore. Another reason was to see what price he could extract for the information he knew she wanted.

"How you doing, Lester?" Will asked politely as she greeted him at the door to the restaurant.

"I'll be doing a damn site better once we get out of this weather" he shot back, as the wind almost blew them off the steps. "At least it's not raining right now. I wish this storm would hurry up and get here. Heard it's still just gaining strength and spinning like a top off the coast of Georgia." he said as he held the door for her and entered, admiring her long legs and tight backside. Inside the restaurant, the loud whir of the restaurant's wind turbine quieted. "I can't believe they haven't tied that thing off in this breeze. It's spinning like the prop on a Cessna about to take off."

"How many in your party?" a bright young woman asked, cutting off the conversation.

"Two for lunch please" Will replied.

"Right this way" the woman motioned and showed them to a table up a half flight of stairs, on the railing overlooking the main bar and seating area. The restaurant is open and airy, but the attraction behind the bar are the huge stainless-steel brewing vats, where the beer is made. It's a fascinating view of a working brewery, and the beer is the attraction of this pub feel restaurant. From their table, Lester and Will had a view of it all.

"Perfect" Will offered as she sat and took a menu.

"Mind if I take off my jacket?" Lester asked politely, before sitting, and when Will nodded, he peeled off the light blue seersucker suit jacket and hung it on the back of his chair. Lester propped a pair of reading glasses on his nose and started to peruse the offerings. "Care for a cocktail with lunch?"

"Counselor, that sounds like a great idea! I'll have a Cosmopolitan, and to be clear right up front, I asked you to lunch, so this is my treat. Got it? No fighting over the check. Ok? Now you order our drinks while I go to the ladies for a minute." Will got up and walked past Lester and back down the stairs to the restrooms, certain that he was watching her the whole way. She didn't need to use the restroom, she just wanted to "pique" his interest. She wore a tailored mint green suit with a pencil skirt that came a few inches short of her knees, a beautiful lavender silk blouse that revealed her impressive chest with the top few buttons undone. Of course, she wore her four-inch heels that matched the suit, showing off her tight backside and accentuating her incredibly long, tan, toned legs. She also towered over the man, which gave her an extra advantage, since, when standing next to each other, Lester's face was looking right into her bosom. God had given her some gifts and she wasn't afraid to use them when she needed. She wasn't attracted to the man, but she knew that distractions, and liquor, eased the tongue and made getting information easier.

When she returned to the table, she gave his shoulder a little squeeze and then slid back into her chair, folded her long tan legs under the table, and put her napkin in her lap. Lester noticed she'd touched up her make-up, re-applied her lipstick and unbuttoned another button on her blouse so her tan chest was easily visible from across the table. The drinks were delivered, and food was ordered. Will went for the pan seared scallops on a mushroom risotto, which wasn't on the lunch menu, but she asked the waiter to see if Chef Tony would make them for her. Lester ordered the shrimp and grits. They sat for a minute, sipping their drinks, and enjoying the view of the restaurant and bar below them. Will saw the waiter talking to the chef and, when he looked up at the table, she smiled and waved and mouthed 'thank you'. Chef Tony smiled back, and she knew she'd get her scallops! Will knew there were advantages to being tall, athletic, and stunning. Men would do anything for her, just hoping to get the chance. She played the game, but they never succeeded. Tom Moore raised a good girl, and she was saving herself for the love of her life.

"Now, Lester, I know you are wondering why I asked you to lunch, and I bet you probably have one or two guesses already, don't you?" Will cooed softly. "But I'm not much of a game player, so I'll just be right up front with you, Ok?"

"Ok" Lester returned with a suspicious look.

"I want your business. I want to write the insurance on your law practice and you personally. I've known you casually for a few years and realized I've never just come out and asked you for it. You own your office building in Manteo, you have a lovely home on the sound in Kitty Hawk and a very nice cottage on the beach in Nags Head. You've also got some rental properties scattered around North Carolina, and of course the usual assortment of cars, boats and other toys. I know you've been with Roanoke Insurance for years, and they were recently swallowed up by BB&T Insurance and have had a lot of staff turn-over, so it seemed like a good time for us to talk."

Lester sat stunned. He had been completely broadsided by this, since he assumed she would be discussing the Ralph Midgett estate and probate. He had been appointed executor of the will and was handling the arrangements to disperse the assets according to Ralph's stated wishes. "Well, I'm flattered. Yes, of course. This probably would be a good time to discuss everything. My relationship with Roanoke Insurance is pretty much shot since all the fellas I used to deal with there have retired after the sale. BB&T brought in a couple of hot shots from Charlotte to run things and they just rub me the wrong way. Not beach folks, if you know what I mean."

"I do, Lester, and that's why I thought we should talk. I've met those boys and I know just what you mean." Will had met them, but just in passing, enough to say hello and welcome at some civic function, and both men were about her age, but she loved playing the southern belle and she could see she was reeling Lester in. "Well, now that that's settled, why don't we make a time for me to come by and review over everything so we can give you topflight service?" She said as she removed her smartphone from her purse and opened to her calendar. "Would sometime early next week for you?"

Lester was fumbling with his jacket, trying to get his iPhone out. "Ugh, yes, I think so. If I'm tied up in court, I can have my office manager pull everything together for us. Let me see here. Ugh, well, looks like we're in luck. Would Tuesday afternoon work?"

"One o'clock?"

"Yep. Great!" They both tapped at their phones for a few seconds to enter the appointment.

"Perfect. Now, let's enjoy our lunch" Will smiled as the waiter delivered the two beautiful dishes and asked if they needed anything else. "I'm good. You need anything Lester?"

"Would you like some white wine with our lunch to celebrate our business dealings?" he smiled across the table as Will's face lit up with seductive joy.

"Why not. Sounds perfect. You choose." Will picked up her fork and pretended to be examining her food while she listened to Lester order the wine. When he was done and the waiter left, she looked across at him and said softly, "Thank you." Then they both began working on their lunch in earnest.

"So, Lester, how are the kids? You have two, right?" Will inquired while chewing on her tender scallops.

"Yes, Sam and Scout. Sam's twenty-three, just graduated from Elon and headed to Winston Salem to work at Reynolds Tobacco. Scout is twenty-one, finishing up at Furman with an accounting degree, and I hope she'll come back here and work for me, but we'll see. Knowing her, she'll up and move to London or Paris or something. She's definitely her own person."

"Wow, you must be proud. Sounds like you did a fabulous job raising them. I gotta ask though, Scout? Is that her real name?"

"Ha!" Lester laughed loudly, loud enough so people looked. He blushed a bit and then answered "No, heavens, that's her nickname. Her real name is Jean Louise Finch, same as the character in 'To Kill A Mockingbird', so we just naturally called her Scout. She never minded as she got older, so it just stuck. In a lot of ways, she's very much like the character in the book. Since 'To Kill A Mockingbird' is one of my favorite books and movies, it worked. And yes, I am a proud Papa. You know what? We even named our black lab Tom, our yellow lab Boo, and our beagle Dill after the characters in the book."

"Okay…. Give me a minute, it's been a while since I've seen the movie and longer since I read the book." Will scrunched up her brow in concentration and leaned forward resting her elbows on the table. It took all of Lester's will power to not look at her chest since it were provocatively displayed just above her lunch plate. "Tom… black lab… oh, Tom Robinson, the character that gets tried for raping the girl?"

"Wow. Very impressive." Lester cheered with just a hint of blush over his face. Will was not oblivious to his double.

"And Boo would be Boo Radley, the quiet neighbor who saves Jem. And Dill was… Dill… a beagle… Dill. Well, I'm in a pickle over Dill." Will laughed and Lester almost spit out his mouthful of grits.

"Dill Harris, the young boy who spent the summer with his Aunt across the street and played with Jem and Scout." Lester answered with a laugh. "Dill was a tough one, no doubt about it. But our beagle was sorta the runt of our litter, and Dill was as well, so it fit."

The waiter came and checked to see about dessert after they both had finished their meal and bottle of wine, and Will insisted they split a chocolate lava cake with some coffee. They both settled back in their chairs and smiled contentedly.

"So, did you do work for Tom Mills? That was tragic what happened up in Corolla." Will said quietly to break the silence.

"Yes. I did. He'd have me help with things from time to time." Lester answered evasively. "Did you do business with him?"

"I did. We had just about everything. Life, disability, and health insurance through the bank and then personal life and all his property and casualty. He was a good and longstanding client with us. We heard Currituck County ruled it a murder, since there was no gun found at the cottage." Will and Lester sat quietly shaking their heads disbelievingly. "Any idea why someone would want to kill a bank branch manager, Lester?"

"Well, I know that Tom made some enemies with his banking practices, particularly with developers. Tom was tough, and he protected the bank like it was his money. Even when things began to loosen up in the last couple of years, he was still squeezing people, and some of them didn't like it much." Lester dipped into the lava cake with his spoon and sampled a bite.

"Ok, I can see that. But do you think his death and Ralph's murder were related?" Will gently probed.

"Oh, well, I don't know." Lester showed concern on his face when he thought for a second. "Timing seems pretty suspicious though. But Ralph hadn't been a part of the bank for years, so I don't see that as a connection."

"Are you handling Ralph's estate?" Will asked as she dipped into the cake for another bite.

Lester blew on his coffee and looked down his nose and offered a nod. "Yep, I am."

"Did you write the wills for Tom and Ralph?"

"No. I referred them both to a firm in Charlotte that handles estate planning and such. That's not really my specialty. I maintained copies of both wills, Ralph's, and Tom's, but that's only because I was appointed Executor in each of them." Lester offered cautiously.

"So, have you scheduled the reading of the Will? I don't really know how any of that works!" Will spoke over her coffee, her beautiful full lips ready to caress the cup for a sip, her big blue eyes looking seductively up at him.

Lester licked his lips and swallowed hard. His mouth was suddenly dry and his palms sweaty. He coughed "Well, no, we have a lot of work to do before we can read the Wills publicly. There has to be a full accounting of assets, we have the Pflieger CPA firm working on that, and then records have to be filed with the courts, notices posted, etc... It could be a few months before we make the Wills public."

"So how does Mrs. Midgett keep going if all the assets are tied up in probate?" Will asked with the appropriate concern, already knowing the answer.

"Well" Lester grinned and shoveled another piece of cake into his mouth. After swallowing he said "that's where you come in. The life insurance Ralph had doesn't go through probate, so she has that money as soon as the insurance company pays out. Of course, she also has her own accounts which provide her substantial funds to tide her over. Tatiana has no worries there."

"Oh Lester" Will chuckled, "Seems the lava cake erupted on your cheek! Lean over here." Will reached across the table and very gently wiped the chocolate off his cheek with her thumb and then seductively licked the gooey goodness off herself, all the while looking at him with her big blue eyes. At that, Lester let out a faint groan, and Will knew the lava cake wasn't the only thing that erupted on Lester.

They both sat for a few minutes, Lester slightly red from embarrassment, Will very satisfied that she was able to control the powerful attorney, and then Will's phone buzzed and broke the silence. After a quick glance at the screen Will said "Lester, I hope you don't mind, but I need to run back to the office. I'll get the check and pay downstairs. You stay and relax a bit." With that, she stood and walked toward the stairs, but before she descended, she turned and smiled at Lester, saying "see you Tuesday." On the way down the stairs she reread the text message and typed a reply 'on my way.' Lester sat and happily watched as all the men in the restaurant watched Will stroll across the room.

EIGHTEEN

"Ok, Angie, whatcha got for me?" Will was feeling pretty chuffed with herself after her lunch triumph, and it was expressed in the smile in her voice.

"Well, don't you sound happy! I guess the lunch with Mr. Finch went well?" Angela knew it had. She'd worked for Will long enough to read her moods, and she could hear that she was in a very good mood.

"It did. It did indeed. Make an appointment for me on our calendar for next Tuesday at 1pm, his office in Manteo. I'm fairly certain we're getting a new client, and I really want to bag the whole account."

"Great Boss, way to bring home the bacon! Want me to run the usual background searches and compile your research?"

"That's OK. You keep after the Midgett case. I got Lester wrapped around my pinky." Will chuckled.

Angela blushed. She knew what that meant. "How bad was it Will?"

"I think Lester enjoyed his lunch more than most."

"WOW. Just WOW. You are a bad girl. LOVE IT!" Angela sung the last words in joyous delight.

"Just business, Angie. Just business." Will chuckled. "I'll be at the office in a few minutes. Let me drive. The rain and wind are really something. I need to concentrate on the road."

"Ok. I'll see you in a few." Angela hung up the line and offered a silent prayer. The weather was worsening, and lives were in danger.

A few minutes later the office door swung open and Will stroll in triumphantly but soaked to the bone from just running across the parking lot. "Days like this I wish we had covered parking." She exclaimed. 'Maybe I should look into that open space down the road. They have parking under the building, and having the offices raised off the ground would be good in the event of flooding' she thought to herself while she dropped her purse and took off her raincoat in her office. She slipped out of her heels to give her feet a break and leaned over the desk to hit the office manager's intercom button "Angela, let's make a note to contact the leasing agent for the space down the street. Maybe it's time for an upgrade!"

"Boss, you have a call on line 3. It's your dad" the receptionist called over the office intercom.

"Thanks Nicole! Got it" Will called back authoritatively. "Hi dad! Everything Ok?" she shifted her tone to her sweetest concerned daughter voice.

"I'm good Wilma. Just wanted to check on my baby girl." Tom Moore came back.

"Dad! Thanks, but I think I'm your only girl…. I'm your only child that I know of any way…. And I stopped being a baby about thirty-five years ago."

"Don't matter. You'll always be my baby girl, and I'll always worry about you… and you are my only child. Period. Between working and caring for you, what time did I ever have for foolin' around? And best I can remember, you were born an adult." They both chuckled for a second.

"Ok, ok, don't get defensive Dad. Just teasing you some. Listen, Daddy, thank you for your help with the Midgett – Mills cases. Your connections got my Angela on the inside with the Sheriff's office. I'm working the interviews and she's diving into the research. Feels like 'Nancy Drew' around here. Makes the boring old insurance office hop with excitement."

"Well, just remember, you aren't the police, so don't get caught on the wrong side of their investigations. You've got feds, local and the county sheriff's all working those cases. Don't get caught steppin' on toes." Tom cautioned. "You know how prickly the feds can get when they think a civilian is mucking around in their case. I bet you heard that enough from me in the thirty years I worked for the Bureau."

"I will Daddy. Angela and I are being careful." Will cooed sweetly to her father.

"Good. Listen, when are you coming to visit? Can you get here this Sunday? We could do brunch at the Country Club. You could bring your clubs and we could grab eighteen too. Been a while since you showed your old man how good you are. What do you say Wilma? Make your dad happy." Tom knew all he had to do was ask, but he missed seeing his baby, and even though she was only 80 miles away, she had her life, her business, and her "interests" that kept her plenty busy.

"Dad. I'll come for lunch, but have you looked at the weather lately? That storm is pounding us, and I don't feel much like playing golf in a monsoon."

"Ok, yeah. Got me there. It's been blowing pretty good here too. So, Lunch? See you about eleven?"

"Yep. I'll see you then. Look, Dad, I gotta run. Angela is giving me the stink eye. Love you. Bye." And Will hung up.

"You need me? Thought I heard my name." Angela appeared in the doorway with her typical helpful look on her face.

"No, just used you as an excuse to get off the phone with my dad. If I didn't, we could talk all afternoon long. Ever since he retired a few years ago, he forgets that I have to work!"

"Ok, well can we talk? I've got some more to share." Angela closed the door to the office and took a seat. "The Sheriff is still waiting on the Crime Lab in Raleigh to process the evidence collected at the two murder sights. I was told that it could be a few weeks before they get anything definitive, but they were able to collect some evidence that might lead them to the killers."

"Oh, so they are thinking more than one killer?" Will rocked back in her chair with a pensive look as she spoke.

"Well, they are working on the assumption that Tom Mills and the Midgett Mansion murders were by separate killers, but they have not ruled out that they all were done by the same person." Angela replied. "Boss, there's something else I wanted to discuss too, but it's kinda personal."

"Of course, Angie. What's up?"

Angela sat awkwardly in her chair. She felt a bit like the schoolgirl tattling on a classmate and it made her squirm inside and out. "The thing is, when I was at the Sheriff's office the other day, Betty Thompson pulled me aside to mention how much she enjoyed lunch with you, and how much she was looking forward to your next meeting. I got the feeling, the strong feeling, that she wasn't just being polite. I think she's interested in you, like, as a date."

Will let out a full belly laugh "Really!" she exclaimed. "What a relief. I was worried you had a medical issue or family crisis or something."

"I know it's kinda trivial, but I wasn't sure ... forget it. Forget I said anything. I'm sorry." Angela felt embarrassed and ashamed. "I shouldn't have put myself in the middle of your personal life."

"Angie! You didn't! Betty did when she talked to you." Will shot back quickly. "Don't think a thing about it. I appreciate you telling me. That will make my life much easier now when I'm talking to Sheriff Thompson."

Angela was relieved and felt a bit emboldened. "Oh, ok. Well, when you do talk to her again, could you put in a good word for me with Deputy Strong? I'd really like to see him socially."

"Angela!" Will blurted out. "What about your husband? Is there something I should know about there, I mean, as long as we're sharing?"

Angela looked down into her lap. She couldn't bear to look at her friend, her boss, and discuss the pain she felt. Her hands were folded together, and she was unconsciously picking at the dead skin on her cuticles. "Well, you see" she started quietly, "Glenn and I haven't really been together for a while now. He hasn't moved out, but he's always traveling with work, and doesn't even come home most weekends. I'm really alone, even with all my fur babies. I think I started rescuing dogs and cats as a crutch for my loneliness." Tears started to well up in the corners of her eyes. "I'm sorry. You don't need to hear this. I feel so ashamed." She began to sob as she slumped in the chair.

Will moved quickly around her desk to comfort her friend. She sat next to her and put her arms around her, holding her close and stroking her hair. "It's Ok. It's Ok Angie" was all she could say.

"I don't love him anymore, and I don't think he loves me" she offered between sobs. "He doesn't even call me at night, and I can't remember the last time either of us said 'I love you' to the other. Even when he comes home, he's not really there. Stays in his office or goes out to hang with friends. It's been years since we've gone on a date, and I think we only have sex on his birthday!"

"Angie…. It's Ok. Let's get you cleaned up and I'll buy you dinner tonight. We can talk it all out and get you …" Will wasn't quite sure where she was going with this, but she knew she had to help. Angela was her friend, one of her best friends, and to see her hurting like this, to hear the pain in her voice, Will knew she had to do something. Will remembered back to when she was a little girl, and how her father would get melancholy thinking about his wife abandoning them. She remembered the pain in his eyes, even though he tried to maintain a brave face. When she tried to comfort him, he'd always say 'character isn't about getting knocked down. It's about getting back up'. That was one of the many lessons he taught her, and at that moment she needed to pay it forward.

NINETEEN

After a delicious meal at Josephine's Sicilian Restaurant in Kitty Hawk, Angela asked Will if she'd like to come back to her place for dessert or coffee? Angela lived right around the corner around Mile Post 4.5 in an ocean front cottage that was a bit of a local landmark. Her grandparents built the place in the mid 60's when round was cool, and it fast became known as the Round House. A bit tired and worn looking, it was still charming, and had a lot of sentimental appeal for Angela. The red paint could use with a fresh coat, but she was reluctant to invest in much renovation when the next big storm could take it out to sea. Several of the cottages north and south of her had been taken, or seriously damaged in recent years, and when the ocean got angry, the high tide line would reach to the bottom of her steps. Angela and Will parked their cars in the small area just off the beach road. Angela's ten-year-old Subaru Outback fit nicely, but Will's monster Cadillac Escalade SUV was a snug fit, with the front bumper nudged into the sand dune and the rear bumper just clearing the white line on the road behind it.

"Are you ready for this?" Angela asked reluctantly.

"Angie, I've been here before. I know the drill." Will was comfortable with dogs and cats, always liked them, but Angela's pack could be a bit overwhelming. As they climbed the stairs to the elevated house, the roar of barking became more fevered. When Angela put the key into the front door, turned the lock and pushed in, they both entered single file, as the police enter during a raid, and then bedlam erupted. A yellow lab, a black lab and a husky all danced around Angela and Will. A corgi jumped between them, everyone begging for attention. Two short hair house cats, one stocky grey male and another fluffy brown female stood on the back of the couch vying for affection, and a large Maine coon cat sat in a chair off to the side, as if he was the Lord of the Manor. "When did you get the husky?" Will shouted with a laugh, as she was buried in kisses from the dogs and lost in a cloud of fur.

"Oh, I guess I didn't tell you. I rescued her from a shelter near Greenville about two months ago. She is a real sweetheart, and so gentle with everyone. Those two love to sleep with her, nestle into her thick fur and make muffins. She just adores them." Angela nodded over to the two housecats on the couch. Angela made her way into the small kitchen to put the coffee on. She stopped to look out over the raging ocean outside, the tops of the waves were being blown off by the strong northeast wind. The tide was out, but the water was still high on the beach. 'If I want to get these dogs walked before dark, I need to get to the beach soon" she thought. "Hey, Will, you want to help me get these guys out for a walk before darkness sets in?" Angela said as she turned to see Will sitting on the floor, surrounded by dogs, and cats, and fur.

"Sure, if they will let me get up." She said jokingly, as she tried to untangle herself from the mound of fur, and affection.

"I gotcha Will. 'Walkies?'" Angela said quickly, and at that, the 4 dogs shot to the back door and began a dance of excitement, tails wagging, each trying to get closer to the door than the next, as if to say, 'me first!' "All right. Everyone got their collar and tags?" she asked the dogs, expecting an answer. "Right! Let's stay together" she pleaded as she opened the door and they raced out onto the deck. Angela and Will followed and watched the herd shuffle down the back stairs and on to the beach. The two ladies followed, although the strength of the wind caused them both to struggle to stay upright and be heard, even when shouting right next to each other. "I wish this storm would hurry up and get here!" Angela shouted.

"If it's this strong now, I shudder to think what it will be like when it hits!" Will shot back. "Wonder if we'll have a mandatory evacuation?"

"Well, I know I'm leaving if this storm is coming here." Angela replied. The dogs were all sniffing and staying close. A couple did their evening business and Angela walked behind to pick it up. She noticed a lone figure running on the beach, coming down from the north and thought to herself 'you gotta be dedicated to run in this weather'. As the figure approached, she could see it was a man, a big beautiful man that she knew and lusted after. "Hey Jack!" she cried out with a wave.

"Hey yourself!" he answered as he broke stride and moved toward the two women. Jack was wearing high end running shoes, running shorts and a high vis day glow orange tank top. His body glistened with sweat, but he wasn't breathing hard, since he ran on the beach almost every day. His physical training was a carry-over from his days in the military, and his broad shoulders and chest, tight waist and rippling athletic muscular limbs were impressive, especially on a six-foot four-inch frame. At thirty-two, he was every bit the eye candy that women adored. "You two on pup patrol?" he asked laughing. "Me too!" as his two dogs moved up behind him. "Thought I'd get in a run after work. I know we won't have the time for that when this storm hits, and these two need the exercise." Will had already dropped to the sand and was stroking the beautiful golden retriever and white great pyrenes. They were almost oblivious to the other dogs, who were checking those two out, as dogs do.

Angela stood among the excitement, hers and the doggos, and quickly offered "Hey Jack, I just put a pot of coffee on at the house. Want to come have a cup with us?"

Jack looked at her with his beautiful blue eyes and then looked down at the sand, almost embarrassed, so un-Jack Strong-like. "Well, if you don't mind the company." He said almost too quiet to be heard over the roaring wind and waves. Jack knew Angela liked him, and he knew she was married, and he also knew the mental image of her had kept him restless at night. Angela didn't hold a candle to the stunning beauty of

Will, but between the two, Jack liked Angela more. She was cute, sweet, smart as a tack, just like Will, but she was less threatening, more accessible, and he liked that she had a softness to her personality and her body. "My coming over won't cause you any trouble, will it?" he said looking straight at her big green eyes, full luscious lips, and sweet rounded smiling face.

"No!" She shouted, looking quickly away to her husky, who had decided it was a good time to try and mount the great pyrenes. She rushed over and pulled him off of her, and then turned to Jack and Will, who both were laughing uncontrollably, and said, "Let's get into the house so everyone can settle down." With that, they all walked back to the house, climbed the stairs to the deck and pushed into the house.

"So, this is where the super sleuth lives, huh? Your lair! Much better than a bat cave." Jack chuckled. "Very nice. Very cozy. Very neat and organized! How do you do it with 4 dogs?"

"And three cats!" both Angela and Will shot back simultaneously, and then laughed together. Jack stood with his mouth agape in utter disbelief.

"Is cleaning all you do?" Jack asked with real interest and amazement. "How do you stay on top of all the fur? I have tumble weeds of fur floating all over my house, and I just have the two dogs."

Angela poured the coffee and put some milk and sugar on the table. "I have a great vacuum, a Dyson that I use for a big cleaning every weekend, and I have two rumba vacuums that run every day to help me keep ahead of it. The biggest mess used to be the litter boxes, but since I've trained the cats to use the toilet, I just flush when I get up, and when I get home and before bed."

Will laughed at that. "I thought something was different. The air is so much cleaner and fresher. You can't even tell you have cats now. Nice work Angie! Cat whisperer!"

"Are you freakin' kidding me? Trained the cats to use the toilet? No way! Seriously?" Jack asked with bewilderment and amazement in equal measure. "Color me impressed!" With that, everyone melted into laughter. Each picked up their coffee. Jack sat on the sofa, Will sat on the floor, surrounded by the dogs, who had all collapsed on the floor to sleep together, and Angela sat on one of the kitchen chairs across the room. The muffled roar of the ocean outside and the creaking of the house from the wind were the only things that interrupted the silence. That, and the snoring from Winston, the corgi, and Apollo, the great pyrenes, who had snuggled together in a most incongruous pairing.

Angela smiled over her coffee at the sight of her dogs and cats cuddled up with Jack's two big boys. "You wonder why people can't get along as well as these guys." They all nodded in agreement. "Any closer to an arrest in the Midgett case, Jack?"

"Well" he began a bit cautiously.

"Jack! It's just us girls! You can tell us" Will shot back quickly. "Hey, it's not like we haven't been helping with the investigation."

"Come on Jack." Angela pleaded.

"Ok, but nothing gets back to Sheriff Thompson, Ok? I mean, if it does, I could lose my job." Jack responded with a boyish grin and a wink. He knew the Sheriff wouldn't mind him sharing details with these two, but he wanted to be clear that nothing could leave the room.

Will and Angela both shook their heads in agreement, and Will said, "Pinky swear!" with a broad smile that showed her perfect teeth. Angela leaned in and hooked pinkies with her, and Jack did the same. Laughter erupted as they all fell back into their seats.

"Oh, we disturbed the sleeping beauties!" Angela mocked, and a couple of her pups looked up from the floor at the group, almost asking 'what's the ruckus about? Can't you see we're sleeping here?'

"So, let's see…" Jack started with a summary of details so far. Angela knew most of it, but she liked watching Jack systematically review each bit of information. Will had gotten bits and pieces from Angela, Betty Thompson, and Lester Finch, so she was glad for the recap. "The intel you provided us Angela, was super helpful. We were able to narrow our suspect pool because of it. Nice work eliminating those with motive based on social media posts. We cross referenced that to financial transactions and phone records and we were able to strike most of those from our suspect pool. The remaining few have been assigned for interviews. Before I left the office today, we had almost everyone accounted for and first interviews scheduled. As you know, some of the suspects are out of town, so we needed to coordinate with local law enforcement for preliminary interviews. If we find anything promising there, we'll be making personal visits for follow up interviews."

"So, anyone looking particularly promising?" Will asked quizzically.

"Well, yes, but I don't think I should go into those particulars right now. We have a lot more work to do before we can point fingers."

"Ok, but …." Angela came back but was cut off by a quick look from Jack.

"We don't want to drag anyone needlessly through the mud just because they had a beef with, or didn't like, the victims. That wouldn't be professional, and frankly, borderline negligent. We don't need the lawsuit for slander or defamation. Some of the suspects are pretty powerful players in local or regional politics, and really well connected." Jack offered solemnly. "Who needs that publicity?"

"So, you've settled on a motive? Or at least the primary target was Midgett and not Kelly Fuco?" asked Will.

"Well, early days yet." Jack came back "Based on the location we assume that Midgett was the target and Fuco was collateral damage, but we haven't discounted the possibility that Fuco was stalked there and Midgett was collateral. The scene, as gruesome as it was, didn't provide much evidence of the killer. The murder weapon was left but didn't appear to have any fingerprints. There were no obvious shoe prints in all the blood, and no trace hairs or fibers that didn't belong there. This was obviously a well planned and executed murder."

"Something that got me" Angela said quietly looking at the great pyrenes curled up with her corgi, "was that this big fella was there, but didn't react! None of the staff mentioned the dog barking. There was no sign from him that something was wrong. Was he drugged, or did he know the killer?"

"You know, we've thought of that. I had his blood tested before I adopted him to check for sedatives, and the vet didn't find anything. Clean as a whistle." Jack responded "that has us thinking more towards someone Midgett knew and knew well. I can't see Apollo sitting by while his owner is hacked to death by a stranger."

"Apollo? Is that your name for him?" Angela wondered.

"No. That was his name when I got him. Mrs. Midgett gave me all his records. He answers to it, so I wasn't going to confuse him. Besides, it works with my crazy little girl there, Molly. Molly and Apollo, my babies now." Jack offered with a smile.

Angela looked at the pile of fur on her living room floor and smiled. She loved animals, her own and those she met on the street. She'd rescued stray cats, rabbits, dogs, helped injured birds. She always thought being surrounded by animals was preferable to people. "Jack, what will you do with Apollo and Molly when the storm hits? Do you want me to evacuate them with my crew?"

Jack sat stunned for a moment "I hadn't even given that any thought. I suppose I'll be pretty busy then and they won't be safe if the island floods. Can you handle a couple more?"

"Look at them Jack. They've blended right into the pack. Easy peezy." Angela responded with a wave to the room.

"Angie, My dad lives over in Edenton and he's already told me to come. He's got loads of room, a big yard, and he'd love the company. I'll call him and let him know. He'll love it." Will offered with the confidence of a daddy's girl who knew he'd help out.

"Ok then. Let's keep our fingers crossed that we won't need to evacuate..." Angela said.

"... but it's good to have a plan." Jack finished her thought and smiled warmly.

Will sensed that it was a good time to leave Angela and Jack alone, so she made her goodbye's, hugged Angela, kissed the dogs, snuffled the cats, and grabbed her purse and bolted down the steps with a scream and into the safety of her car. The wind was stronger, more forceful and the gusts were swaying road signs. The rain had picked back up and was coming in sheets. It was a dark and stormy night.

Angela watched her friend and boss drive off and turned from the front door to walk back into the house. Jack was standing behind her, and she almost walked into him. "Oh, sorry, didn't see you there." She said apologetically.

"No worries. Didn't mean to startle you."

"Listen, the weather is really bad right now" she said as she hooked her thumb over her shoulder in the general direction of 'outside'. "Want another cup of coffee and wait to see if it calms down before I run you back to your car? It's not that late yet, and I would sure enjoy the company. I mean if you don't have plans. I'm sure you have someone to get home to, and I don't want to keep you. It's just so nasty outside, and..."

Jack laughed, held her shoulders with his strong hands and looked deep into her green eyes. "Angela, I have everything I need and care about right here. I can stay as long as you need me. I just don't want to cause you any trouble. I don't think your husband would be too happy having me here, do you?"

Angela felt her legs go wobbly, and her stomach churn. She knew she'd have to address all of this, but she didn't think it would be so soon. "Can we sit down? I need a drink, and not coffee. You want something?"

"I do. Have any bourbon?"

"Would Gentleman Jack work? I have Woodford Reserve too." Angela responded as she walked into her kitchen and pulled two tumblers from the cabinet.

"Jack works just fine, thanks. You need some help?"

"Jack, you have no idea!" Angela called out with a laugh. "Do you have a degree in psychology, cause I need all the help I can get." She walked back into the living room with the glasses and ice. "Liquor is in the hutch over there" she motioned across the room to the far wall, and Jack walked over and opened it.

"What do you want?" Jack asked over his shoulder while looking at the selection of spirits.

Angela chuckled to herself and said, "I'll have what he's having."

"What's so funny?"

"Oh, just thinking of "When Harry Met Sally", the diner scene."

Jack paused for a beat and then erupted in laughter. "Meg Ryan. Fake orgasm! That was hilarious. Of course, I only saw it on the TV. I wasn't born when that movie came out."

"Neither was I!" Angela shot back "But I still love movies, especially older movies... the classics. I curl up and watch them most nights."

They filled their glasses with ice and bourbon and sat back on the couch to talk.

"Jack, my life is a mess. I got married right out of high school and I've been miserable ever since. He's not the person I thought he was. He's not mean. He doesn't lay a hand on me. Well, actually that's a big part of the problem for me. We aren't intimate. He travels constantly with work, he makes an OK living, but I think he likes the travel, and he stays away weeks at a time. And when he's home, he goes out with his buddies and fishes. I'm just really lonely." Jack shook his head in understanding but remained silent. He knew she needed to talk, and he wasn't going to say something that might upset her more. They both took a sip of their drink. "Look, I know we've just really met. I don't know that much about you and I'm sorry I'm dumping on you like this..."

"Hey, it's Ok." Jack said quietly. "Can I be honest? I don't really have a lot of friends here, and I really like you. I liked you the first time I met you." Jack reached across the couch and touched Angela's hand. She took his hand and he leaned toward her, their eyes locked on to each other, when the house suddenly shook with a shudder. The dogs all awoke and began barking which sent the cats all into a bedroom to hide. Angela bolted off the couch and went to the back door and flipped on the floodlight. The ocean was raging, eating large chunks of beach with each wave. The wooden furniture on her deck had been thrown to one side and sat in a pile.

"I need to get that furniture off the deck" Angela squealed in a panic "and I need to drop the storm shudders. I guess it's time to batten down the hatches."

Jack and Angela moved quickly to secure what they could. Movement outside was difficult given the strength of the wind and the blowing fine grain sand. When they made it back inside, they both were raw from the elements.

"Angela, why don't you pack a bag and come to my house. My place is up on a bluff overlooking the sound in old Kitty Hawk Village. Let's get away from the ocean. You can stay there until an evacuation order comes, Ok?"

Angela didn't contemplate the offer long. She ducked into her bedroom, pulled a suitcase, and filled it with clothes, and then went into the bathroom and loaded her toiletries into an overnight case. "All set" she said when she emerged back into the living room. "Let me get the kitty carrier loaded and then we can pack everyone into my car. Oh, Jack, do me a favor and put some cans of cat food in a shopping bag. They are in the pantry over there" she pointed to the door in the kitchen.

"Got it! Where's your dog food?"

"They eat dry food. It's in the big bag on the floor of the pantry."

"Ok, I'll grab that too! Where are your car keys, I'll load your car?"

Angela flipped her keys to him, and she began loading the frightened cats into a large crate. "Ok, you guys ready for an adventure. Everyone got collars and tags?" she asked to the dogs who all were milling around waiting to be taken to the car. "Ok, y'all wait here. I'm going to get these guys in the car first." She picked up the crate and headed for the door. It flung open when Jack bounded back into the room.

"I got that. You stay here and get everyone's leash on. Glad we're going. It's crazy out there now." Jack grabbed the crate and headed back out into the darkness. Angela watched from the window as he got her babies situated in her Outback. She turned to the dogs and began putting their leashes on when Jack reentered the house. "Great. Let's get this circus on the road." The tone of Jacks voice was even but forceful. He was in full commando mode now, and that made Angela quiver with excitement she had not felt in years.

TWENTY

"Sheriff Thompson" Betty answered her phone.

"Sheriff, this is Jack. The weather is deteriorating fast. Do we need to rally the troops and get into the command center?"

"Jack, you sit tight. I'll make some calls and get back to you. Alert the other members of the team to stand by and be ready for a lengthy deployment."

"Roger. Copy that." Jack clicked off the call and turned to Angela. "You might want to call Will and see if her dad's ok with everyone showing up on his doorstep. We could be getting an evac order tonight."

Angela grabbed her phone and hit speed dial. "Will? I'm with Jack. We left the beach and moved to his house, but he thinks an evacuation could be ordered tonight. Yes. No. Yes, I've got everyone here. Ok, I'll call you back when we hear more. Ok. Good. Thanks, Will." She hung up. "We're good to go. Her dad insisted, no question. Will's calling the rest of the office staff to see if they need a place to get to, and she's extended that offer to any family that's here too. I'm calling my folks now." Angela went into the next room to chat with her parents while Jack watched the Weather Channel. The storm had changed, and it was a monster. It was now moving up the coast and headed for a direct hit on Cape Hatteras, and then the expected path would take it just off the coast as it moved north. Jack knew that meant the OBX would get pounded. Seriously pounded. He'd been through two tours in Afghanistan, but this enemy had him really worried.

"Angela, we'll hunker down here until we get more from the Sheriff and Emergency Management. If we can wait, we'll evacuate you in the morning. Traveling at night in this weather would be crazy." Jack spoke while studying the TV, not knowing if Angela was even listening.

"Mom and Dad have already boarded up the gift shop and house and are headed to my aunt in Raleigh." Angela called out from the bedroom. That was a relief. Angela's parents were natives to the OBX and had ridden out many a storm in their sound side home, but this storm was different, and Angela was happy to hear they were being sensible this time. The lights flickered as she walked into the living room. "Ugh, Jack, you have a generator?"

"Actually, yes. It will automatically kick on when power goes out." He said reassuringly. "That was one of the 'perks' that attracted me to this house. The previous owners built it to withstand a force five hurricane and put the bells and whistles into it. It's a smart house that I can control from my iPhone. Automatic storm shudders, generator, the works."

They both looked out of the living room windows at the rain and wind lashing the trees and houses. It was a scary sight. They could see lights in the distance, so the power was still good on the island, but no one knew how long that would last.

Jack was the first to break the silence "Let's try and get some sleep. The dogs are safe. The cats have hunkered down, and we have a LONG day ahead of us tomorrow. You take my bedroom, and I'll sleep here on the couch so I can keep an eye on things."

"Jack! You'll never get any sleep out here. You're the one who'll have the long day tomorrow. I just have to drive an hour inland, and then I can relax." Angela was having none of Jack's bravado. She knew how difficult the next several days would be for him. Regardless of his training in the Seals, he needed some rest. "You've got more than one bedroom. I'll take the guest bed. You sleep in your bed. No arguments.

Got it!"

"Yes ma'am. Roger that." He snapped back with military precision, and then chuckled at Angela's resolve. "All right. Let's go to bed." They made their way to their bedrooms, with dogs following behind. Winston, the corgi, followed Apollo into Jack's bedroom. Angela and Jack stood outside their doorways watching the scene.

"Well, I guess they're an item now!" Angela laughed. "But, seriously, Jack. Thank you for taking us in tonight. I appreciate the help."

"Don't mention it. You'd do the same. Try and sleep. See you in the morning. Good night."

"Good night." Angela walked into the room and stepped over the dogs, who had already staked their claim to available floor space. As she undressed, her mind wandered away from the raging storm outside to the raging torrent of feelings she had for the man in the room next door.

TWENTY-ONE

"Wilma Ruth Moore! You made it!" The voice of Tom Moore boomed out across the front lawn as Will emerged from her Escalade and stretched her back. She looked lovingly at her father, who was dressed in worn jeans and a polo shirt. He stood a shade over 6' tall and was still trim, even after a few years removed from his FBI days.

"Hi dad! You look good. Retirement definitely agrees with you. Can you help us corral the tribe?" Will turned as Angela pulled in behind her.

"Hi Mr. Moore. Thank you for letting us stay. I promise to clean all the fur before we leave!" Angela exclaimed as she walked to greet her host.

Tom and Will hugged and then he gave Angela a fatherly hug. "Angie don't worry about it. I love the company. Now, let's get you unpacked." Tom grabbed the cat crate from the rear of the Cadillac while Winston and Apollo hopped out of the back seat. Angela's other three dogs climbed out of the Outback and ran after their human and into the house.

"The wind doesn't seem too bad here." Will commented as she pulled her luggage from the car and walked toward the house. "Has there been much rain?"

"Oh, it's been coming in waves. We're having a little break right now but earlier you couldn't see the road it was so heavy." Tom explained as he walked back to the cars to get another load.

"Mr. Moore don't worry about my stuff. I got it. You go in and visit. I'm right behind you." Angela pulled her two bags from the car and wheeled them up to the house just as a few drops of rain began to fall. "Wow, Mr. Moore, you have a lovely home!"

Angela stood on the wrap around porch with robin's egg blue paint on the ceiling of the classic white southern home with dark green shutters. She looked into the entry foyer which bisected the house down the middle and had stairs up to the second level toward the rear of the house. Off to one side was a library with floor to ceiling bookshelves stocked with leather bound classics and more current hardbound favorites from Grisham, Patterson, King, and Follett. Opposite that was an office, which had the usual equipment, but situated on some spectacular furniture. The focal point of the room was the partner's desk with opposing executive chairs. Off to one side was a large gun safe, and there were several antique handguns mounted on the walls. Both rooms have rounded bay windows with lush window seats in each, and a view of the front garden beyond the porch. As Angela walked toward the back of the house, the large family room / kitchen appeared and beyond that, she admired the screened porch that covered the back of the house. The view was an expansive area of grass and pine trees that backed up to a golf course. It was beautiful. The dogs had all congregated on the cool slate floor of the porch and were sleeping peacefully after the excitement of arriving. The cats were laying on a sofa there enjoying the solitude like they owned the place. Will and her Dad were in the kitchen.

"Angela, leave your bags and come eat. We're about to make some lunch for us. I'll get you settled after you've had something to eat. I'm guessing you didn't have a proper breakfast this morning."

"No, I didn't. Not sure about Will, but it was chaos for me trying to pack and get off the island so lunch would be great. Mr. Moore, can I help?" Angela asked as she came toward the granite counter in the middle of the room.

"You sit. And call me Tom. I used to supervise kids younger than you, and they called me Tom. Ok?"

"Ok, Tom. I appreciate the hospitality. Will, is anyone else from the office evacuating here?"

Will looked up from slicing some fruit and cheese for a platter "Hummm. I spoke to almost everyone. They were all evacuating, but they had places inland to get shelter with family or friends. The only person I didn't reach was Nicole Dorcas. She's the cute girl who works reception for us now Dad. You met her when you came by last time."

"I did. Very cute. Very sweet. Very southern." Tom said without judgement.

"She has family in Raleigh she goes to visit on the weekends, and her boyfriend has folks in Durham, so I'm guessing she's gone there." Angela chimed in.

They settled around the kitchen island and nibbled on the charcuterie platter that Tom and Will created as the rain began pouring down and the wind blew it sideways onto the porch, scattering all the animals back into the open floor plan family area.

TWENTY-TWO

The Command Center was humming with activity when Sheriff Thompson walked in at 6:30am. "Tink? Jeff? Did y'all go home?"

"No ma'am" they answered simultaneously without looking up.

"My ex took the kids to her cousin's in Greenville" Deputy Tink Taylor continued "they're safe so no reason for me to go home. Too much to do here."

Deputy Jefferson Daniels explained, "Boss, my folks bugged out a few days ago to stay with family in Charlotte. Making a mini vacation out of this storm. They took my sister and brother with 'em, so I'm good. Rather keep working anyway. Between the storm and the Midgett case, there's just too much to do. I got a little shut eye on the floor of the conference room."

"Anyone seen Deputy Strong or Jennifer Jennette this morning?" Betty asked as she scanned the room. "And where's Tim Cudworth?"

"I heard from Jennette. There was a tree down across the road in Colington and she was stuck waiting for the fire department to move it. That was about an hour ago, so she should be here any time now." Deputy Taylor offered. "Haven't heard from Jack. I think Cudworth is on patrol in Kitty Hawk, Sheriff."

"Sheriff, Tink and I have been running down leads on the Midgett case. We have a theory."

"Jeff, that's great, but right now we need to manage this storm evacuation. Let's get back to the Midgett case when this storm quiets down." Betty Thompson looked at Deputy Daniels reassuringly and he nodded his understanding.

"Hey everyone! I've got Duck Donuts!" Jack boomed as he walked in carrying several boxes of warm fresh donuts, and a cheer went up from the exhausted troops. "I'll drop them in the break room. Help yourselves."

"Glad you could join the party, Jack" Betty shot a smirk and the corners of her mouth turned up ever so slightly.

"Had to get my pups to safety and batten down the hatches. I'm here for the duration now." He shot back with no apology.

The Command Center was state of the art, with stations for every concern and contingency. Monitors for weather, emergency services, power, hospital services, Red Cross, road conditions, and more lit the room with flashing red and green indicators. Traffic cameras were on other monitors to check on the network of bridges that connected the islands to the mainland and each other. The Coast Guard, National Park Service and NC Fish and Wildlife all had people crammed into the Center. The Sheriff ran point, but everyone had a role. They were going to have to survive on donuts and coffee and whatever MRE's they have in storage for a while.

Sheriff Thompson stood up on a desk in the middle of the room "Alright, people, we've got folks all over the county who will need our help. Get word to Jennette to work Colington and Kill Devil Hills and Tim help with Kitty Hawk. Tink, you're from Mann's Harbor, so you get there and keep it safe. Jeff, you're from Roanoke, so you work this island. I'll take Nags Head. Jack, you handle Duck and Southern Shores. Keep in constant contact. Let's get into our cars and get out there and help get people out of their houses and into shelters, or off the island altogether. This Command Center will coordinate communications and help us work with local emergency services. Let's stay smart and stay safe."

TWENTY-THREE

The storm is now located 300 miles east of Ocean City Maryland... The TV weatherman reported. After almost twenty-four hours of being lashed by the near hurricane force winds and massive full moon high tide, the storm of this century was moving away from the Outer Banks. The dawn broke to a spectacular day. The wind was calming, the sun was bright, and the air was dry and crisp. It was a Chamber of Commerce day, except for the destruction and debris left by the storm. The Sheriff's Office deployed once the storm passed and made their way around the county to assess the damage.

"Ok, let me get a sit rep from everyone." Sheriff Thompson called out on her radio. "Jack?"

"Have not seen much damage. Road from Duck through Southern Shores is clear."

"Great! Tim?" Sheriff Thompson called.

"Sheriff, we have flooding on the beach road near the Black Pelican. I've alerted NCDOT and I'm parked just north of the area with lights on. Looks like some of the road washed out and the dune is completely gone."

Damn, thought the Sheriff, every time there's a storm that area floods and the road gets taken. "Ok, Stay on station and wait for back up. I'll send Jack to coordinate. Jennifer, give me some good news please?"

"Sheriff, there are some trees down on Colington but KDH looks good."

"Good. Jennifer, you approach on the beach road from the south and block traffic when you get to the flooded area. We don't need any fools trying to run through standing water. Jeff, how's Roanoke?"

"We're Ok here. Just some debris blown around but looks peaceful. No flooding here."

"Got it. I need you to run down to Hatteras. We've got a section of 12 that washed away. There's a new inlet to the south so block traffic. Tink? What's happening on the mainland?"

"All quiet here. No damage, no issues. Roads are quiet."

"Roger that. Good to hear. Meet me back at the Command Center. Everybody, keep hydrated and check in with your families so they know you're safe, and you know their ok."

"Sheriff?" the radio crackled.

"Yep. What's up control?"

"Report of a disturbance in South Nags Head. You're the closest to the scene. Can you respond?"

"Roger. I'm on it. Send me the details" Betty wasted no time in accelerating her Charger through Whalebone Junction and down Highway 12. Her computer screen blinked the address and it flashed into GPS mode to guide her to the location. "What's the nature of the disturbance?"

"Neighbors have called in seeing a naked man waving a gun outside a house. They report he's screaming "I killed my Dad." The neighbors cannot identify the man." The command operator reported in a calm controlled voice. "Do you want back up Sheriff?"

"Let me get on scene and assess the situation. I can always retreat and call in the cavalry if it escalates."

The Sheriff drove down Hwy 12 into South Nags Head. On her left were the row upon row of cottages that made this a quiet vacation spot for so many. On her right was the endless sound side marsh, which extended down the barrier islands over 50 miles. With lights and siren going, she whirled into South Oregon Inlet Road, made the sharp left curve, and then accelerated to the right at South Seagull Drive.

When Betty rolled up to the South Bodie Island Court address, it didn't take her long to find the problem. The midnight blue Charger rolled to a quiet stop about one hundred yards from the naked man holding a rifle. He was tall and lean, athletic looking, like a man who worked outdoors for a living, not ripped but very well put together. He had brownish blond hair pulled into a short ponytail and a pleasant, rugged angular face with stubble from day old growth and a thick mustache. His broad chest and muscular arms were covered in tattoos and his skin had a healthy glow from a tan. From this distance, Betty thought this guy could be a model, or a porn star.

Sheriff Thompson didn't have the car siren on now, but she kept the lights flashing to get everyone's attention. Using the bull horn in the car Betty calmly asked "Please, put the weapon down on the street and back away."

The man had a crazy confused look in his soft brown eyes, which Betty assumed was why he was naked, but she kept focused on him, hoping he would comply. She repeated her instructions "Put the weapon on the ground now!"

"Hey police lady, I killed my daddy. I ain't scared o' you. You want my gun? You gonna have to come take it from me!" the naked man screamed at Betty.

"Ok" Betty replied, "but tell me where your daddy's body is first. That'll make it easier for us to bury you both at the same time."

"Well, shoot, you don't mess around, now do you Ms. Policewoman. I like that." The naked man crowed with a smile on his face as he bent over to lay the rifle on the street. 'Whatcha want me to do now?"

"You need to back up and then lay on the ground face down." The Sheriff commanded through the bull horn.

Surprisingly, he did, sort of. "I don't want to burn my willy on the pavement. Can I lay down over there in the sand?" he asked politely as he gestured to an area to his left.

"Sure. That will be fine but move slowly. What's your name, anyway? Since you don't have any ID on you that I can see, you need to help me out now." Betty asked while she put the still running vehicle in park, opened her door and got out once the man was away from his gun. She clicked the safety on her service weapon, just in case, and kept her hand on it ready to draw if needed.

"I'm Ralph Midgett. The bastard son of Ralph Midgett!" shouted the man as he got on the sand next to the road.

"And you say you killed Ralph Midgett?" Sheriff Betty qualified.

"That's right. I shot him dead!" Ralph Jr. replied.

"Well, Then I guess I need to arrest you for murder." Betty said calmly. "Put your hands behind your back for me so I can put handcuffs on you."

He did, and she read him his rights while he lay on the sand. She noticed that he was as nice to look at from behind as he was from the front, and that the tattoos went all around his broad back in an intricate pattern. They weren't violent or satanic. They were art, beautiful, full color works of art on his skin.

"Now Ralph, where are your clothes? Why are you naked in the middle of the street in South Nags Head?"

"They started itching me, almost to the point I felt like my skin was on fire, so I stripped 'em off over yonder under my house. I thought the

Lord was punishing me for killin' my daddy." Ralph Jr. said with a soulful look on his face and some moisture building up in his eyes. Betty could see this man was troubled, but she was convinced he didn't killed Ralph Midgett.

"Ok, Ralph, let's walk over there and put your pants on." It was then that Betty noticed Ralph seemed to really like her, since, when he stood up, his little soldier was stiff at attention, and it wasn't little at all. "Right, clothes. Now!" Sheriff Thompson muttered as she walked with him over to the house and gathered up his clothing. He sat on the steps to his house and she helped him put on his pants without incident, although his erection did not subside and made Betty's mocha skin blush when she pulled up his trousers and zipped up his fly. 'He could do porn,' she thought to herself while being careful to not pinch his ample member in the teeth of his zipper.

Standing this close to him, Betty noticed he didn't have the usual signs of alcohol or drug intoxication. She also noticed that she was aroused and a bit flushed. Ralph was behaving himself like a perfect gentleman, albeit one who was in handcuffs, and under arrest, and had confessed to murder. But, damn, he was fine to look at and got her hot. She needed to move things along before her fantasies got the better of her professionalism.

But then, he bent over and kissed her on the cheek and whispered "Thank You. Thank you for noticing me. Everyone looks at me like I'm invisible." Sheriff Thompson stepped back and looked into his face and saw tears. She quietly said, "Let's go. I need to get your statement and get you processed." Then she took him by the arm and began walking to her car. When she opened the back door and helped him climb inside, she said, "You're welcome, Ralph."

TWENTY-FOUR

"Hey boss? Did you hear they arrested Ralph Midgett's killer?" Angela called out toward Will's office.

"No! Who is it?" came the shout from behind her desk. Will had just gotten back from lunch with clients and was taking off her linen jacket and placing it on the hanger. She was, as always, dressed to kill, but professionally. Her linen suit was yellow with a pencil skirt that came to just above her knees. With that she wore a silk blouse with a beautiful floral print in pastel colors with the top three buttons undone, and yellow 4" heels. Her make-up was reserved, but her lipstick drew attention to her sensual mouth. Her trademark blond hair was pulled into a tight ponytail that swished when she walked. She looked like a gorgeous ice cream cone that everyone would want to lick.

"It was... Damn, I didn't see you come in. You left here in jeans and a tee shirt and come back dressed like that! I hope to god you didn't pay for your lunch?" Angela said standing in the office doorway.

"Oh no. They paid. And they will keep paying. Count on it." Will chuckled with a broad grin showing her perfect white smile. "I got those boys at JLJ Realty eating out of my hands. As long as I show 'em some leg, bat my baby blues, laugh at their off-color jokes and give 'em a peek of these" she said as she leaned over her desk, "they will always be mine." She and Angie then laughed as Will pulled out the six-figure premium check from her briefcase. "I love my job!" she exclaimed. "Now, let's get this into the bank before somebody robs us."

Angie took the check and spun on her heels to leave, but then realized why she came in. Turning back to face Will, Angela said "Hey, Ralph Midgett killed Ralph Midgett, can you believe it?"

"What?" The shocked look on Will's face didn't require words, but she questioned "Can you run that one by me again?"

As Will plopped into her office chair Angie told the story "Talked with my connection in the Sheriff's department and they told me that Sheriff Thompson arrested Ralph Midgett for the murder of Ralph Midgett. Seems Ralph was quite the "playa' before he settled down."

"That man was always a player, even after he "settled down" Will interrupted using air quotes.

"Well, he had an illegitimate son about thirty-five years ago with a waitress who worked at Owens Restaurant. He didn't want to get married at that time, so he paid her to keep it all very quiet. She was on the beach for summer work and went back to the mainland after Labor Day. She had the baby but told Ralph she would only keep quiet as long as he kept paying support for her and his son. To spite him, she gave her son his full name. She passed away in a one car accident when the boy was twelve and her parents raised him after that. When he turned eighteen, they told him everything that they knew, and he moved to the island. Now, as you know, there are a ton of Midgett's living around here, so no one knew that the boy was Ralph's son, and he never said. He worked odd jobs, construction and maintenance, and then, in a twist of fate, got a small business loan from Outer Banks Bank to start his company."

"Midgett Maintenance?" Will asked with some shock in her voice.

"Yes. Got it in one. Well played." Angie joked.

"That's our account, isn't it?" Will asked sheepishly. She knew all of the big accounts and handled them personally, but the smaller accounts, she only had a vague knowledge of. That's why she paid her people so well. They kept the little fish happy while she fried the big fish.

"It is. We've had them since they opened, and he's grown the business nicely. I could see in a few years, that account will come up on your radar. Of course, getting sent to prison for murder might put a full stop to that."

"So, your contact in the Sheriff's office. Did he tell you about the evidence against Ralph Jr?"

"How do you know it's a HE? I have girlfriends too." Angie protested sheepishly.

"Everyone knows you swoon for Jack Strong, Angie! Geez, I think even your husband knows!" Betty laughed.

"Don't say that. Not even joking. Glenn can never know. I'm filing for divorce and I want it to be as quiet and uncomplicated as possible. We've already agreed to split and he's letting me keep the house without a fight since it's my family property. Everything else is pretty much fifty-fifty, except my fur babies. I get to keep all the kids. He actually told me he never really liked having all of them!" Angela just shook her head. "It's like he never really knew me."

"I'm sorry Angie. If you need some time, a vacation, get away for a while..." Will offered.

"No. God no. I love working here. My work, this place, keeps me sane. I'll be fine. Not like he was around all that much anyway. But thank you for the offer." Angie smiled with a hint of moisture forming in her eyes.

"Well, about the evidence? Whatcha got?" Will asked cheerily. "Give us some juicy news."

"Oh, right" Angie righted herself and cleared her throat. "He confessed."

"What!?!?"

"Yep. Jack… er, my contact told me that he was naked in the streets of South Nags Head waving a gun. Sheriff Thompson talked him down, disarmed him, and got him dressed. He confessed right there in the street! Said he shot his daddy. He shot Ralph Midgett."

"Wait… Ralph was butchered! He wasn't shot!"

"Yep. They are holding him on the weapons charge, and public indecency, and having a psychological evaluation done, but Betty and Jack both know he didn't kill Ralph Midgett. They also asked him to give them a blood sample to test for paternity, just to prove his story. Ralph had no problem with that, so we'll find out soon enough if he really is Ralph's son."

"Well, that could throw a monkey wrench into the reading of the will. Between the wife, his one living ex, and his two kids, now three, there will be some pie slicing. But with his assets, everyone should do Ok." Will mused.

"Hey, let me get to the bank and get this deposited!" Angie said as she headed for the door.

TWENTY-FIVE

"Hey, Mom, this is Jenn. Call me when you get this message. I haven't been able to speak with Stevie for a while now and I'm getting nervous too. I love you! Bye." 'The storm did a lot of damage in the Norfolk – Virginia Beach area but it was unlike Steve Lawrence to not communicate with me or mom,' Jennifer thought after hanging up. 'Maybe it was time for me to work the phones and track him down. He's probably holed up in a cabin in the mountains with no cell service and some pretty young thing having a 'storm vacation'. If he is, then he is just like his father!'

TWENTY-SIX

"Sheriff Thompson" Betty answered crisply.

"Hey Betty, this is Will Moore."

"Well hello there. What can I do for you?" Betty asked playfully.

"Ok, well, it's late on a Friday, so I'm sure you already have plans, but I was wondering if you'd like to catch drinks and dinner together?" Will asked sheepishly.

"Oh, oh…" This was an unexpected pleasure and Betty was knocked back and wrong footed for a second. She quickly regrouped and switched into smart ass mode. "Ok. You thinking tonight, just fun, and casual? Or do you want to sweep me off my feet with a proper Saturday night date? You know, wine me and dine me?"

Will chocked on her bottled water and coughed with that unexpectedly frank response. "Give me a minute to recover" she wheezed. "Damn girl, you got me."

"Sorry. Smart ass is kind of a default setting for me." Betty was ginning like a Cheshire cat and feeling pretty good. She was hoping to hear from Wilma Ruth again. She thoroughly enjoyed their lunch together and she wanted to see if the feeling was mutual.

"So, what time should I pick you up tomorrow night?" Will was going all in.

"Seriously? I hope you aren't a love 'em and leave 'em kinds girl, Wilma. I'm too emotionally fragile for that!" Betty said with a chuckle. "If you aren't a one and done playa, why don't you pick me up at seven thirty tonight and we can discuss where we'll go for our big date tomorrow night over some drinks and beach music? You do play double headers, don't you?"

"Oh, Ok. I see what you're doing. Will you bring your handcuffs? I've been known to get frisky." Will was enjoying this immensely. She loved a person who could be as playful and fun as her imagination would allow, and she seems to have found one in Betty Thompson.

"Of course. Can't leave home without them."

"Text me your address. I'll swing bye at seven thirty and we'll have some fun. Oh, and this is my treat. No arguments. I don't want to have to get rough with you, at least not in public."

"Damn girl, I thought you were fun." Betty shot back, and they both laughed lustily. "Ok, your treat. Thank you, and Will, thanks for calling. See you soon. Bye."

"Bye."

They both hung up and smiled contentedly with a playful twinkle in their eye and butterflies in their stomach. Each in their offices, comfortable in their executive chairs, commanding million-dollar budgets, and both feeling like teenage girls with the excited anticipation of something new.

Betty picked up her phone, opened the text app and sent Will her details and then rushed out of her office before anyone could stop her. She needed to get home and change. She had a date!

TWENTY-SEVEN

"Wow! How do you do it? You look amazing!" Betty said as she stood aside her front door and let Will saunter in. Betty admired the sheer cream linen blouse with a thin blue pinstripe and the short white skirt that showed off Will's amazing tan smooth legs, which ended at her white deck shoes. She complimented it all with some beautiful jewelry. A simple silver chain necklace with a single aquamarine stone dropped seductively into her cleavage, two large silver hoop earrings adorned her pierced ears, a simple silver band on her thumb and a silver bracelet watch finished her look. Will had her hair pulled back into her usually ponytail tied with a pink scrunchy and just some evening eye shadow, blush, and pink lipstick. She didn't wear much make up. She didn't have to. "Well," Betty said excitedly, "come on in, I just want to grab my lipstick and a clutch. I guess since we'll have cocktails, I should bring my license too. Lord listen to me. Thirty-nine and babbling like a teenager."

Will spun around and looked appraisingly over her date for the night. "Thank you kindly, missy. You look pretty special yourself. Nice to see you out of your uniform." Will drawled in her sweetest southern accent as she strolled into the house. Betty had chosen to wear a white crotched V neck crop top with a sexy white lace push up bra underneath, showing off her beautiful breasts and tight belly. Riding low on her hips was a tan denim mini skirt. Betty thought her outfit just glowed against her mocha skin. A beautiful turquoise necklace adorned her neck and dangling silver earrings hung from her pierced ears. Some flip-flops with cute sparkles and jewels and a toe ring on her left second toe finished her look with style. Betty wore almost no make-up, letting her god given beauty shine through, but she did love wearing red lipstick when she was going out. "I like your place, Betty. How long have you lived here?"

The condo was located on some reclaimed marsh land on Roanoke Island not far from the causeway to the beach or the mainland. It was newer construction, the second floor of a three-story block, with each unit taking up the entire floor, three bedrooms, three and a half baths, in twenty-four-hundred square feet. Decorated in a relaxed home style with casual furniture and pictures and mementos from Betty's life and travels, it had a fabulous view of Currituck Sound with the shock of brilliant sunrises every morning, and the twinkle of beach lights dancing on the water every night. It was homey but not corny. It was tasteful, but not flashy. It was Betty.

Betty finished putting her lipstick on, popped it into her clutch purse and turned to Will. "Oh, I bought here right after I moved to the island. I got it for a steal as a foreclosure. I like it for the location. Easy to work and easy to the beach, but relatively quiet and private, especially off season or during the week. Most of the units are rentals for folks coming to enjoy the sport fishing which is usually on the weekend. It's nice, but now that I'm Sheriff I'm looking for someplace with a bit more privacy. I can't afford anything close to where you live. Everyone here leaves me alone, but sometimes the noise from weekend partygoers makes it tough to sleep."

"How do you know where I live?" Will asked sharply. Betty shot her a 'seriously' look and Will grinned. "Oh right, you're a cop. Got it. Hey, cut me some slack. You certainly don't look like a cop right now!" They both chuckled in amusement, and then Will said "Hey, wait. You have something on your lip" and put her hands up to hold Betty's face.

"What? What is it?" Betty protested.

"My mouth!" and Will leaned in and kissed her deeply and passionately. Betty's arms wrapped around Will's slim waist and pulled her close. Will ran her fingers through Betty's hair and pulled her head back so she could caress her neck. Both of them could feel the electricity and the heat.

"Well, that was an unexpected, but thoroughly enjoyable and welcome surprise. Is that how you say 'hello' to all your dates?" Betty blurted out, with a huge smile on her face.

"Ok. Ok. I'm sorry. That was truly, um, impulsive." Will stuttered in reply, feeling a bit embarrassed and wrong footed, as a blush rose up on her cheeks. "But listen, let me be clear, I don't date. I've lived here for a while now, like 14 years, and I can count on one hand the number of 'dates' I've been on. Seriously. I don't date, but I felt like you were different, and I needed to see…"

"Hey, Wilma, don't apologize." Betty cooed softly, "I loved it. I've never had anyone sweep me off my feet before, and, girl, you rocked it." Betty stepped in close and looked up into Will's beautiful blue eyes, put her hand on her cheek and kissed her softly, slowly, then passionately. Then she whispered "Now, since you've started this fire, are you gonna let it burn, or put it out? I mean, seriously…" She batted her eyes playfully as she looked into Will's beautiful face

With that, the passion floodgates opened, and they both dissolved into each other's arms and surrendered to their basic instincts.

"Oh my god! You've ruined me!" Betty exclaimed with sweat pooling on her belly as she reclined back in the overstuffed chair. "I don't think I can stand up right now. My body is just a quivering mass of jelly!"

Will looked up at her, with a broad smile and a wicked twinkle in her eyes. "Glad to be of service, my lady. I was hoping you enjoyed that as much as I did?" She caressed Betty and felt a shiver of delight pulse through her body.

"Oh, shut up and kiss me, you saucy wench!" Betty exclaimed deliciously.

"Hey!" Will said with a start, "when did you cut your hair? I like it a lot. It's really sassy. That style looks great on you. Short in the back and longer in front, really frames your face and shows off your long lovely neck" she said as she snuggled in to kiss her neck and lips.

"Thanks! I had it done yesterday. I just got tired of dealing with long hair, especially going into summer. I've worn it long for so long, I'd forgotten how a haircut can really brighten my look." Betty was enjoying the attention and the relaxation washed over her like a warm summer breeze. She hadn't realized how tense she'd been lately, or how much she missed the physical and emotional intimacy of a lover. "Hey, are we still doing dinner?" she asked with a chuckle. "It's like 9 o'clock. I better put my skirt back on and you need to go to the bathroom and fix your make-up if we want to be seen in public. It's been a long week and I need some food and beer. How about you?"

"Let me go freshen up." Will said as she rose up and started to stumble away. "Oh, hey, where is the bathroom? I completely forgot where I was. Do you have that effect on all your lovers?" she asked coyly.

"It's through that hall there, last door on the right, and, no, I don't. It takes someone special, I guess." Betty responded while testing her legs to make sure they still worked. 'Glad I still have some flexibility,' she thought as she replayed some of the activity of the past few hours in her mind. "Right, let's get dressed and go eat."

"Hey, this is my date, so I'll drive!" said Will as she came back down the hallway. "I don't want to push, but you want to finish the evening at my place later? Just asking in case you need to bring anything. No pressure, but I really don't want this fun to end and I have nothing planned for the weekend but wining and dining you beautiful lady."

"Well, I think we know each other well enough now, so, yeah, I'm definitely up for more, but I really do need to eat." Betty said as she moved closer for another kiss. "Where are you taking me? Casual fun tonight, remember?"

"Yep, let's head to the car and I'll see where the spirit takes us." Will said as she spun around and headed for the door. Betty picked up her bag and followed to set the alarm and lock up.

"I thought you drove an Escalade?" Betty asked with a puzzled look on her face as she walked down the steps to the parking lot. Will was standing next to a Porsche 911 Carrera convertible with the top folding down electronically. She was holding the passenger door open for Betty.

"I do! This is my play car. The Cadillac is my work car." Will explained in a casual matter of fact way. "The insurance agency has done really well. I have a great team and we all like to work hard and play hard."

"I noticed, especially about the play!" Betty chuckled as she slid into the passenger seat. "So, where you takin me to fill my belly? I need to refuel and recharge if you want any more out of me tonight."

"How does Tortugas Lie sound?" Will offered as she walked around and climbed into the driver's seat and started the car.

"Awesome! Great casual atmosphere. Right on the beach. Plenty of cold beer and excellent food." Betty said excitedly. "I heard they were on that Food Channel show with Guy... oh, what's his name?"

"Yeah, Guy Fieri. Diners, Drive-ins, and Dives is his show. Yep, he's done a few of the places here. Coastal Cravings, where we had lunch, and the Outer Banks Brewing Station are the others I'm familiar with." Will eased the Porsche onto the Causeway heading toward the beach and quickly got up to speed. The night air was cooling, but after the workout they just had, it felt good. Some jazz played on the sound system and gave a relaxing vibe as they speed along, turning north at Whalebone Junction and rocketing up the by-pass highway. This early in the season, and this late at night, there was little traffic on the roads. Will looked across the car and saw Betty with her head back against the seat rest. "You falling asleep over there?" she asked while taking her hand and touching Betty's thigh.

"Nope. But I am seriously relaxing." Betty came back with a sideways glance. "This is really nice. I cannot remember when I've been this comfortable with someone else. Thank you for asking me out." She smiled and put her head back. Will gave her thigh a gentle squeeze and smiled.

They drove in silence as they passed Jockey's Ridge on their left. The darkness enveloped the massive mountain of sand and the sky briefly blew up in stars with little surface lighting there. Will reached into a cubby and pulled out a headband and silently offered it to Betty, since her hair was whipping from the breeze. "You are a full-service date, aren't you?" Betty quipped.

"I aim to please." Will smiled back, and then downshifted to slow for the light. She indicated a right turn and easily cornered on to Barnes Street to cut across the island for the beach road. After another right, and two blocks driving, they pulled into the restaurant parking lot. Will hopped out and circled to open Betty's door, but the passenger door was already closing when she got there. "Hey, it's a date, remember?"

"Sorry." Betty gave her a quick peck on the cheek and looked around cautiously. "I'll try and do better."

They both walked into the front door and were greeted warmly. "Hey Sheriff! Hey Will! What brings you two out so late?" called Richard Welch, co-owner of the restaurant from behind the bar. Even this late in the day, the feel of the restaurant was laid back Caribbean. You almost expected Jimmy Buffet to come strolling in.

"We're hungry. Can we still order?" Betty asked with a smile.

"Hey, for you Sheriff, I'm happy to fire up the grill. What can I cook you?" said head chef Dereck Bellinger as he walked out of the kitchen. The bar area still had several regulars nursing their drinks, but the restaurant tables were already cleared, and the chairs flipped on top.

"Gosh, fellas, y'all are the best!" came a warm response from Will. "You know, such great service won't help you on your premiums next year, but it will be much appreciated by the OBX Insurance Agency."

"Don't worry Will. I'll cook for you too." Derrick said with a chuckle.

"Hey, would you be able to throw a combo steamer platter together? We could split it?" Betty suggested to Will while asking Derrick.

"Sounds good" Will responded. "Clams, Shrimp and Crab legs?"

"Comin up. Just give me a few. Have a drink on the house while you wait." Derrick said while turning back into the kitchen and pointing at Richard.

"What's your poison ladies?" Richard asked as the two women sat at the bar.

"I'd love a gin and tonic with lime. Do you have Hendricks gin?" replied Will immediately. "That's always my go to drink when I want something refreshing." She offered to no one in particular.

"Make that two" came Betty's reply. "I need to help wash this week from my memory, at least for this weekend."

Richard began making the two drinks, and Betty interrupted "Can you put them in tall glasses please?"

"Ok. Tough week, huh? I saw some of the news. Big storm! Bank robbery. Double murder. Naked man with a BIG gun!! Sure hope it didn't go off while you were arresting him, Sheriff." Richard laughed loudly as the others at the bar all joined in.

Will was confused about the laughter and jumped in "What's so funny?"

"Well," Betty started, "the fella I arrested yesterday was naked and he had a gun."

"A BIG gun is what we all heard Betty. A really big gun!" Richard shouted, barely able to contain himself as the others fell all over the bar. Even Derrick was cackling in the kitchen.

"Ok, he had a really big gun." Will said with a puzzled expression. "But you disarmed him, right Betty. I mean, you got his gun off him and no one got hurt, right?"

The bar roared with laughter and Betty's face blushed. "I think what Richard is alluding to, was that the gentleman in question was rather well endowed, and he became quite erect when I was arresting him. A good portion of his manhood showed above his jeans when I pulled them up. He was freakin huge!" At that, everyone fell over laughing. "…. like a horse! I mean, DAMN!" and the small crowd roared.

"So, I never saw who this fine specimen was. Who was it Betty?" asked Richard as he handed over the two drinks.

Betty shot him a quick, serious look, and said calmly "That information will not be released to the public." And with that, everyone went back to nursing their drinks. "Richard, when each of these gentlemen decide to leave, I know you'll be calling them an Uber. I'm not a fan of drunk driving, and I don't want to have to call one of my deputies to come and breath-a-lize each of them in your parking lot."

"Copy that, Sheriff. Roger Wilco. 10-4" Richard straightened with a mock salute and turned to see Derrick coming out of the kitchen with a nice steaming plate of seafood. "Here are a couple of roll ups for you two and I'll snag each of you a plate for your bones." He also set a basket of warm rolls, hushpuppies, and butter on the bar. "Enjoy ladies." He turned and popped a couple of beers for himself and his partner and fell into conversation at the end of the bar, leaving Betty and Will to eat.

Will went straight for the crab legs and cracked them like an expert, withdrawing the delicious meat from their shell. Betty worked on the clams, dipping each in drawn butter and sliding them down her throat. They both shared their catch, and worked together to eat the wonderful seafood, but avoided the potatoes and corn. Will couldn't resist a hushpuppy, but that was her only carb. With the last of the shrimp eaten, and a pile of shells left on their plates. They both sat back satisfied and finished their second Hendricks and tonic.

"Hey guys, let us let you close up. We're stuffed to the gills. Thank you for a delicious meal" Will called down the bar to the owners, who were working on their 3rd beer while reviewing the receipts for the day.

"Sure I can't get you some dessert? Maybe a Toasted Turtle to share? Best coffee drink on the beach!" Derrick shot back without getting up. Richard wandered over with the bill and picked up the black AMEX card offered by Will Moore, ran the receipt, and returned with the slips and a pen. "Thanks for stopping in Sheriff, Will. We enjoyed the company."

Will gave a quick look at the bill, added an obscene tip, and laid the pen on the bar. "It was our pleasure fellas. Always enjoy the food here! Thanks for staying open for us."

"Boys, get home safe now, hear?" Betty said with a smile on her face. Both men laughed since she was 20 years younger than either of them, but they understood her duty as Sheriff. "Night guys. See you soon." Will and Betty headed for the door and the deserted parking lot. The restaurant sign was already dark, and Will's Porsche was the only car around. All they could hear was the sound of the ocean crashing on to the beach just across the road. The sky was ablaze with stars, and a cool breeze blew through their hair while they leaned against the car. Both ladies had contented smiles on their faces as they looked up the road. "I can't remember the last time I've had this much fun." Betty said quietly without altering her gaze. "Think you want to do it again, Wilma?"

"Humm. I do" Will whispered as she looked at her watch. "How about tonight?"

"Yep. Works for me. How about we go home and snuggle in bed and get some sleep so we're ready for our big date?" Betty looked up at her companion and laughed. "But give me a kiss first beautiful."

FLIGHT

Will gladly complied.

TWENTY-EIGHT

"You stay in bed and sleep in, sweetie. I have something I need to do every Saturday morning. I won't be gone long." Will whispered as she kissed Betty on the cheek. Betty hardly moved but gave a brief wave of understanding as she pulled the pillow closer. Will threw on some shorts and a sports bra and running shoes and headed to the garage. Once inside the Escalade, she opened the garage door, started the engine, and reversed out into a spectacular morning. The sun was just coming up over the treetops and the air was crisp and clean. Spring was definitely starting to bloom. Will put her window down and enjoyed the breeze as she drove out her gate at the end of her driveway and onto West Kitty Hawk Road, through the marsh and past houses and businesses all shrouded with old trees covered in fresh new leaves. Just past the Kitty Hawk Police station, she swung right into the church parking lot. Holy Redeemer By The Sea had been Will's church since she moved to the OBX. She was born and raised catholic, and her dad had instilled in her a duty to give back to the community through the church. She liked the relaxed atmosphere at this parish, and Father Bill was an easy man to talk with, a good listener, and only offered advice when it was sought.

Will was surprised to see the priest walking outside when she pulled up. "Morning Father." Will called to him as she climbed out of her car.

"Top of the morning to you, Will. Must be Saturday morning if Will Moore is coming to church!" the priest called back. "I won't stop you or interrupt your routine with idle conversation. I've got miles to go before

I sleep, so..." he trailed off as he continued to power walk around the church lot.

The doors to the church swung open automatically when she approached, and Will smiled. She'd been coming every Saturday morning for years, and the priests all knew to open the church early so she could worship. Inside she walked to the back of the church, near a small chapel and approached the votive candles, where she lit a candle and kneeled down to pray.

"Heavenly Father. Please protect my mother, wherever she is. Watch over her and guide her. In the name of the Father, and the Son, and the Holy Ghost." She made the sign of the cross, using her right hand to touch her forehead, chest, left shoulder, and right shoulder, and then brought her hands together and bowed her head. She quietly said an Our Father, Hail Mary and Glory Be prayers, which she learned as a very young child and would repeat almost daily ever since. When she finished, she quietly got to her feet and left. This was her routine. Every Saturday morning. Almost no one knew, not even her dad.

When she got back to her car, she looked up at the piercing blue sky and a small tear rolled down her cheek. "I miss you momma." She caught Father Bill walking on the far side of the lot and gave a wave. "Have a great day, Father!" she called out.

"You too, my child. May God be with you" he replied without missing a beat.

Easing the Escalade out of the lot, Will took a right and went down to the light, where she made a left and drove up the by-pass. Her thoughts drifted back to last night and she thought a little treat, an indulgence would be in order, so she pulled into the Duck Donuts parking lot and walked into the small storefront shop to order. "Morning Cassie, Jim! Been busy?"

Cassie looked up from behind the counter with a warm smile. She was an older woman who'd lived a hard life but turned a corner when she came to work at the donut shop. She enjoyed the work and it showed in her service and dedication. "Good morning Will! We don't see you around much. I guess that's why you stay so damn skinny!" the woman's voice boomed across the small room. After a lifetime of smoking and drinking, her voice was more a rasp or wheeze, but she was warm and pleasant. "You want a bacon maple glaze for the road?"

"Ah, yes ma'am! Actually, make it two, and two key lime with coconut, and two chocolate glaze with sprinkles!" Will said gleefully.

"Well, all right then. That's what I'm talking about. What's got you so frisky Ms. Will?" Jim shot back from the donut making station, where customers can watch their donuts made fresh to order. He was a quiet man, polite and hard working. Cassie never had a bad word to say about him, but truth be told, if Cassie had anything bad to say about any employee, they didn't work there anymore. Will stood shocked to have heard the man speak. She wasn't a regular customer, but when she did stop in, he usually just smiled and made the donuts.

"Well, Jim, er, well. I don't know" she stammered. "I guess it's just a glorious day and I'm glad to be here with y'all."

"Well, we're mighty glad you're here too, Ms. Will. You always brighten up the place whenever you come in. Just wish it was more often, is all." Jim turned back to his work and started to whistle a tune quietly.

The smell of fresh baked donuts lying next to her on the front seat of the car as she drove back home was making her crazy. Last night's late dinner was wonderful, but they both kept away from the rolls, boiled potatoes and corn on the cob and just ate the seafood. "A girl has got to keep her figure" she thought, and then laughed at the realization of the calories they burned off before and after dinner. A few donuts would be good for the carbo loading needed to sustain them through the weekend, she gleefully rationalized.

Climbing the stairs from the garage into the kitchen, Will was rendered breathless. Standing next to the coffee pot with a warm mug of fresh brew was Betty, wearing a sheer cream-colored teddy and a smile. Except for the hair on the top of her head, her skin was beautifully smooth and hairless. "Can I buy you a cup of coffee stranger?" she cooed playfully as she blew on her cup to cool the drink before taking a sip, all the while looking devilishly over the rim at Will's blue eyes. It was obvious that the passion and excitement from last night had not subsided, and Will made the snap decision that the marble kitchen countertop was as good a place as any to continue their play. She dropped the box of donuts on the table, the thought of eating them now a distant memory, and advanced on Betty, who obliged by putting her mug in the sink and hopping up on the countertop as Will arrived for a warm and tender embrace. "Good morning, Princess." Betty whispered after their sweet kiss.

"Good morning, beautiful" replied Will as she moved in for another full-mouthed kiss. Betty then reclined back on the cold marble and arched her back. The pleasure was more intense than anything she'd ever felt before. Once the waves of pleasure subsided she smiled and said, "Now, you said something about coffee?" Will chuckled, as she reached into the sink to retrieve Betty's mug. "Oh, you take it black!" she exclaimed as she made a face after sipping without looking.

"Um, yeah!" Betty said. "So, do you!" as she waved her hand from head to toe.

"Well, you're more a creamy mocha with lots of sugar!" shot back Will with a laugh.

"Ok, girl, I'll give you that." Betty replied, "but right now, please don't ask me to move, cause my legs are rubber. I feel bad. I've lost count of how many times you've done me. What can I do for you?"

"Hush" Will said as she put a finger over Bettys lips. "You are doing it baby, trust me, you're doing it."

Will handed over the mug, topped up with fresh coffee, and reached into the cupboard for her mug. She tipped in her coffee, added a splash of sweet creamer, and popped it all into the microwave for a few seconds. "I like my coffee hot, just like my woman!"

They both roared, and Betty had to fight to not spit out her coffee. "Warn me next time you're going to make me laugh!"

"Consider yourself warned." Will said while retrieving her cup and taking a sip. "Hey, I hope you like donuts" she said as she reached for the box on the table.

"Seriously!" Betty shot back. "You're offering donuts to a cop? Cliché much?"

"Oh my god! I am so sorry. I didn't even think." Will cheeks blushed with embarrassment as she set the donuts down on the counter next to Betty.

Betty flipped the box open and squealed "bacon maple glaze!!!" Before Will knew it, the donut was in Betty's mouth and another orgasmic wave came over her face. Her lashes fluttered and her eyes rolled back in pure joy. "Thank you. Thank you. Thank you" she murmured while chewing. "These are my absolute favorite. You are the devil, aren't you? You tempt me with sex and food, my two greatest weaknesses. I am your slave! You own me now."

"Well, that's not exactly PC, now is it? But I'll take it." Will roared. "Can I have another kiss?

"You can have it all, Wilma, as long as I can have that second bacon maple glaze donut!"

"Definitely, but then I'll have to work those carbs off you." Will grinned.

"Promise?"

"Promise."

Just as they began to embrace, Betty's phone rang with a very distinctive ringtone. "I need to get that sorry." Betty said as she hopped off the counter and rushed to the bedroom to get her phone. "That's my Dad calling. Hold that thought."

"Who uses 'Who Let The Dogs Out' as a ringtone for their father?" Will muttered as Betty walked back into the room.

"Ok, Dad, what time you think you'll be here? Ok. Ok. No worries. Can you give me a sec? Thanks" Betty put her hand over the microphone and looked at Will dead on. "Can you have lunch with me and my mom today? They are driving down from DC and Mom wants to treat me. I think she wants to talk. I could use the moral support, please?" Will looked stunned for a moment but then smiled and shook her head.

"Sure! Sounds fun!"

"Ok, Dad? Oh, Hi Mom. Yes. Let's lunch. Right. Dad said you'd be here around 1:30. I'll meet you at your house. Oh, and mom, would it be ok if I bring along a girlfriend? Yes. No. NO! Mother, stop. Ok, yes. See you at 1:30. Love you. Bye." Betty disconnected the call and saw Will standing by the glass doors looking out over the lawn, and the Albemarle Sound beyond. This was the first time Betty was awake enough to notice the fabulous house she was standing in. When they got home last night most of the house was in darkness and, frankly, she had other things occupying her mind.

The kitchen was the central hub of the first floor with a formal entrance hall, dining room and sitting room to the east. To the west were a wall of glass doors that opened to a large covered porch. Between the two was the open area for casual dining and entertaining. The Master Bedroom was on the south west corner of the house with the en-suite, and the staircase to the upstairs and garage below was on the north end of the house with a powder room. There was also an elevator! 'Seriously? An elevator! Damn, this girl has done well for herself.' Betty thought.

The main feature of the house, the reason for it being here, was the amazing view. To the North you could see the Wright Bridge leading off the island to Point Harbor. To the south you could just see the faint outline of Roanoke Island, but the money shot was straight out. The Albemarle Sound stretched for 50 miles uninterrupted all the way to Edenton. It was magnificent. "Wilma, I am so sorry. I never expected that call, and if you don't want to go, I completely understand." Betty offered as she walked across the room to Will.

"What? No. Don't even give it a thought. Betty, if your momma is anything like you, we'll have a great time. I'm ok with it if you are." Will said, looking into Betty's hazel eyes and holding her face. "Don't sweat it girl. Life is too short." After a sweet kiss and a wink, Will straightened to her full 5'11" and stepped back a bit, taking in Betty fully. "Now, I have a question for you. Who gave you permission to use my birth name? My daddy is the only one who calls me Wilma, and when he's mad, he gives me the full Wilma Ruth Moore treatment. I've heard you say it several times now. So?" Will stood full on, locked on Betty's face.

"It's your damn name, girl. I didn't ask permission because your parents gave you the name and I'll call you whatever the hell I want. Got it?" Betty responded with a steely edge to her voice, as if she was commanding the troops at the office. Her nostrils flared slightly. Her jaw was set tight and her gaze what straight and true. There was no give in her posture, as she puffed out her chest and seemed to rise beyond her 5'6" frame. "Am I clear Wilma?"

"Yes ma'am! Crystal!" came the response, followed quickly by an exhale of a full breath Will didn't realize she was holding. "Damn, you are hot! I am jelly inside right now. You can call me whatever you want, just as long as you call me."

"Good. Now why don't we finish our donuts and coffee, we can shower and then you can run me back to my place so I can change to meet my mom."

"That's a plan, but only if we shower together." Will added with a devilish grin and a wink. "And I promise I'll keep to the schedule. Promise…"

TWENTY-NINE

"Ok folks, the Sheriff is taking this weekend off. This is the first weekend she has not worked in months. Hell, it's the first days she hasn't worked in months. She needed a break, and she deserved it. I know everyone hates working on the weekend, but until we close the Midgett murder, there are no days off. I know the storm threw us all back a bit, and I want to personally thank each of you for your dedication. Some of you had to leave family, and we all had to leave friends to work and safeguard this community. Thank the Lord, Mother Nature cut us some slack. Now, we're a new unit, Criminal Investigations, and Sheriff Thompson has put me in charge of this murder investigation. I hand-picked each of you to join me and the Sheriff is looking for us to close this case, and I aim to do it. Am I clear?" Jack didn't wait for an answer. "Good. let's go around the room and update what we've got. Tim, what have you gotten on Ralph's kids?"

"Jack, so far I've arranged an interview with the daughter when she comes into town for the funeral. She is supposed to arrive tomorrow for the Monday funeral. I've scheduled an interview tomorrow at 5pm here." Tim Cudworth said with a monotone like he couldn't be bothered. "I have not been able to track down the son. Both his mother and sister have been unable to reach him, and they say that's unusual. I'll need some help tracking his credit cards and phone records."

"Tim," Jack shot quickly, "I need you to look at the possibility that Ralph had more than just the two legitimate kids we know about. Finding out about Ralph Midgett Jr on Thursday made me realize that our murder victim could have been steppin' out before or even while he was married. Let's coordinate with Jeff on the accounting. He may have regular monthly payments going to women as under the table support. Also, check the court records for any civil filings against him over the past 40 years. And everyone, if you schedule an interview here, I want to sit in on them, got it?"

"Got it, boss" Tim said with no joy.

"Ok Tim. Listen, as long as you're interviewing the kids, why don't you handle the mother too. See if she's coming to the funeral. You can get the whole family in one go then. Jennifer, can you assist Tim with his computer work? And fill us in on your investigation into Kelly Fuco's known associates or adversaries." Jack Strong inquired.

"Where do I start?" Jennifer said with a chuckle. "Kelly Fuco was a popular person, which is to say she made a lot of enemies. Right now, I have 27 complaints made by her or about her from the Raleigh PD. There were a handful here from local PD and a bunch more in Florida... Tampa, Orlando, Jacksonville. All of them are domestic related. Either she beat up a boyfriend or the boyfriend beat her, allegedly. Nothing ever went to trial, and she seemed to move on to the next one, or they moved on from her, before it escalated. I do have her visiting psychiatric hospitals twice for bi-polar depression, so that explains her erratic behavior. I gotta say, she has a bunch of folks who would want her dead, but so far most have solid alibis for the timeframe of the murder. I'm still chasing a few down, but I'm not thinking there's our killer here. Just my gut."

"Thanks JJ. Keep on it. No loose ends. Ok, Big Man. Whatcha got for us, Jeff?"

"I've been running down the business angle. I know Ralph was retired, but I don't think guys as successful as he was truly retire. He made a lot of enemies here locally with his bank, but as he grew, he made even more and bigger enemies throughout the state, and really the southeast. I made some calls to a forensic accountant in Norfolk, and with the Sheriff's permission, she's agreed to work with us on business and banking records. I'm ok with numbers, but it's her area of expertise, and if we can uncover something, I want to make sure we can make it stick in court. I've gotten Mrs. Midgett to sign off on a personal accounting, and I'm waiting for the current owners of the bank to agree to the same."

"Well, Jeff, I hope you don't hold your breath on that one." Tim chimed in. "Bankers are slimy bastards and their lawyers, well, we all know about them. I've got $20 says you don't get the bank to agree."

"I'll take that bet Tim" said Jeff confidently.

"Count me in too!" said Jack.

"I'm in." said Jennifer with a nod to Jeff, as if to say 'I got you bro.'

"So, Jeff, when does your accountant start with us?" Jack enquired. "We need fresh blood around here." he said while staring at Tim.

"She will work remotely and bill for her time," Jeff replied confidently, "but the Sheriff may make her an offer if she works out. Financial crimes are really big, and we don't have the manpower, or the brain power to work them properly. She's young, but ridiculously sharp, and she did express an interest in moving to the OBX, so, we'll see how it goes."

"Tink, what have you been able to uncover?" Jack asked as he spun around in his chair to face the slim deputy leaning against the door frame.

"I've had the pleasure of interviewing the current Mrs. Midgett and exploring her background, which has led me all over Europe, virtually, of course. I don't leave eastern North Carolina, as y'all know. As many of you are aware, eastern Europe is full of, humm, shall we say 'bad actors' of both the terrorist and organized crime varieties. Well, Tatiana Midgett, born Milanovich, and her family have strong ties to both. I've been working with Interpol and various national police agencies, as well as our State Department and the British Intelligence Service. It's been slow going, mostly due to politics and the time difference, but I'm making steady progress. There are a few interesting characters I'm bringing into focus. Naturally, I'll ask local law enforcement to do any interviews, unless you want to fly to Serbia, or Bosnia, or Croatia Jack?" That brought a welcome laugh from the group.

"Thanks, Tink. I think I'll pass on that for the time being." Said Deputy Strong. "Maybe Sheriff Thompson will want to go. She could meet Jason Bourne there. Or James Bond?"

"Or George Smiley?" came a voice from the back of the room. Everyone whipped their head around to look at Angela Peterson sitting quietly against the wall with a laptop propped on her knees. "George Smiley?" she repeated. "Tinker, Tailor, Soldier, Spy… nothing? Come on people! John LeCarre thriller? Seriously? Great book. Great movie. Still nothing? Ugh… I give up. Troglodytes."

"Angela, we don't all have the time to read, or watch British movies, or whatever…" Jack jumped to the defense of his team. "Angela has been helping us pull information together and I've been feeding you some of her work for follow up. She helps when she can on loan from the OBX Insurance Agency."

"Jack! Seriously? An insurance agent is helping us solve crimes. What is this? A Nancy Drew novel? Geez…" Tim shouted as he threw up his hands in mock disgust.

Before Jack could respond Angela shot to her feet "Tim, I'll have you know that we employ two retired FBI agents who help us investigate all sorts of insurance fraud, and we serve those cases up to local police on a platter, signed, sealed and delivered express mail. Most of the details you shared with the group today were provided by me. My leg work, so…"

Angela was about to say something she definitely would regret, so Jack jumped in and cut her off with a look and a stop sign hand gesture. "Tim, I think you owe Nancy Drew here an apology, and be quick about it."

Sheepishly, Tim acquiesced "Sorry Angie. Really. Please don't jack up my premiums this year." That got a roar from the group. It always felt good to put Tim in his place. Everyone knew he was the anchor man on this team.

"I can't make any promises, Tim, but thank you." Angela regrouped and sat back down. Then, she asked a question. "Y'all considered that the bank robbery, and the murder of Tom Mills, and the double homicide at the Midgett Mansion are all related? I've been kicking that around and I can see a connection. Any chance we can get a peek at the FBI file on the robbery and the Currituck County Sheriff's file on the Mills murder?"

"What's the connection?" Jack asked.

"The Bank" everyone in the room responded at the same time.

"Bingo" Angela shouted! And with that the room flew into a renewed flurry of activity.

THIRTY

"That was the best shower I've ever had!" Will said as they both stood in the bathroom and toweled off.

"Well, it was a pretty 'dirty' shower, but I could get used to that! But seriously, your bedroom and bathroom are bigger than my whole house! You have a spectacular property here." Betty said. "I am in awe."

"Thank you." Will blushed. "As I said before, I'm blessed with a great team who work hard, and I'm blessed to have been in the right place at the right time. When I bought this property, the backside of the island was just an afterthought. The house that was here was little more than a shack. I was able to pick it up for pennies. I built the breakwater and the dock, and then started working with an architect and design team to make my dream, my vision, a reality. I knew that this was going to be my forever home, so I wanted to make it mine. I've got four acres here of complete privacy. I can sunbath by the pool and never worry about anyone seeing me. I can assure you that no one heard you last night or this morning. We could make love on the grass under the moon light and no one would know. This is a dead-end street that stops at my dock. I've got a security gate and full security monitoring, cameras, motion sensors, lights, so if anyone even tries to come on the property from the land or water, I know about it instantly right on my phone."

"Maybe later you can give me a tour? Right now, we need to hustle over to my place so I can change."

"Deal. Let me just throw on some clothes and we'll get going. What should I wear to meet your parents?" Will stopped cold at the realization of what she just said.

"Hey Wilma, it'll just be my mom. Dad has a meeting he's running to, and we're doing super casual. Remember, they are driving down from DC right now, so... casual. We'll probably just pop over to Duck Woods and have lunch there. Dad's a member and mom loves the new clubhouse and grill. Shorts and a polo, can't go wrong."

"Ok, cool." Wilma said as she went into her walk-in closet to pull something together while Betty went into the bedroom and scavenged for her clothes from last night. About five minutes later Will walked into the bedroom in white tennis shorts, a pink polo with pink Sperry docksiders and a pink scrunchy holding her ponytail. She'd put diamond studs in her ears and had a diamond tennis bracelet on her left wrist and her silver thumb ring on her right hand. A thin shmeer of pink lip gloss was all the make-up she wore. "How's this?"

"Wow. Just wow. Maybe later you could give me a tour of that closet!" Betty stood, almost dressed but wearing only one flip-flop. "Any idea where the other flop went?"

"The closet? Definitely. The flip-flop, I have no idea." Will said as she scanned the room. "Wait a minute. I think I see it under the curtains." She walked over to the huge wall of windows looking over the lawn and the water beyond and pulled back a curtain to reveal the errant footwear. "Hey, do you have a dock across from your unit, just across the parking lot? I thought I saw it when I drove in last night."

"Yeah. It's a community area so you can pull your boat in to load and unload. I don't have a boat, so I just watch other people do it."

"Well, I do, and with it being a Saturday with rental check outs and check ins, I'm bettin' we'll make better time on the water than land, so let's go." Will scooped up her keys, set the alarm and headed downstairs to the garage with Betty following close behind.

FLIGHT

"If we're taking a boat, what are we doing in the garage? Do we have to launch it?" Betty asked with some confusion.

"Over here." Will called as she walked past the vehicles. "Hop in."

"A golf cart? Seriously, what don't you have?" Betty gaped in wonder. A small garage door in front of the cart opened and they shot out on to a gravel path as it closed behind them. They sped down toward the dock and boathouse, and when they got a bit closer, Betty could see a gleaming dark blue hull bobbing gently under the boathouse. "Good god, that boat is huge!"

"It's a Hinkley 37 Picnic Boat. I just took delivery last year. She may look old fashioned, but she is state of the art modern. We'll be over at your place in 15 minutes" Will bragged as she shot Betty a sideways glance and a wry smile. "What can I say? I work hard..."

"and you play hard. Got it." Betty finished her sentence and they both grinned.

"Can't take it with you, so enjoy it while you can." Will pulled the golf cart right up onto the dock next to the boat and hopped out and motioned to Betty to 'come aboard'. She climbed onboard and pushed the start button. The twin Yanmar 370 V8 diesels roared to life and as she slid into the captain's chair, she slowly eased the boat in reverse. It glided effortlessly out of the boathouse and, once clear of the structure, she spun the wheel and the yacht pivoted in its own space.

"How'd it do that?" Betty yelled in amazement over the engine noise. "I have never seen a boat do that before."

"She has twin Hamilton HJ274 jets. It's like a really big jet ski. Sit down and hold on. I'm guessing you're gonna like this" Will shouted as she pushed the throttle down and the boat responded with a roar as it began to sprint across the smooth water. Once the boat began to move forward, the automatic hydraulic bow planes lifted the boat, so it was flying across the sound at forty plus mph. "What do you think?"

"Ridiculous! I love it." Betty shouted with an enormous grin on her beautiful face. Will returned the smile, and then leaned over to give her a kiss. Will then looked at the GPS and plotted her course to Betty's doorstep. Then she relaxed and watched her new friend enjoy the ride.

As scheduled, Will throttled back to enter the canal next to her building, slowly navigating under the Ballast Point Drive bridge and then turned hard to port to glide up past the community pool. She executed a perfect pivot to point back the way she came and then crawled to starboard and docked behind the clubhouse. She put the engines in neutral and hopped off on to the dock to secure lines fore and aft. "We won't be here long, so I won't go to any great length to tie off the boat more than this." She told Betty as she came back on board and shut the engines down. "Let me just set the security system, and we'll be good to go." Almost exactly fifteen minutes from leaving the boathouse they were on the dock and walking across the parking lot to Betty's building. Once inside, Will could see her baby gleaming in the late morning sunshine from the kitchen window. Betty scampered into the bedroom and quickly peeled off her clothes and then searched for the outfit she thought would look nice, for herself, her mother, and her lover.

"What do you think?" Betty asked as she came from the bedroom dressed in a lovely pink and green floral print spaghetti strap sundress that fell to mid-thigh and moved seductively when she walked. She carried a soft pink cardigan sweater and had white tennis shoes with a pink swoosh on the side. She had the same chunky bag she carried last night, and it didn't look right with her outfit.

Will debated for a minute, looking critically, and then said, "I love the dress, the sweater, and the shoes, but the bag just doesn't fit."

"I know. I get it, but I don't have another concealed carry bag that would work with this look." Betty answered truthfully to a puzzled Wilma.

"Huh?"

With that, Betty withdrew her S&W MP 9mm from the side pouch of her bag.

"Oh right!" Will exclaimed. "I keep forgetting you're a cop."

"Yep. 24/7/365. The only time I'm not carrying is when I'm naked."

"Ok." Will stepped back and said "You look seriously bad ass with that gun. Damn girl, now I can see why Ralph Jr got such a thing for you!"

"Well yeah!" Betty chuckled. "But don't go rootin' around in my purse. I've got a tactical knife and can of mace in there too, along with some tampons and tissues, cause, ya know, I'm a lady."

"So, is that the only concealed carry purse they make?" Will asked naively.

"Oh, hell no." Betty laughed. "Trust me, in concealed carry states, half the women on the street are carrying serious protection. I just haven't shopped for one because I haven't needed to. Like I said. I don't date much. You're the first person in a long time that I've wanted to dress up and look pretty for."

"Well, I'm flattered," Will said, "and I know how you feel. It's mutual. Ready to head back and meet your mom?"

"Let's do this."

They walked out of the unit, down the stairs and across the parking lot to the boat. This time Will didn't have to ask Betty aboard, she helped untie the bow while Will got the stern and then they both hopped on board. Betty sat to the port side while Will fired up the engines and eased the boat down the canal from the captain's chair. Instead of navigating under the roadway, Will went straight down the canal and out into Shallowbag Bay, where she opened the throttle and cruised home. It was a glorious day for a cruise, but that would have to wait for later. Lunch with Momma came first.

With the boat put up on its lift and secured, Will and Betty went back to the garage in the golf cart and traded it for the Escalade. "Tell me where I'm going, Betty, so I can plug it into the GPS."

"I can get us there but let me check my phone for the address... Ok, 69 South Dogwood Trail, Kitty Hawk. It's just past the clubhouse for Duck Woods."

"Oh, ok, got it. Want to give your folks a call to make sure they've arrived?" Will asked quietly.

"Hey. Speak of the devil. Mom just texted that they've arrived. I'll let them know we'll be along shortly, pending any traffic snafus." Betty responded while focusing on her phone.

The garage door went up and the Escalade cruised out of the garage. The gate had already swung open and they slid easily out on to the road as the gate closed behind them. As they passed the Kitty Hawk Dog Park Will asked, "I wonder if Jack or Angie have taken the dogs for a good run today."

"I don't know about Angela, but I know Jack is working straight through until Ralph Midgett's killer is caught. He's got the whole team working today. Bill Anderson has been hot on my tail for a break, so it's balls to the wall until the case is closed." Betty offered without a smidge of guilt. "In case you're wondering, I gave myself the weekend off and Jack and the team agreed. They work a schedule. I work around the clock. I've needed a break for a while and it's just serendipity that you came into my life when I needed it most.

As the light changed on the by-pass and Will sped up past Sea Scape Village and Golf Course and then the urgent care medical facility, Betty relaxed and reached for Will's hand. "All this is kinda new for me, and it's happening really fast, but I feel really blessed to have you in my life. Thank you for calling and asking me out."

"Well, I feel the same way, so thank you for saying yes." Betty felt a chill and goose bumps on the back of her neck. She leaned across the wide car and gave Will a big smooch on her cheek. "Oh, hey this is the turn just up here. Right, just after the ball field at the elementary school. Yep, then it's just a little bit past the clubhouse."

The car pulled into the driveway, and Will and Betty got out and walked up the front path. The house was a lovely four-sided brick, two story traditional home with dormer windows on the second floor and a small entry porch up a few stairs. The first floor was elevated to avoid any issues with flooding, which was always a concern from a storm, like the one that just rampaged through the area. It was a lovely home that backed on to Jean Guite Creek which flowed to Currituck Sound. The yard was landscaped and well maintained, obviously by a service, since this was a second home and the owners had just arrived. Without thinking, Betty sprinted up the steps, opened the door and called out for her mother. "Mom, I'm here. Where are you?"

"Oh child, I'm coming. Just hold your horses." Lizzy Thompson came barreling down the hallway from the bedrooms with a huge smile on her face and a full head of steam. She was not a small woman, about five feet five but almost two hundred pounds. She had dark skin and tight curly hair that she kept in a short afro. Her face was round with a broad nose, smallish ears, and expressive brown sparkling eyes. Her mouth was pleasant with full lips, and rarely stopped moving. She dressed comfortably in a full flowing ankle length cotton dress with wide flowing sleeves and a squared collar. It was a beautifully colorful print mixture of rich blues and reds and golds in an African tribal pattern. She wore a lovely heavy gold chain around her neck, gold hoop earrings, her gold wedding and engagement rings and a pair of gold sandals with red, blue, and green jewels and sparkles in the straps. "Oh, there you are. Girl you look thin. Are you eating? Just like your father. Work yourself to the bone. Gimme some sugar baby girl. I need a hug." Realizing there was a guest present, "Oh, I'm sorry. You told me you were bringing a friend." Lizzy turned quickly to face Will and extended her hand. "Hi, I'm Betty's momma, Lizzy Thompson. It's a pleasure to meet any friend of Betty's. She's very particular about who she calls a friend, so you must be something special!"

"Mrs. Thompson, I'm Will Moore, my daddy calls me Wilma Ruth Moore, Ruth was my momma's name, but my friends call me Will. Believe me, it's all my pleasure to meet the mother of this wonderful woman. I am honored to be her friend. I can see where she gets her personality and her zest for life." The charming salesman came out in Will and she dazzled Lizzy and Betty.

"Ok, you two. Y'all are making me blush here, and that's not easy for a black girl!" Betty jumped in. "Momma, do you need any help with your bags or anything? If you need anything up high, take advantage of this one while you can." Betty joked as she hooked her thumb over her shoulder at Will.

"No. No. You two sit a bit and let me just finish freshening up after the drive. I won't be but a minute." With that, Lizzy spun around and bustled back down the hall.

"Your Mom is a house afire. Wow. I'm out of breath just watching her. Does she..."

"All the time." Betty finished Will's sentence. "My dad has a full-time job just getting her to slow down. She's one of those people who just isn't happy if she isn't doin'."

"It's early days, but I don't know anyone who is like that!" Will flashed her beautiful smile, and Betty blushed a bit.

"Well, maybe, just a little. But I'm not near as bad as she is." Betty protested.

"Who's bad, Betty?" Lizzy asked as she blew through the room on the way to the kitchen.

"No one, Mamma. Can I get you anything?"

"No, Betty. I'm fine. Just need to get a drink for my blood pressure pills. I didn't take them this morning because I'd already packed them. Lord, some days I think I'd forget my head if it wasn't screwed on. Ok, girls, let's go to the Club and have us a club and Long Island iced tea!"

Will shot Betty a look of horror and mouthed 'I can't', so Betty calmly said "Momma, I think I'll just stick to unsweet tea for lunch. How about you Will? Feel like goin' on a bender? Just remember, I'm the Sheriff in these here parts, and I'll slap the cuffs on you and throw you into the ..."

"All right missy, you made your point. I'll control myself... this time. But it's all your fault Betty, bringing such a lovely young woman along for company. She just swept me off my feet." Lizzy looked at Will dead on as she climbed into the front passenger seat of the Escalade and gave her a playful wink.

"I do declare Miss Scarlett... Momma, you kill me." Betty didn't see her mothers' wink as she climbed into the back-passenger seat, but she caught Will's wide eyes in the rear-view mirror and knew there was more to this story.

"So, how long have you two been together?" Lizzie asked innocently as the car rumpled down the street to the Club.

Both women had a shocked look, as if caught by the teacher, and they locked eyes through the rear-view mirror. "What are you talking about Momma?" came Betty's incredulous reply. "Wilma and I are friends."

"Sweet child, you know I've been married to a detective for 40 years, right? I was raised by a cop. Your grandfather was the first black detective in the DC police force. My brother and your father were partners a long time ago. That's how I met Tim. I've learned to observe enough to see when two people are more than friends." Lizzie offered in a very matronly tone.

Will sat shocked in the driver's seat with her mind spinning, worried that being called out might put an end to something that only just started. She had no idea how Betty's parents would react to their daughter dating a woman, let alone a white woman.

"Momma! I think your intuition is way off here, and you're embarrassing me in front of my friend. Now, please apologize so we can have a nice lunch together." Betty wasn't using her commander voice, as she did with Will earlier today, but she was a little too sharp in her tone for Lizzie's liking.

"You watch yourself, Betty Thompson! Remember who you are talking to. I will not be spoken to like that by my daughter. Am I clear?" Lizzie snapped as she turned to look Betty dead in the eyes.

"Yes ma'am. Crystal." Betty replied with a huff.

Wilma had pulled into a space at the parking lot of the Club and had the car in park, but kept it running. "Ok, you two. Betty, you owe your Momma an apology for trying to lie to her. And Lizzie, how did you know? We just started dating like yesterday!" Will had turned in her seat to face both of her passengers.

Lizzie reached across the center console and put her hand on Will's. "Child, there were a couple of things, easy things really. First, the way you two look at each other reminds me of how Tim looks at me still to this day. Second, I've known this girl her whole life. Seen her in good times and bad, highs and lows, and I've never seen her more relaxed and comfortable around someone that she is around you. Third, I know my daughter pretty well, even though we've got some miles between us now, and I can tell you for a fact I have never had lunch with this girl when she's wearing a sundress! And" she looked right at Betty now, "you look radiant girl, just beautiful!" A tear leaked from Betty's eye, as she looked down at her hands in embarrassment. "But the biggest clue, and easiest, was when I saw Will." Both women looked at Lizzie and then at each other with a puzzled expression. "Lord!" Lizzie shouted, "pull down your visor and look at yourself." She commanded. "You are too beautiful, and way to put together, to walk around with lipstick on your cheek, especially the shade that my daughter is wearing. So, she must have just kissed you before you came to the door, and you were too love struck to realize you are wearing the evidence of your deceit." With that, Will's head slumped on the steering wheel, and Betty just roared with laughter.

"Lizzie, you rival Sherlock Holmes!" Will said as she leaned across the car to give her a hug. She whispered "thank you" in her ear. "Now, let's go eat, and I've changed my mind, I do want a cocktail." She said confidently as she looked at Betty getting out of the car.

"Me too." Betty chimed in as she helped her mother hop down from the vehicle. "And, Momma, I'm sorry. I'm sorry for what I said, and the way I said it." They hugged tight, and Betty kissed her momma on the cheek and said "I love you… There, now I've branded you too!" and the three ladies all laughed and admired the lovely pink lipstick kiss on Lizzie's cheek.

"I'll wear my brand proudly!" Lizzie exclaimed.

"Good. Now, Wilma, get over here and give me some sugar!" Betty said in her most playful commanding voice. Wilma obliged and left a lovely pink kiss on Betty's cheek. Before she could turn away, Betty grabbed her arm and pulled her in for a sweet kiss smack on the lips.

"Alright! That's what I'm talking about girl! In front of God and country. Excellent!" shouted Lizzy for all to hear. "Praise Jesus! I think my girl has found love!"

"Momma!"

THIRTY-ONE

The Dare County Sheriff's bullpen was a buzz of frantic activity as all the deputies worked to figure out the connection to the OBX Bank and the three dead bodies. The adjacent conference room walls became the "murder board" where pictures of the crimes and suspects were being arranged and connections made to locations on a world map. It was all too much for Commission Chairman Taylor, who'd popped in to check on progress of the prominent murder victim's case. "What in the world?" the Chairman exclaimed.

"Yep, exactly. Don't worry Barney, the Sheriff's got this. She pulled on one thread and an entire underworld cloak of secrecy is unravelling." Explained DA Anderson, who never missed an opportunity to impress the Chairman. "Seems our quiet little bank is at the center of money laundering, drug trafficking, human trafficking and terrorists. Can you believe it Barney? We're gonna be famous!"

"Well, I'm not sure that's what I want to be remembered for... but, like any good politician, any fame is better than no fame at all." The Chairman quietly joked to his District Attorney. "I'll leave you to it. I'm headed over to the restaurant for the night. We're just getting to that part of the calendar where we should be crowded on a Saturday night now. The season is just around the corner. Tell the Sheriff we're all proud of her, Bill." With a pat on Bill's back, a sharp smile and a wink, Barney walked to the door and left.

"It ain't over yet, but damn it's exciting." DA Anderson quietly said to himself as he continued to watch the frenetic movements of the

Sheriff's team.

Jack Strong sat in his office next to the bullpen debating whether to send the Sheriff and update on their progress. There had not been a break in the case, per se, but the direction had shifted, and she might want to know what she's walking into on Monday morning. He thought that she might need to use some of her old FBI and Secret Service contacts now that the scope of the investigation has gotten global. He picked up his phone to send her a text when Jeff poked his head in the door. "Deputy Daniels, what can I do for you?" Jack said without looking up.

"I called the forensic accountant in Norfolk and sent her the personal account details we have for the Midgett's. She's keen to get to work on them right away, and since we're focusing on the bank, I thought we should just move ahead a couple of days early. You good with that?"

"Excellent. Good work Jeff. Keep me posted on what she finds."

'Jack?" Tim Cudworth asked. "I set an interview with the first Mrs. Midgett for the same time as the daughter tomorrow, at 5pm. We only have the two interview rooms here, but we could always go upstairs to the courthouse or over to the jail to get the room and keep everyone separate, assuming the son turns up. What do you think?"

"Still nothing from the son? Steve Lawrence, wasn't it?" Jack quizzed.

"Nope, but Jennifer has helped me access phone and credit card records on him. He's gone totally quiet since the day of the murder."

"Hummm. Ok, look at his activity in the week leading up to the murder. Look for suspicious transactions and recurring calls. Run it down." Jack instructed. "And Tim, good work. I think you're on to something there." Before Tim could leave the office, Jennifer appeared at the door. "JJ, got something to add?"

"Yes, I do. I did some digging into Steve Lawrence's bank accounts. Now this may be nothing since he's in commercial real estate and the commissions are huge, but about a week before the murder he had a $250,000 wire transfer drop into his savings account from a bank in Croatia."

Jack and Tim both looked at JJ and neither could speak. "Holy Smokes." Jack bolted from his chair and went into the conference room. He studied the map, and then turned in the doorway and shouted "Everyone! We've uncovered a significant clue that could break this case wide open. Tim and Jennifer can explain. I need to let Sheriff Thompson know." With that, Jack strode across the room and back into his office and closed the door. He stood for a second to gather himself. His hands were shaking. In all his years of sniper training and deployment, he'd only experienced this sensation once. This wasn't killing Bin Laden, but it was damn close. He took measured breaths to calm himself. He knew there was a long way to go, but he was certain they were headed down the rabbit hole and they were gonna kill the head of the snake. Jack picked up his cell phone and started typing a text to his boss.

Outside in the bullpen, Tim and JJ were explaining what they found, and you could hear a pin drop. DA Anderson, standing off to the side sipping what had to be his tenth cup of coffee, could be heard mumbling "Holy Smokes."

Jack popped out of his office a few minutes later, and there was a determined buzz around the room. "Ok, people. Tink, you need to work from Eastern Europe back to here. I know. I know. Virtually. Interpol. MI5 CIA. Get them all involved. We could be looking at a terror network. Tim, you, and Jennifer need to track Steve Lawrence's exact movements leading up to the murders. JJ put Kelly Fuco's contacts on the back burner for now. We know a lot of men wanted her dead, and probably a few women too, but this lead takes priority. The son could be the killer, or he could have contracted for the killing. Jeff, I want you to help Tink, and also work with Suzie Chin to track money at the Bank. Get the Treasury involved. I'll get the Sheriff to use her Secret Service contacts to help you there and Angie, you could get your FBI guys involved too. Whatever you normally pay them, the county will pick up the tab. Got it?"

"Got it Jack." Angela beamed.

"Let's go people!" Jack shouted as he went back into his office.

Tink leaned over to JJ and asked, "Who's Suzie Chin?" which earned him a 'I-don't-know' look and a shrug.

THIRTY-TWO

"The funeral is tomorrow Momma and we still don't know where Stevie is. I'm really worried now. It's not like him to just disappear for both of us. I usually talk with him a few times each week, more lately with what's been going on." Jennifer Lawrence lamented.

"I know." Carol said. "I speak with him almost every day. Sometimes he just calls to tell me he loves me. That's it. Thirty seconds, a minute tops, and now I haven't heard from him since the murder. I don't know what to do. Should we call the police? Report him missing? I really don't want any more police. Bad enough I have to meet with the Dare County Sheriff on Sunday. Are they talking to you too, Jenn?"

"Yep. I have a meeting set for 5pm."

"Me too." Carol squealed.

"Ok, mom. This isn't a social. The police are questioning us about dad's murder. You need to get a grip."

"I realize, honey, but at least we can get it out of the way together and put all this unpleasantness behind us. Your father made nothing but trouble for us when he was alive, and now that he's dead I was hoping we could..."

"Just let sleeping dogs lie?" Jennifer finished her mother's thought.

"Well, yes. Exactly." Carol grew quiet and they both drifted off into their own worlds sitting in Carol's room at the White Doe Inn. "Have you ever stayed here before?" Carol asked out of the blue.

"No, mother. I checked online for something in Manteo that would suit us. It's close to the funeral home and offers us some privacy. Best of all, it's away from that monstrosity of a house Dad lived in, or his 'grieving widow'. The less time we have to spend around her, the better. The scheming dog! Did you know she's a chain smoker? All those eastern European mail-order brides are. Her clothes wreak of cigarettes, and the linens, pillows, cushions and curtains in that house will need to be burned when she's gone."

"I guess Ralph's standards slid as he got older, fatter and less attractive. Lord knows, his only redeeming feature was his wealth. Nice to know he's paying for all this" she said as she gestured around the lavish room. "This is lovely. You chose very well Jenn. Very well indeed." Carol sat proudly in the large cane chair in the mint green sitting room near the fireplace. "I booked in a 90-minute massage for tomorrow after breakfast. Have you considered it?"

"No, but that does sound delightful. Did you confirm with the front desk or is it an outside service you've engaged?"

"I contacted the front desk and they took care of it for me. Someone will pop in here at noon, so I'll be indisposed for a couple of hours. Oh, I do hope they send me some strapping young body builder for me. Yummy! Oh, wouldn't that be fun." Carol fantasized and drifted off into her make-believe world.

"Yes, well I think I'll go down now and arrange one for me as well. I hope you don't mind, but I've made plans for dinner with a lovely gentleman I met last night. He's quite charming and very handsome and has the most divine accent. So, I might be otherwise engaged tomorrow morning as well. Should I stop by, say 4:30pm to pick you up for our meeting?" Jennifer suggested with an entitled air.

"Huh? What?" Carol said with a start as she returned from her fantasy. "Oh, yes. 4:30 would be excellent. Have fun tonight and do be careful dear. I worry so about you and your playing with strangers. Give us a kiss."

"Yes, mommy, I'll be careful." Jennifer kissed her mother's cheek and walked out of the door with a wave good-bye.

THIRTY-THREE

"That was a delicious lunch, and Will, I invited you, so you really shouldn't have paid. It was very sweet though, so thank you. Can I buy you two a coffee? I need to talk to Betty, but it's nothing we can't discuss together." Lizzie offered as the table was being cleared.

"Are you sure, Mrs. Thompson? I can always disappear for a while so you two can talk privately." Will said as she slipped her black AMEX back into her purse. "And it is always my pleasure to pay for such delightful company."

"Ok, that didn't come out right. You make us sound like we're hookers!" Betty laughed, and then Lizzie realized the meaning as well.

"Oh, my, yes... are we dirty girls?" Lizzie whispered playfully. Will and Betty shot each other a shocked look, both remembering their shower together earlier, and then doubled over laughing.

"I'm sorry. Y'all know what I was trying to say." Will said with a broad grin showing her perfect teeth. "Charlie?" Will called to the waitress, "can you bring us some coffee please?"

"Yes ma'am, right away" the young girl spun around and hurried off to fetch the request.

"So, Will, you're very familiar with the staff. Are you a member here?" Lizzie enquired diplomatically.

"Yes ma'am. My company purchased a corporate membership. That allows my employees to use the place too, which is a nice perk for their families, the pool, tennis courts and golf, but they can also use it to entertain clients. The membership, I'm happy to say, gets a lot of us. I use the clubhouse for entertaining and the golf course for relaxing. I use the tennis courts to win. I played in college."

"Oh!" both Lizzie and Betty said together. Betty then shot her mother a look and commented "Remember, this is new for me. I'm learning right along with you!"

"That's Ok. There's a lot of ground to cover after 35 years. Anyway, as you can imaging, when I showed up at ECU my freshman year, the volleyball, basketball, swim, and tennis coaches were all after me to walk on to their teams. I'd played all of them in high school, and at five feet eleven inches short, they saw what I could bring to their teams without having to commit to a scholarship. You see, I was offered scholarships to play basketball at Clemson, TCU and Boston College, and volleyball at Georgia Tech, Virginia, Western Kentucky, and Ohio State, but I always knew I was going to ECU. That's where my parents went to school, and it's pretty close to Raleigh, where daddy spent his last years with the Bureau."

"Will's dad was career FBI" Betty volunteered proudly as she looked at her mom and Will. "I know some stuff, but I'm loving the story. Sorry to interrupt."

Will gave her a wink, and picked up "So, I decided to swim, because I love the shape it keeps me in, and I played tennis, because I love to compete, and tennis was my best sport. At least I thought so. I worked my way up the team ladder to where I was playing #2 singles and #1 doubles my senior year."

"Wow, that's impressive" Lizzie said with a sincere look.

"Thank you…. Charlie? Did you forget our coffee?"

"Um, I'm sorry Ms. Moore. I'll bring it right now, on the house."

Charlie hurried over with three cups and saucers and then scampered back for the coffee pot, which was a large traditional silver service, complete with matching cream and sugar. It was quite elegant.

"Very nice Charlie. Thank you. Sheriff, would you be so kind to pour while I excuse myself to the ladies?" Will said while getting up. "Back in a flash."

Lizzie waited until Will had disappeared before she spoke. "She is delightful! You look very happy, and I couldn't be happier for you. I cannot wait to tell your father. I saw what the job did to him, and I've worried that you were headed down that road too young. Oh child, tell me how you met."

"Ok, mom. You breathe for a minute and I'll talk. I'm glad you are happy. I really am, but let's not get too far out over our skis, shall we? Will and I are still new, and there's miles to go before we sleep. She's very successful, very driven. I'm the same. You know what conflicts can arise from those personalities clashing! Although, I have to say, early indications are good. We have a lot in common, and a lot of differences, but the best thing is her heart. You always told me to look at how someone treats a waiter or a dog. 'If they are mean to either, they are no good.' Well, I can tell you, she treats everyone with kindness and respect, and I have it on good authority from my top deputy that she loves dogs. But, like I said, early days...." Seeing that Lizzie was about to interject, "I know I'm not getting any younger. Can we at least wait for the 'Tim Test'? Dad has a way of seeing things that mere mortals seem to miss."

"I will grant you that. He can be 'other worldly' with his intuition." Lizzie agreed.

"Other Worldly... Oooooh, tell me more" Will giggled as she pulled out her chair. "Sorry, it took a minute more than I expected, but, as they say, it happens! But all better now. Have you two had a chance to chat?"

"Oh, gosh no. We spent the whole time talking about you, sweetie." Betty and Will almost spit out their coffee at Lizzie's honesty. "But I guess I really should get to the reason I asked you to lunch. Betty, how would you feel if your father and I moved here full time? He's gotten his business to where he can operate from virtually anywhere, and I am just sick and tired of dealing with DC. I'm selling my business and looking to open something similar here. What do you think?" Lizzie had been so nervous about broaching this subject she didn't even look up from her hands playing with her coffee cup. When she finally did, she saw the enormous smile on Betty's face and tears running down her beautiful cheeks.

"Oh, my God momma. That would make me so happy. Oh, I was so worried there was something wrong. I have been a nervous wreck inside." Betty gushed.

"Well, Tim thought you'd worry. That's why we called you so early. He didn't want you to have to sleep on it, and we didn't feel it was something we should tell you on the phone. Now, there's still details to be worked out, but we're selling the house in Potomac and buying a condo in Alexandria so when he has to go to DC for meetings, he won't have to stay in a hotel. I've already got several buyers for the business, so I came down to start scouting new locations here."

"Ok, well, between the two of us, you have pretty much every contact on the island." Betty blurted out. "Oh jeez. I'm sorry Will, I just threw you in without asking."

"Betty! Really! This is your mom. Of course, I'll help. Contacts are my life. You are right, between the two of us, we should be able to get you in front of all the best people, and help you avoid those you need to avoid. Don't worry Lizzie, we got you." Will exclaimed before taking a sip of her coffee. "Now, help me out. What kind of business are you looking to open?"

"Hey, I guess that would help" Lizzie joked. "I own a deli, but it's also a specialty shop, carrying meats and cheeses, crackers and baked goods, jams and preserves, from all over the world. We do breakfast and lunch and catering, and close by 3pm every day. I got the idea after the girls flew the coup and Tim still had several years to retirement. I've always loved to cook and bake, and specialty food items from around the world were kinda my jam. Literally! Lord," she said pensively, "that's been 20 years." She sat back in her chair with her hand to her cheek shaking her head in disbelief.

"Ok. Off topic here, but girls? You have sisters?" Will gave a surprised look to Betty and then turned to address her mom "Lizzie, remember we're new."

"Yeah, one. Veronica. Vicki. She's my younger sister by two years. She still lives in DC. Lawyer. Married with two kids. I'm the black sheep of the family." Betty deadpanned.

"Oh, cry me a river!" shouted Lizzie. "We've always loved you girls the same, and we always will. You don't like how we treat you; you can pack your things and leave!"

"Damn, momma, you never change. That was the same speech you gave me when I was ten and got mad because you got Vicki a new barbie and didn't get one for me." Betty joked.

"It was her birthday!!!" Lizzie cried out. "Her birthday!"

Will went from shocked face to hysterical laughter in a New York minute, and both Thompson women enjoyed the moment.

"More coffee?" Lizzie beamed as she lifted the service to pour everyone another cup. "This is too fun to end." She said to mutual agreement. The girls blew on their coffee, took a sip, and looked at each other and nodded. 'We got this,' they thought contentedly. It was then that Betty's phone vibrated, and she saw a new text had come in from Jack Strong.

"Excuse me. I need to reply to this." She stood and walked to the Grill bar to have some privacy while she read the note.

All good. Team gr8. All pumped. On the scent. May need ur contacts in SS & FBI. Going Int'l. Even DA excited! DO NOT CALL OR COME IN

'Wow', she thought. 'Jack is a natural born leader. I knew I made the right call on him.' She floated back to the table. "Seems Jack has everything under control, and it's getting pretty interesting. Says the investigation is international. He's like a bloodhound when he gets a scent, so I expect there will be real results when I get in on Monday." Sitting between them, Jill got a squeeze from her mom and a kiss from her lover.

THIRTY-FOUR

The next morning the team dragged into the bullpen. They were exhausted, but no one called out. They were running on adrenaline and coffee. Well, Jack and Tink downed Red Bull, but everyone else drank coffee. Last night was a long night of running down leads, sifting information, and prioritizing strategy. The murder board looked like a who's who of euro-trash underworld. I doubt Ralph Midgett ever knew his third wife's family, or how they made a living, but it was becoming clear that he was targeted because he owned a bank, and Tatiana was the bait he swallowed hook, line and sinker.

Today would be more of the same, except today there would be interviews. Serious, face to face, make them sweat, read them their rights interviews. Or so everyone thought.

"Suzie Chin, nice to meet you. I'm Jack Strong, leading this investigation for the Dare County Sheriff's department. Welcome to the Outer Banks!"

"Thank you, Jack Strong." She shook his hand and added, "my, you certainly are… strong." She giggled and blushed.

"Right, well Jeff tells me great things about you, and your work for us yesterday has really moved mountains for us, so let's find you some place to work and I can leave you to it." Jack looked around the room for an open cubical and walked her to one that seemed to have the most promise, as in, least debris piled up in it. "Will this do? Deputy Daniels, you here yet?" Jeff's head popped up. "Come introduce yourself to Suzie Chin, and then clear this crap out so she has a place to work."

"On it boss. Hey Suzie, I'm Jeff. Nice to meet you finally." They shook hands, and Suzie just gawked at the mountain of a man. Suzie was not a tall woman, just a shade over 5 feet tall so she was a good 18 inches shorter than Jeff, which meant her head came up to his pectoral muscles. She was not slim. She had a sweet round face with round glasses that complimented her round body. She, however, was insatiable around men, and the bigger, the better as far as she was concerned. Between Jack and Jeff, she was in heaven. JJ was the first to notice the new kid ogling her man, although Jeff didn't know he was yet, but he would, and now it would be sooner than later.

"Hi Suzie. I'm Jennifer." She said sweetly as she shook her hand. She then leaned in close and whispered, "hands off lady. He's mine." Then she stepped back and said, "Welcome to the team!" to a stunned Suzie Chin. "Let me walk you around and introduce you" JJ said as she took her by the elbow and walked her away from Jeff, who hadn't noticed the confrontation because he was carrying boxes of records off to the conference room. "Hey, Tink, this is Suzie Chin." JJ cooed as if nothing happened.

"Hi Suzie. Nice to meet you. I'm Tink Taylor. I'm working the European connections. Your work on the financials is really opening doors for me with Interpol and British Intelligence."

"Thanks. Nice to meet you."

"Hey Tim, meet Suzie Chin" JJ continued the tour. "You'll love Tim. He's a real sweetheart.

"Hello. Nice to meet you Suzie." Tim shook hands but looked confused. He began to speak to her, but she was already moving along, and he was left with his mouth open wondering what that was all about.

"Here, let me get that for you Tim" Angela pushed his mouth closed as she walked by, and he snapped out of his daze and sat back down.

"I take it you are Suzie Chin" Angela suggested as she approached from behind, catching the two ladies unaware. They both spun around, and Suzie was nose-to-nose with Angela. "I'm Angela. You met Jack, right? Big and Strong... well, he's mine, so don't mess with him or I'll mess you up. Got it? Am I clear?" she said in a whisper.

"Um, yeah. Ok. Whatever. You two ladies finished marking your territory? I got work to do." She shot a look at JJ and Angie and walked back to her cubical.

"That went well..." Angie mumbled. "I hope she's not some ninja."

"Don't worry. I bet you can take her. Besides, she does cyber stuff, so she'll probably just trash your credit and get your car repossessed." JJ patted Angie reassuringly on the shoulder and walked back to get more coffee.

"Folks! Hey, if I can have your attention for just a minute," Jack shouted to the group. "First, Thank you for all your excellent work yesterday. We have really moved this investigation along. I'm not going to single out any one of you right now, because this has been a total team effort, but I gotta say, I am proud and impressed by each of you. Let's remember, our goal is to catch the killer of Kelly Anne Fuco and Ralph Midgett Sr. If we expose an international crime ring and terrorist organization, well, that's just icing on the cake." A huge roar for the group and a round of applause. It wasn't the Saint Crispin's Day speech from Henry V, but it worked.

Tim was the first to approach Jack "Great speech Jack" he deadpanned. "I've been trying to get Jennifer Lawrence and Carol Lawrence to confirm today at 5pm. I got Carol, and we're set, but I can't get Jennifer. I'll keep trying but wanted you to know." Jack nodded and Tim walked to his desk to keep working. He and Jennifer had unearthed a treasure trove of details on the two kids and their mom and he needed to sift through it all to organize his thoughts for the interviews later.

"Jack? Jack." JJ moved into his eyeline. "I've pulled records on both mother and daughter going back a month before the murder. Seems they both were getting large deposits into their accounts from overseas, and there was a steady stream of phone calls from Tatiana Midgett to Carol Lawrence. My gut tells me that Tatiana was the point man arranging the hit for the family back in Eastern Europe, and they used Carol and the kids to run cover for them."

"Ok. Good work. I want you to pull everything that Tink has on Tatiana together with what you've found and let's ask her to come in for an interview here. Try for today at 5pm. If Carol Lawrence and Tatiana Midgett happen to see each other, even better."

"Got it boss. On it." JJ spun around and looked for Tink. "Tink? You here?" Deputy Taylor popped up and signaled and Jennifer speed walked over to him.

"Hey Jeff, got a minute? Step inside." A few seconds later the big man moved into Jack's office and closed the door.

"Yeah Boss?" the deep baritone voice of Deputy Jefferson Daniels crooned.

"How's Chin doing?" Jack asked as he sat in his chair and motioned for Jeff to do the same across from him.

"She's killin it, Boss. I mean seriously talented stuff. We've gotten information, legally mind you, that we would have spent months tracking down. Everything she's got for us is Gold Standard. Take it to the bank."

"So, what you're telling me is, she's Ok?" Jack asked stone faced.

Jeff tilted his head a bit and looked eye to eye with Jack. "You messin' with me, ain'tcha Boss? Yeah, you messin' with me." Jeff began to chuckle which sounded more like a rumble from a rockslide, and Jack broke into a deep grin, which showed off his dimples. Angela was sitting across the room working on her laptop when she looked through the office window and saw Jack's big grin. She melted.

"Ok Jeff. Here's what I need you to do. First, go home and change. Comfy casual beachwear. Then leave your cruiser and take your personal car. No high speed chases. Nothing crazy. Just recon. We're going to stir the pot, poke the bear, swat the hive, whatever you want to say, and I'm guessing Mrs. Midgett is going to flinch. You know the parking lot on Chicahawk Trail?"

"Yep, just before Hwy 12, right?

"That's the one. If you park as close to the beach as possible in that lot, you will have a clear view of the entrance to the Midgett Mansion. You stay on the radio and we'll let you know when you might expect movement. If and when she goes out, you tail her and log everywhere she goes."

"I'm on it Boss like white on rice!"

"Good man Jeff. Remember to take plenty of water and snacks, and an empty bottle to pee in. Call me when you're in position." Jack said to Jeff's back as he was leaving the office.

"Jack, we have a situation" Tim called from his desk just outside Jack's office. Jack shot out of the door as Tim stood to meet him. "We have another body. A young woman washed up on the beach near Oregon Inlet. Initial ID from Nags Head PD is Jennifer Lawrence. A fisherman found her when he went to set up for the day. It was called in around 8am. Strangled with a thin wire and dumped in the ocean. Probably took a fishing boat out before sunrise and disposed of the body. They didn't factor in the onshore breeze, current near the inlet and the tide. She had not been in the water long, so the fish hadn't picked her apart yet. Cora was called to the scene and estimated time of death around 3 am. She reported that the body was nude, and she had sex last night, no DNA, but there was some flesh under her fingernails and Cora's running that to see if we get any matches."

"Have Nags Head notified Carol Lawrence yet?" Jack asked

Tim shook his head, "and I told them not to. I let them know we'd handle that, and they were fine with it. You know, who wouldn't be. Worst part of the job."

"Right. Ok. Can you get over to the morgue and get some photos from Cora. Scene of the discovery, close up of the face, you know the drill. And keep this buttoned up. The first time I want her to hear about this is from us in the interview later."

"Got it boss." Tim rocked out of his chair, stretched his back, and walked briskly out of the bullpen.

Jack sat watching this and thought 'I cannot remember ever seeing him move that quickly. Damn, he must be into this.' He shook his head in disbelief and sat back in his chair. 'Well,' he thought, 'the rats are nervous and they're deserting the ship.'

THIRTY-FIVE

"Morning princess!" I let you sleep for a bit, but it's 9am and a glorious day outside Will gently rocked Betty and then kissed her.

"Oh, no... I have awful morning breath. Don't kiss me. I'll kill you from the stench." Betty protested with one eye open. "On second thought, you look so good in that bikini" she exclaimed as she flipped Will on her back. Will offered no resistance. After a few minutes of heart pumping activity, she went limp, and Betty gave her gentle kisses all the way up her body until she pressed against Will, who moaned again deliciously.

"Good morning princess!" Betty grinned. "What's on the agenda today?"

"More of the same, I hope." Smirked Will in reply as she stroked Betty's body and kissed her neck.

"Definitely works for me, lover. Definitely."

"Why don't you put on your bathing suit and we can go lounge by the pool and eat some fruit for breakfast and enjoy this glorious sunny day." Will whispered to her. "The weather report is for clear skies and highs in the mid to upper 80's with just a light breeze out of the southeast. I fixed a platter and I've got a full pot of coffee in an insulated carafe already down there. All I'll need is you, and I'll be set."

"Ok. I'll meet you down there. Let me just brush my teeth and put on my suit and I'm ready."

"Ok, see you down there. I've got sunscreen, and hats, but you need to bring your sunglasses. It's really bright when you're near the water like this." Will cautioned while she adjusted her top and walked to the door. Betty watched that lovely bottom sway through the door and quietly said "I've died and gone to heaven. I truly have."

Not more than five minutes later, Betty came bouncing down the stairs from the balcony in the cutest little white string Brazilian bikini and matching white sunglasses and flip-flops. She had on gold drop earrings and a gold ankle chain, with a big gold watch bracelet. The white and gold against her skin was breathtaking, and Will dropped her glasses to get a better look. "That is a bikini!" Will shouted across the pool. "Give me a twirl so I can see the whole thing!" Betty obliged without breaking stride, like a practiced runway model. "Oh, you better watch out. I might just steal that one for myself. Hey, before you get too far, turn around and go through that door. There are a ton of hats, ball caps, floppy sun hats, whatever you like."

"Ok, thanks," and in a flash Betty was back with a big white sun hat with a broad brim and a cute pink ribbon around the base. "Does this work?" she called out as she circled the pool to the deck loungers facing back to the house. "Does this hat make my butt look big?"

"Nope. No, it does not. Honey, get over here."

"Will, you were right about the privacy here. We really could get naked and nobody would see us." Betty said as she rocked up to a lounger and dropped her phone on the table. "Oh sweetie, this is really spectacular. Thank you for making this a weekend to never forget." She bent over Will and kissed her, softly at first, and then more passionately, cupping her head in her hand. "Oh, you make me dizzy" as she stood up and stretched her arms high above her head. Will reached up and raked her manicured nails down Betty's brown body, causing her to shudder in delight. "Oh, Wilma Ruth Moore, you are a bad girl, and I love it!"

THIRTY-SIX

"Yes, Jeff. You in position? Great. Sit tight and I'll let you know when things should start poppin'." Jack hung up the phone and called out to the bullpen "hey Tink? You ready to call Tatiana Midgett and arrange that interview today?"

"You bet boss. I'm dialing now." Jack showed up behind Deputy Taylor to ease drop on the conversation. "Hello, this is Deputy Tink Taylor with the Dare County Sheriff's department. Can I speak with Mrs. Tatiana Midgett please?" He covered the mouthpiece and said "they are going to get her" …. "Yes? Um, ok. Right. I understand. Can you tell her it's extremely urgent that I speak with her now? We've had some developments in the murder of Mr. Midgett that we need to discuss." Covering the phone again he turned to Jack and said, "she's standing right there arguing with the housekeeper!" Back on the phone "Excuse me? Oh. Indisposed? Oh." Tink gathered himself and then spoke slowly and plainly "I've spoken to Tatiana several times. I know her voice. She's standing right next to you. If you do not put her on the phone immediately, we will have no choice but to come and arrest her for obstruction of justice. Am I clear? Oh, hello Mrs. Midgett! Thank you so much for taking my call. Yes, I'm sorry about the timing. Yes. Ok. Well, the reason for my call, as I explained to your housekeeper, we've had some developments in the case and we need you to come to our office today, 5pm, to review some of the evidence and help us understand how these pieces fit. Oh. I see. Ok. 5:15 then. Very well. We're happy to accommodate. See you then. Right. Bye. Wait. What? Oh, I don't think that will be necessary, it's completely your choice. Ok. Bye." Tink hung up the call and smiled to the deputies who had joined Jack to listen to the call. "Got her! Bet she runs like a rabbit"

"What was that bit at the end of the call?

"Oh, she just asked if she should bring her lawyer? Usually guilty as sin question." Tink answered smugly.

Jack was already speed dialing Jeff's number. "We are good to go. Be ready to move. Remember, Follow. Document. Report. Leave your phone on so we can track you. Happy hunting Big Man!" Jack hung up and looked across the room. JJ, can you bring up Jeff's tracker on the big screen please? Who's getting the popcorn? Anyone want to take bets on her first stop?"

"Jack? I got Tim on line 1. Are you available? He sounds really excited!" the voice over the intercom chuckled.

"I got it. Thanks. Tim, it's Jack. Are you Ok?"

"Jack, I'm with the coroner and she's pretty pleased with herself. I'll put her on."

"Hello Jack, this is Cora Mae. Are you sitting down? I've got some important discoveries here. I haven't had time to write my report, but I figured you needed this ASAP."

"Thanks Cora. I appreciate that. Whatcha got for me?" Jack responded expectantly.

"Well, first, the young girl is definitely Jennifer Lawrence. As you already know, she was strangled and dumped in the ocean. She appears to have put up a pretty good fight before dying, and I was able to recover skin from under her fingernails. I'm running a DNA match in the universal database, but that may take days. However, I can tell you her last meal was quail salad and orange pecan stuffed Cornish hens and numerous Cosmopolitans. She was very drunk. She also had a healthy amount of, well, let's just say she has had a very active night. I've run the test and it's all from the same man. She did just about everything a man and a woman can do. Again, all from the same man."

"Goodness, she had a big night!" Jack said in amazement.

"Yep", Cora continued, "and it appears that the dinner was first, and the sex came after. Now, I did some checking, and unless they drove all over the county, the only restaurant you could get the quail salad and Cornish hen is 1587."

"Hold a second Cora." Jack stood up and shouted, "JJ here! Now!"

"Boss?" Jennifer responded immediately.

"Get over to 1587 and get their receipts for last night and find out who paid for a quail salad, Cornish hen and cosmopolitans. Man and woman on a date. Take a picture of Jennifer Lawrence. We need a description of her date pronto!"

"Got it." She shouted as she flew out of the door.

"Ok, Cora. Nice work."

"Oh, Jack, I'm not done with you yet." She said with a smile in her voice. "What's the old saying, save the best for last? Well, I was asked to help in Currituck on the Tom Mills case, so I did the autopsy. Well, when I did the autopsy on Ralph Midgett, a curious thing came up. They both have the same blood type – AB negative. That's the rarest blood type in the US, so that got me thinking. I ran DNA on both, and are you sitting down?"

"Oh my god! Tom Mills was Ralph Midgett's child?"

"Yes sir, Jack-o-boy o-boy.! How about that." Cora crowed with delight.

"Thanks Cora. You've hit a home run today. I'll buy you a drink when this is all done." Jack offered.

"Thanks Jack, but I haven't had alcohol in 25 years. Coke? Definitely."

"Deal. I gotta run. Tell Tim to hustle back." Jack hung up the phone to find Tim standing in the doorway.

"Pretty great stuff, huh Jack?" Tim beamed.

"Yep." Jack acknowledged. "Not sure how that tidbit of Tom Mills fits into the puzzle, but we'll need to chew on that."

JJ rushed back into the bullpen and slammed into her chair, fingers flying on the keyboard. "Come on. Come on." She mumbled in frustration with the computer. "Faster!"

"Jenn, what's up?" Jack demanded.

"I got the receipt. The hostess remembered the couple right off. Said they stayed for about two hours. Leisurely dinner. Lots of drinks, especially for her, and lots of laughter and the usual date stuff, petting, pawing, kissy kissy, the usual. He paid on a card and left a generous tip. That's why they remembered him. The bill was $175, and he left a $125 tip! The hostess said there was a reservation, but the name given was not the same as the name on the card. I'm running the card and the name now. I think he got cocky and made a mistake and used his own credit card!" Jennifer said enthusiastically.

"Wow, great work!" Jack turned as his phone buzzed, pulled it from his pocket and answered, "Hello, Jeff?... Really?... Ok, stay on it." He hung up and turned back to JJ. "Anything pop?"

"Oh yeah! Anatoli Milanovich is his real name. He arrived from Croatia Wednesday, according to Customs. He entered through Kennedy in NY. I've got his picture, bringing it up and printing everything out for the file. His credit card shows activity in NY, DC, and here, including the charge for dinner last night and a boat rental from the Wanchese Marina. I'll take this picture over there and confirm he rented the boat and see if he's returned it yet. Back in a few." she said as she bolted out the door.

"Jack, I'm sitting right outside the White Doe Inn and I just heard a call on the radio that there is a body and they need assistance. I've got my badge and gun, so I'm responding. See you inside in a few..."

Jack never got to say anything to Jeff, but he called out to anyone listening in the bullpen that he'd be at the White Doe Inn. When he got to his car, he called the coroner and asked her to meet them with a CSI team. Two minutes later he screeched to a halt and raced into the bed and breakfast. Jeff was in the lobby with Tatiana Midgett, and she was hysterical.

"They killed her! They killed her! And I'm next. Oh God, what have I done!"

Jack nodded to Jeff, "Read Mrs. Midgett her rights, cuff her and process her back at the station, but put her in an interview room. I'll be along later. Charge her with obstruction and lying to investigators for now. Where's the body?" Jeff indicated down the hallway and Jack started walking.

Bob and Bebe Woody owned the White Doe Inn and have run this beautifully restored bed and breakfast for the past 25 years. They were standing outside the guest room Carol Lawrence previously occupied. "Hello. I'm Deputy Strong. Sorry we have to meet in these circumstances. Seems you have a lovely home."

"We do" Bob said, "and we've never had anything like this before."

"I'm sure. Thank you for closing the wing off so the crime scene is preserved for our investigators. Did you give Deputy Daniels your details, and your statement?"

"We gave him our business card and said we'd be available whenever he needed us, but he had his hands full with that hysterical woman." Bob explained.

"Ok, thanks. Well, before I go into the room, can you briefly tell me what you saw or heard leading up to Deputy Daniel's arrival?"

"I'll let Bebe tell it. I was in our apartment and came running when she called me."

"I was working the front, checking the books, when that woman came rushing inside and asked where Carol Lawrence was staying. Well, it's against our policy to discuss guest accommodations so I told her I'd ring the room. I picked up the phone and dialed the room number, and, well, she must have noticed the number because she took off running down this hall. We aren't very big, so you could hear the room phone ringing from my desk. I got up immediately when I realized that no one was answering, which was odd because the guest, Mrs. Lawrence, had ordered a massage for 12 noon, so she should have been in her room. The woman was frantically beating on the door, and I asked her to please quiet down as she was disturbing the other guests, some of whom had come out to see what all the fuss was about."

"Yes ma'am. And then what happened?" Jack motioned to keep going.

"Well, I have a master key, so I opened the door. That woman rushed in before I could stop her, after all, it was possible she was taking a soak in the tub after her massage and simply couldn't answer the phone or the door. I was calling to her when that woman screamed and flew out of the door. I saw all the blood and, well, I needed to excuse myself. I called Bob and he came and called 9-1-1. I must say, I was very impressed with your Deputy Daniels responding so quickly, and on his day off too."

"Ma'am?" Jack asked, a bit puzzled.

"His dress. He's not in uniform!" She responded incredulously.

"Right, yes. He was undercover today. Tasked with following Mrs. Midgett. That's why he came so quickly but thank you for noticing. I'll be sure to let Jeff, er, Deputy Daniels know you appreciated his response. Well, right, if I could ask you both to wait in the lobby, the CSI team should be along to process the scene and the coroner will be here to handle the body. Also, we can give you some information on very good cleaning services who specialize in blood removal. Thank you both. I'm going to pop on some booties and gloves and take a quick look around."

"Thank you Deputy Strong. We'll leave you to it then." The Woody's both walked away to the lobby, obviously shaken by the events of the day, and worried about the effect this might have on their business.

'Right then, Jack. Seen it all before. Fresh body so shouldn't smell' Jack psyched himself up before going into the room. The door had been propped open with a door stop. Jack made a note to confirm with the Woody's if they did that. The bed was not made and looked as if it had been used more recently than last night. The bathroom had the look of use as well, with all the bath towels on the floor, damp, and water beads still visible in the shower and tub. "Did the killer wash up before leaving?' The adjoining sitting room had some of the furnishings moved to make room for the massage table. Indentations in the carpet told where chairs and tables customarily sat. The massage table was facing the windows overlooking the garden. The body was face down on the massage table, but covered in a sheet, as if the massage had ended. Mrs. Lawrence had her arms posed by her side and her face resting in the table horseshoe, provided for comfort when lying face down. The only indication that the woman was dead, aside from the enormous amount of blood, was the knife wound on her neck that almost decapitated her. Jack was careful not to disturb anything, especially the blood and the corpse, but at first blush, there didn't appear to be any bloody footprints or fingerprints. 'The techs will scour the rooms thoroughly and if there's anything useful, we should know soon enough' Jack thought while shaking his head. "Hey, Cora! This is getting to be way too regular. I'll leave you to it."

"Thanks Jack. CSI is right behind me. We will keep you posted on what we find."

"I think we both will be burning the midnight oil tonight." Jack noted. "Take care of yourself Cora Mae. You look as exhausted as I feel."

Without replying, Cora walked over to the body and began her examination.

"Mrs. Woody? I didn't ask, but does the business provide the masseuse?" Jack inquired as he was leaving the lobby. Bob and Bebe were sitting in the room off to the side, trying to make sense of it all.

"No, we contract out. They bring their own table and are expected to return everything as they found it." Bob responded for his distraught wife. "I can give you their contact details, if that would help?"

"Yes, thank you. If you could email that immediately, and then I will respond with the names of some clean up and removal companies. I realize this has been a terrible shock, but I've seen it before, and it has almost no effect on the business. Sometimes, interest increases because of the notoriety and publicity."

"Thank you, Deputy. I hope so. We hope so. This is our life, not just our business." Bebe spoke through tears as she held her husband's hand.

"I know Jeff gave you his card, but here's my card. If you think of anything, a sound, something that, looking back, didn't seem quite right, give either of us a call. Unfortunately, the CSI team will be there most of the night, but they work quietly, so ... well, I have to run." Jack's phone dinged and when he looked down, he saw the email from the Woody's. "Thank you." He said as he headed out the front door.

THIRTY-SEVEN

Betty and Will lay quietly by the pool, both lost in their own thoughts and basking in the glow of a glorious weekend together. The sun was baking their bodies and moist beads of sweat dribbled from their chests and pooled on their stomachs. They had both dispensed with the formality of a bathing suit and were enjoying the prospect of an unrestricted tan.

"Betty, you are going to think I'm mad as a hatter, but have you enjoyed yourself this weekend? Now, don't blow up. I'm asking because I know this is not how you spend your weekends. It's definitely not how I spend mine. I can't remember the last time I didn't go into the office on Saturday and Sunday. My business is my life. I'm guessing policing is your life, and as you said, that's 24/7."

"Will, let's hop into the pool and cool off and I'll give you my answer." Betty stood and offered her hand to Will, who took it and joined her standing next to the cool blue pool. "Now, get in!" Betty commanded as she pushed Will and laughed as she flopped into the water. "You goof ball! This has been the best weekend of my life. Period. End of story. Hands down. And that's saying something, since I've graduated Georgetown undergrad and law school, accepted into and graduated from the FBI training program, and guarded the freakin President of the United freakin' States!" She shouted across the water. "None of that even comes close to this weekend. OK?"

"Ok. Good. Because this weekend has me rethinking my priorities." Will called out from the pool. "I've been so focused on work; I've neglected a huge part of me. You've opened my eyes, and other things," they both laughed, "and I'm seeing possibilities I never considered before."

"Yeah, well great sex will do that to you!" Betty grinned. "But, seriously, I know what you are saying. Hey. Move back. This is what, a twenty-five-meter pool? Get back to about three quarters of the way from me and spread your legs."

"Betty? What are you going to do to me?" Will asked sheepishly.

"Trust me?"

"Yes"

"Ok." Betty dove off the end of the pool and swam underwater, her powerful shoulder and back muscles rippling as she went through Will's legs, touched the far wall, pushed off and swam back through her legs before popping up for a breath. "Oh man, that felt good," she squealed. "I haven't done that in a few years. I just wanted you to know, you're not the only swimmer in this family."

Hearing those words "this family", made Will tear up. She threw her arms around Betty, and they stood in the water and silently hugged for several minutes in the late afternoon sun. Will whispered into Betty's ear, "Welcome to the family, babe. You and me."

"You and me. Betty and Wilma... Oh god, what have we done!" Betty shouted, and they both flopped about in the water, giggling, and laughing and singing the theme song to their new life. "Flintstones, meet the Flintstones... Yabba dabba do!'

Will swam over to the side and pushed herself up and out of the water, jogged over to their towels, wrapped herself and then brought the other over to Betty as she popped out. "I think your Mom liked me." Will said confidently.

"Ah, yeah! Ya think! I've never seen the woman beaming like that before. She loves you. My Dad will be a piece of cake. If anything, I'll have to make sure he doesn't try to steal you from me." Will shot her a suspicious look, and Betty added "Kidding!"

"Well, my Dad will even be easier. He's former FBI. You're former FBI. It will be like a reunion when you two get together. I'll just play barmaid and watch the show."

"Well, that provides an image I'll play with later." Betty chuckled.

"As a last resort, I can just take my Dad out and whip him on the golf course!" Will said with confidence.

"Oooooh, Kinky. Do you take the cat-of-nine-tails with you when you play golf?" Betty grinned wickedly, as they both enjoyed the joke. "But does your Dad know you're gay? That was the thing that blew me away about my Mom. We've never discussed sex much. The birds and bees, protection, our cycle, that junk, but not preferences. I was stunned that she was happy for me that I was happy, and not being all judgey about who I'm dating and what sex they are. I mean, I've dated boys before in high school, and a few men along the way since law school, but a few women too. I got the feeling from my folks that after 39 years of waiting, they'd sort of given up that I'd get married and have a family. I think they saw me as married to my work, and I guess, in a way, I was."

"My Dad has no idea. He still sees me as his little girl in pig tails and ribbons and bows. I don't know if he's even realized I have breasts. Before you two meet, I plan on having a serious heart to heart about the birds and the bees with him. He's a really good man, sweet, kind, and considerate to a fault, but he's a poppa bear and protective of his cub. It's just been him and me since I was a wee lass, so I get it. But he's also very traditional, very conservative, so I may have to break it to him gently that I like women as much as he does."

"Hopefully, he'll see how happy you are, and, you know, I go both ways, so if you think it would help for me to stroke more than his ego...."

"Betty!!!" Will shouted, and put her hands to her ears., "Lalalalalala......

No! A thousand times No!" and then she shimmied in disgust and stuck her tongue out in a mock vomit. "I think you just traumatized me for life."

"Hey, would you like to go on a sunset cruise on our last night?" Betty asked happily.

Will made a face and frowned. "Last night? It is not. Maybe the last night of the weekend, but babe, we have a lot more nights ahead. Let's go in, shower and change, take a cruise, drink some cocktails and eat dinner on the water. Is that a plan?"

"It is. Perfect."

After washing the chlorine out of their hair, soaping up their bodies to wash the suntan lotion off, and throwing on some fresh clothes, they headed down to the dock. Will wore low cut skinny jeans and a sports bra and white boat shoes. She carried a white cashmere sweater, in case it got cool. She left her hair to dry in the wind and only wore silver teardrop earrings and her thumb ring for jewelry. Betty put on jeans, sandals, and a white tee shirt but no bra. She brought a hoodie to pull on if it got cool.

Will pressed the button in the garage to open the small garage door for the golf cart while Betty grabbed a couple of ball caps for them. Will also pushed the button on the garage wall to activate the hydro lift and lower the boat into the water. They zipped out of the garage and the door magically closed behind them. As they approached the dock, the boat was settling in the water, ready to go. Pulling up alongside, Will pushed the key fob for the boat and the automatic side door opened so they could walk right on.

"You didn't do that before?" Betty protested.

"I was testing you. I wanted to see if you had sea legs and could get around a boat without falling in the water. Now that I know you're good, I can make life easier. Plus, honestly, I was so taken by you, I forgot. Tee Hee." Will scampered on board before Betty could connect with her punch to the shoulder.

"You brat!" Betty scolded.

The engines roared to life and Will carefully guided the boat out of her slip and on to the open water, which tonight was smooth as glass. They both put on their hats to shade their eyes and hold their hair down. Will slowly powered the engines up to get the boat to rise up on plane, and then she throttled her wide open. The ride was exhilarating. The temperature perfect. The company sublime. They were flying across the Albemarle Sound heading due west. After about 5 minutes, Will throttled back to an idle and asked "Cocktails?" Betty flared her eyes and nodded 'yes' enthusiastically. "You keep watch to make sure no other boats come and run us down while I duck below and play bartender." Will opened the hatch, which Betty had not noticed before, and disappeared down into the cabin.

"That's new too! How cool is that! What all is down there?" an eager Betty quizzed.

"Well, there's a refrigerator, a stove top and microwave here in the galley. There's a toilet, sink and shower over there, pointing over her right shoulder, and through there, at the front of the boat, is a queen size bed, closet and storage." The tour complete and the G&T's made, Will reemerged from the cabin, and handed Betty her drink. "Oh wait," as she ducked down below again, only to pop up with a tray of fruits, cheeses, and crackers. "Nibbles?"

"Yes please! What else do you have down there? Side of beef?" Betty laughed. "Anyway, I can't believe I've been on this boat three times now and this is the first you mention a toilet! I almost pee'd myself Friday night and thought I'd have to wet the deck. Now you tell me there's a toilet!"

"Ok. I'm sorry. Remember? New to all this" Will said as she gestured back and forth between the two of them. "Are we good? I mean, are you happy with this spot to watch the sunset?"

"Yes, and Yes."

Will pushed a button to engage the windlass and lower the anchor. She checked the gauge for depth, and when she felt she'd paid out enough chain for a good set, she slowly eased the boat into reverse to allow the flukes to dig into the bottom. Satisfied that they wouldn't be going anywhere, she cut the engine and flipped the mast light on. It was still light out, but she wanted to make sure the anchor light was set before it got dark. Always the insurance agent managing the risk.

"Ok, let's relax and talk. Why don't we move to the back where we can watch the stars light up the sky and enjoy the glorious end to a glorious weekend." Will carried the tray, and Betty took the two glasses. They got comfortable, facing each other, Betty facing forward, Will facing aft. The sun was setting slowly beside them as they quietly rocked to the gentle rhythm of the water.

"I don't mean to be a kill joy, but you know I need to get home tonight. I have my uniform, laptop, work phone, all that stuff, and my car at my place." Betty said suddenly, as if the real world were closing in around her.

"I know sweetie. I'll take you home on this and then run back by myself. Whatever you left at the Kitty Hawk house can stay there waiting for you to return. And I can leave some stuff at the Manteo pad. We can work it out slowly, but that can give us the flexibility to stay either place and still be able to function. Is that too fast for you, Betty? I can get ahead of myself sometimes and I don't want you to feel any pressure."

"I'm good with all of that. In fact," Betty confessed, "I was making a mental checklist of things I should pick up to leave at your house. Is that too fast?"

"Not at all. But one correction, mi casa es su casa. From now on," Will suggested, "the house formerly known as My House is now, either Our

House or the Kitty Hawk House."

"And the condo formerly known as My House is now," Betty announced, "Our Condo or the Manteo House. Clear?"

"Yep. Crystal." Will leaned over and they kissed, softly and gently. "Perfect."

THIRTY-EIGHT

Jack called the team together, not for a pep talk, but a strategy session. Tatiana Midgett was sitting in Interview 1, cameras rolling, sound on, stewing for a bit, and Jack needed to decide how to play her.

JJ had come back from the Wanchese Marina with a positive ID on Tatiana's brother. He chartered a boat, and then bribed the Captain handsomely to allow him to use it privately. Told him he wanted to impress his girl with a midnight cruise.

"Thoughts? Tim?"

"She's scared for her life," Tim started, "and can't stop saying the word DEAL every five minutes. We've got a mountain of evidence, but she needs to fill in the blanks."

"How about we use a soft touch," Tink suggested. "Let's let JJ play the sympathetic role and have Big Man just stand there guarding the door. Honestly, I pee myself sometimes when he's around, and I know and like the guy. No offense Jeff, but you are scary big."

The team chuckled and Jack spoke in agreement, "Tink, I think you are on to something there. I like it."

"Wow, wow, wow. Slow that train down. I've never been lead questioning a suspect before!" JJ interjected. "Help me out guys. This case is huge, and I don't want to be the one to blow it."

"Jack, how about we give her an earpiece," Angela chimed in, "and you can sit in the observation room and help walk her through the interview. Like they did on 'The Closer'" Everyone spun around to look at Angela, each with a question etched on their faces. "'The Closer?' TV show from like 10 years ago? Kiera Sedgewick? Anybody? No? Geez, you guys need to … ugh, troglodytes!" All eyes refocused on JJ

"Better?" Jack said with an intense stare into JJ's ice blue eyes.

"Better." A slight smile crept on to her beautiful face as she locked on to Jack's intensity to steel herself for the challenge. 'I can do this' she thought to herself.

"You can do this, JJ. We got you girl!" Jack encouraged. "Ok, let's pull the paperwork together and get you wired up." Jack looked to Jeff and said, "Go in there and offer her a drink. We need her to want to run to us, more than she already does and do anything we need, to protect herself."

"Got it boss." Jeff left.

"Ok, people. It's showtime." Jack announced, "Let's get this puppy to bed and have it all wrapped up in a nice bow for the Sheriff when she comes back in tomorrow."

"Hey Jack," Tim approached Jack in a lowered voice, "Any idea what the Sheriff has been doing on her first free weekend in months?"

"Not a clue, Tim. Probably sleeping, catching up on Netflix and reading some spy thriller or crime mystery, but you're guess is as good as mine."

"Well," Tim whispered, "between you and me, I hope she had fun." Jack's eyes went wide with understanding but then a broad grin formed.

"Me too, brother. Me too." Jack turned in the doorway to his office and watched his team whirl around the bullpen and conference room, pulling evidence, organizing paperwork, and reviewing pictures. He was pleased. In a week's time, this group had pulled together and was on the verge of cracking the biggest case in Dare County history. Jennifer was in the corner, getting wired up with the earpiece and testing it to get comfortable. Angie was helping her, talking into the headset. JJ's computer dinged and she leaned over to look at the notice and then bolted upright and shouted "He just bought fuel at Oregon Inlet. Anatoli is taking the boat and running!"

She moved into the conference room to study the map. "I put a tracker on his credit cards, and one just popped at the Inlet Fishing Center. Wanchese told me he had a 45 Hatteras sport fish. That has an eight-hundred-gallon fuel capacity. That gives him a range of between 200 and 800 miles depending on his speed. From the Inlet, he can go outside to Norfolk, or inside through the Intercoastal."

"I'm calling the Coast Guard to intercept and detain him." Deputy Taylor called out. "Did you find out if that boat has a tracker on it? High value boats usually have a marine Lo-Jack to make it easier to recover if they are stolen."

"Yes! They gave me the tracker number. Said we can plug it in to this website and it will show us location in real time." JJ crowed as her finger flew on the keyboard. "There he is! Gotcha, you bastard! Ha! He's going inside. Just going wide around Herring Shoal Island. He doesn't seem to be haulin' ass, so my guess is he'll be easy to track down with a Coast Guard Cutter, and their 50 cal deck mounted gun on the bow should get him stopped."

"Coast Guard is on it and they are tracking him now too." Tink informed the room. "They have the Cutter Bayberry in route, and they can get a 'copter up to assist if needed. They want him to get clear of Roanoke Island before engaging. Master Chief Brown said they will take him down when he gets to the mouth of the Albemarle Sound so he's as far from people as possible. He said they will hand him over to us at the Manteo dock. Command will keep us apprised."

You could see everyone was nervous, but it was a good nervous energy, Jack thought. The kind you get after hours of practice and preparation

FLIGHT

gets put to use in the big game. Tatiana Midgett's testimony would be critical, but he knew, they were ready. Jack went back to his office and grabbed a notebook and a few files from his desk and went to the observation room. She's been alone with her thoughts for over an hour, so he wanted to see how she was doing. Her head on the table as Jeff walked into the room, startling her from her nap.

"I thought you might need a drink, Mrs. Midgett" Jeff's baritone rumbled. "Didn't mean to wake you. Sorry. We'll be back shortly."

"Thank you, Deputy." Tatiana mumbled, sleepily rubbing her eyes to wake up. "I haven't been sleeping since the murder, and today has been exhausting."

"Yes, ma'am." He turned to leave but was stopped by her question.

"Will you protect me Deputy? My family is going to kill me. Not the Midgett's. They're all dead now, the Milanovich's. They are here, and they are coming for me."

"You're safe here, Mrs. Midgett. We'll be back shortly." Jeff said quietly as he opened the door and left.

Jack picked up the headset linked to JJ. "Don't go in yet! Give her another 15 minutes. I'll meet you in my office." He watched Tatiana put her head back on the metal table and close her eyes. 'The guilty always sleep' he thought.

Jack left the observation room and caught up to Jeff, "Come with me Big Man." They hustled down the hall and walked through the bullpen to Jack's office. JJ was waiting.

"She's really close to breaking down. Remember the goal is to get not just a confession, but to reveal the entire scheme. We need to know who started the whole thing, names, dates, everything. She is deathly afraid of her family in Croatia, so getting the back story on that will be key. Be sweet, not hard for you JJ," Jack said with a smile and a quick glance at Jeff who nodded in agreement." Be sympathetic, understanding. Let her unburden herself and you just guide her. Ok?

"I'm ready, Jack." JJ said confidently.

"Good. Communications all good?"

"Yep. Heard you loud and clear. I was waiting for you, wasn't I?" Jennifer responded.

"You want to add anything Jeff?" Jack shot a quick look at him.

"It won't be just you and me in the room. The whole team is with us." He slipped his massive arm around her shoulders and gave her a squeeze, "but we make a fine team, you and me, so let's show everyone what you got!" He beamed down at her and gave her a wink.

Jennifer blushed. She'd liked Jeff since the day she walked into work for the first time three years ago. It wasn't just a physical attraction, there was that sure, but it was an emotional connection with the gentle giant. He was like a white night, albeit, very dark skinned, her big black teddy bear and her older brother she never had, all rolled into one. "Thanks Jeff." She leaned into his hug. "Thanks Jack. I'll make y'all proud."

"Would you look at that," Jeff exclaimed, "the little Hispanic, black, Scandinavian girl from Minnesota talking southern! 'Y'all'..." He gave a deep rumbling laugh. "You killin me sista."

All three enjoyed Jeff's humor, but Jack broke up the party. "It's time." Jeff let Jennifer exit first, and Jack came up behind the Big Man and quietly offered "nice work. She's right where she needs to be" as he patted the mountain of a man's broad back approvingly. Jeff walked to catch up to Jennifer and they stood outside the interview room waiting for Jack and the team to get into the observation room.

"Ok" Jack spoke into the headset. "Go." The door to the interview room swung open and JJ entered with Jeff behind her. Tatiana looked up from her chair but didn't get up.

FLIGHT

"Hello, Mrs. Midgett. I'm Deputy Jennifer Jennette." She extended her hand to shake, and Tatiana looked suspiciously as she took it and gave a weak grip. "I think you know Deputy Jefferson Daniels here" she hooked her thumb over her left shoulder, and Tatiana looked up, and Jeff politely nodded. "First, I wanted to offer my condolences on the passing of your husband. I am sure that has been a terrible shock, and this has been a trying time for you."

"Thank you" Tatiana quietly mumbled as emotion started boiling inside her. Her lower lip began to quiver, and tears leaked from her eyes. Jennifer moved the tissue box and placed it in front of Tatiana. JJ sat on the steal chair opposite Mrs. Midgett, put the files and note pad off to the side and reached across the table and held Tatiana's hand.

"You're Ok, now. You're safe." Jennifer's ice blue eyes locked on to Tatiana's sad, brown eyes and they sat quietly for a while holding hands. Bonding. Trusting.

The silence lasted only a few brief minutes, but to Jeff, standing by the door, it seemed like an eternity. He was captivated by the poise and confidence, empathy and emotion JJ showed. 'She was good, damn good' he thought. He didn't show it on his face, not even a hint, but he was glowing inside.

"I can help you Tatiana. We can help you. Can you help us?" Jennifer broke the silence with a simple question that, hopefully would get the floodgates open.

"Yes." Tatiana replied quietly. "I can tell you everything."

Jennifer nodded her head, flipped open her notepad and said, "Before we start your story, I want to confirm that Deputy Daniels read you your rights?" Tatiana nodded. "And you are waiving your right to silence by speaking with us?" Another nod. And you know you have a right to an attorney during questioning?" She nodded again. "And you are waiving that right?"

"Yes", she finally spoke. "No attorney. They will get me killed. I need you. Protection. Witness protection. I need to disappear before they make me disappear!"

Tatiana was getting frantic again, so Jennifer replied calmly. "Ok, let's start at the beginning. How did you meet Mr. Midgett?"

So far, Jack had not said a peep to Jennifer. She was running the show and she was doing brilliantly. He muted the microphone to talk to Tim, who was taking notes next to him. "Let's be ready to run down leads from this story. We need to nail down everything. With Jennifer in there, we've lost one of our best computer people, so we need Angie and Tink to pick up that slack."

"Don't forget the new girl. Chen, chu, hell, Suzie something. She's a wiz on the keyboard." Tim reminded Jack.

"Oh yeah. Chin. Suzie Chin. She's here today? A Sunday and she came in?" Jack asked curiously.

"Yep. She was the second person in the door this morning. She walked in about 7:30." Tim replied.

"How do you know that Tim?"

"Because I was already here. I wanted to get a jump on things. I could feel that today was going to be the kind of day you dream about when you join law enforcement, and I didn't want to miss a minute of it." Deputy Cudworth offered proudly, and Jack quietly smiled.

Tatiana blew out a long breath and relaxed into her chair. "This is going to take a while" she said with resignation in her voice. "It's a long story, and it's not very pleasant."

"Not to worry. We have all the time you need, and we aren't here to judge, we just want the facts." JJ offered resolutely.

"Thank you, but you won't like me very much after I tell you, but if I'm going to live, and live with myself, I need to do this, and it has to be now." Tatiana said with tears filling her eyes again.

Jennifer quickly slipped a glance at the large mirror on her left, knowing that Jack and the team were on the other side. Tatiana didn't notice. She was wiping her eyes and blowing her nose after a good cry. "Ok, we knew Ralph was an easy mark..." Tatiana began.

Three hours later, Jennifer rose from her chair, stretched, and left the room. She shot Jeff a look to indicate he needed to stay and closed the door behind her. Jack, Tim and Tink were waiting in the hall with massive grins on their faces. "You must be exhausted" Tim was the first to speak.

"I'm so proud of you, JJ. You rocked in there. Perfect tone, temperament, everything. Great job!" Jack said as he extended his hand for a brief shake. "I never even thought about using the comm system to prompt you. You were brilliant!"

"Hey fellas! I understand you have a witness that wants to play Let's Make A Deal?" bellowed DA Anderson from down the hall.

"Yep. Let's go into my office and I can fill you in. Tink, why don't you give Jeff a break. Tim, it's way past dinner time and I'm guessing she didn't eat lunch either. You know how hungry people are after confession. Can you get her a sandwich and chips? Jeff, you're with us" Jack instructed as everyone moved to fulfill their duties. Jack offered to let Jennifer lead the way, and she confidently strode down the hall.

When they got to the bullpen, Angie and Suzie Chin were banging away on their keyboards. Angie looked up and said "Jack, the Coast Guard is moving in to take Milanovich down. We can watch it real time on the big screen. They've sent us the link to their onboard cameras."

"Beautiful. Put it up there." Everyone moved into the conference room to watch as Jack turned and shouted across the room "Hey Bill, you'll want to see this." It was getting dark as the sun set over Albemarle

Sound, but the forty-five-foot sport fisherman was clear on the screen. The PA boomed to life, and the spotlight flashed on. *"This is the Coast Guard Cutter Bayberry. Cut your engine and prepare to be boarded."* The boat started to throw off a big wake as it powered up to run, and the Coast Guard responded with a few bullets across his bow. Using the VHF radio channel 16 and the PA, the Captain repeated his call *"Cut your engine and prepare to be boarded or we will sink your vessel."* There was no humor in his voice, and Anatoli Milanovich wisely gave up and cut his engine. As the Cutter moved along side, several sailors manned the port rail with guns drawn and ready. They knew this was a dangerous man and they were prepared to meet resistance. Anatoli climbed down from the fly bridge and obeyed the instruction to lay face down on the aft deck with his hands laced behind his head. He was cautioned that any sudden movements would cause his death. The second in command led a small group to board the fishing boat and handcuffed the criminal while another sailor secured a tow rope to the bow of the vessel.

"Hey, would you look at that?" Angie called out. "The folks on that boat over there got a lot more than a sunset for entertainment tonight. Talk about a front row seat!" Off on the right side of the screen you could just make out the shape of a boat at anchor, it's lone white light shining from its center mast.

THIRTY-NINE

"What a gorgeous sunset! What's the old sailor's tale? Red sky at night, sailors delight. They ain't lying! Spectacular." Betty gushed as she sipped her third drink and reached for the last of the cheese. "I will give you this, Wilma, for a woman that claims to be unfamiliar with wooing, you do a damn fine job of it. Not one wrong step in the past three days."

"Thank you, sweetie, but I really have no idea what I'm doing. I'm just living in the moment and having a blast. I don't want this to ever end." Will confessed. She got up and walked down below to freshen her drink. "Did you like the restaurant last night, Betty?"

"Oh yeah. That was top drawer." Betty enthusiastically responded. "I'd never been there before. Heard about it plenty. I think it's a favorite hangout for DA Anderson. I've heard he's got a thing for the hostess. Seems a little young to me, but, as long as his wife doesn't mind." She laughed. "My crab cake was perfect. All thriller, no filler. And my entrees, the seared tuna, yum! Did you enjoy yourself babe?"

Will shot her a look from the galley door "You couldn't tell? The constant moaning with every bite wasn't a big enough clue? Not much of a sleuth if you didn't deduce that I was in heaven. Can I freshen your drink?"

Betty studied her glass and stood up and strolled over to the companionway hatch, took another slug, and handed her the glass. "Yes please, bar maid. But better make it a light one. I have to return to the real world tomorrow, and I've still got a double murder to solve and a

County Chairman to satisfy."

"What! Maybe you need to rephrase that before the image is permanently burned into my brain. Please tell me you don't with Taylor! He's just gross."

"Sorry. A girl's gotta do whatever it takes to get a head!" and Betty roared with laughter while Will looked in mock shock. "Sweetie do not worry about that. There isn't a barge pole big enough for me to get near that creep. Did you know he made a pass at me not long after I moved here? He told me he really wanted some sweet brown sugar! Can you believe it! Had his hand squeezing my bottom when he said it too. Took every ounce of restraint to not snap off his arm and beat him with it."

"Good god. He tried that with me too, but I told him he couldn't afford me. He scrunched up his face and said, 'I bet I can.' I looked down, I was wearing killer heels that night," Will's eyes flared with pride as she did a little curtsey, "and I squared up on him, got nose to nose and whispered 'I write the sexual harassment coverage for the county, and I know what those policy limits are, and they wouldn't be close to what I'd sue your ass for, Chairman. I would leave you divorced, broke and unemployed when I got through with you. Touch me again and find out just what Wilma Ruth Moore can do.' I saw him physically shrink away from me, and thank god too, because he smelled of bourbon and cigarettes and it about made me puke. He hasn't bothered me again. I also made sure I made friends with his wife and her brother, who's a mean son of a gun and hates his brother-in-law, just for a little added insurance." Will climbed back up on deck and passed the refreshed gin and tonic to Betty as the sun disappeared over the water's horizon in a final blaze of glory. "Cheers" Will said, raising her glass. "To many more sunsets together."

"Amen. I'll drink to that. Cheers!" Betty clinked her glass with Will's and they both took a sip, and then a kiss.

"Will, last night in the restaurant, did you notice that other couple a few tables over from us?" Betty asked. "Maybe it's just the cop in me, but something seemed off about them."

"Yeah, I noticed them." Will replied. "He did seem a little old for her, like 20 years too old, but she seemed to really be into him. She was downing those cosmos like they were water."

"I noticed that too," Betty went on, "but what didn't add up for me was how he hardly ate or drank, and he didn't seem nearly as entertained as she was. He was fidgety. Played with his lighter a lot. One of those zippo's the GI's used in world war two. Kept snapping it open and closed. Remember, right during dinner, with all their food on the table, he tried to light a cigarette, and it was one of those brown foreign cigarettes too. The waitress almost had a heart attack, rushing over to tell him he couldn't smoke inside. He reacted like he'd forgotten where he was."

"When I went to the ladies, and I must say, I was shocked that you didn't join me. I mean, what are girlfriends for?" Will said with mock incredulity.

"It would have looked like we were walking out on our tab!" Betty shouted.

Will laughed and said "Well, it wouldn't be the first time that's happened."

"Will! Don't tell a cop that." Betty pleaded.

"Oh sweetie, don't worry. I always pay." Will chuckled. "Just sometimes I have a 'blond' moment." Betty joined in the laughter and they took another drink.

"So" Betty piped up, "before we went down that rabbit hole, you were saying about passing their table?"

"Oh... yeah..." Will regrouped, "when I passed the table, he was telling her about his boat. We're on an island, so no biggie there, but what was interesting was his accent. Now, I'm crap with accents, so I couldn't tell you where he was from, but I can tell you for certain he ain't from around here, sugar."

"Oh." Betty rolled the ice in her glass and drifted off into thought.

"You know, when you go to the Harris Teeter or the Food Lion during the summer season, a lot of the check-out girls sound similar to him. You know what I mean Betty?"

"Yep. Russian. Polish, Eastern European." Betty pulled out her phone and started typing into a web browser. "Damn."

"What is it sweetie? Will asked reluctantly. "Everything ok?"

"Croatia." Betty said. "Look hear on this map. Croatia was formed when the former Yugoslavia split up. Before that it was a satellite of the Soviet Union. Now, it's one of the most corrupt countries in the world, and the former home of Mrs. Ralph Midgett."

"Do you think this guy was family and came all this way for the funeral?" Will asked. "That is what families do, you know."

"Hummm.' Thought Betty, "Maybe. But my Spidey senses tell me otherwise. Well, nothing I can do about it now. I'll see where we are on the investigation when I get in tomorrow. Maybe our clue will be what breaks the case!"

"Put that phone away. You're interrupting the light show!" Will whispered. "look at all those stars in the east, and the last bit of sun in the west. It's moments like this that make me realize how small and insignificant I am. Praise Jesus, I'm glad I have you to share it with, Betty Thompson."

As Will leaned over to kiss Betty, the crack of a spotlight and the cackle of a PA boomed over the water. *This is the Coast Guard Cutter Bayberry. Cut your engine and prepare to be boarded.*

FLIGHT

"Shoot Will, are they talkin' to us? I can't see a damn thing with that spotlight."

"No," Will said as she moved to the Captain's chair and switched on the radar display. "I should have set this to notify us of an approaching boat. My bad. Come look." She motioned for Betty to join her and as she approached Will slid her arm around Betty's waist and pulled her in close. "See here. That's the Coast Guard and that's the boat they are talking to. We're here in the middle. You can see that if that boat makes a run for it, we are right in the line of fire. Why don't you grab your purse and sling it over your head and slide your hand into that concealed pocket? Also, keep your badge handy. The Coast Guard doesn't stop boats for drunk driving. When they stop a boat, it's serious."

As if on cue, the sound of gun fire echoed across the water.

Betty went to the locker she stowed her purse in and did as instructed. Will ducked below and came back with a marine grade pump action shotgun. "Hey, better safe than sorry. I'm an insurance agent. I mitigate risk all day long."

"You ever shoot that thing?" Betty asked cautiously.

"Yep. At least once a week I shoot. It relaxes me and keeps me sharp. Don't worry Sheriff. I take guns and gun ownership very seriously." Will stiffened in a mock salute and looked over at the radar display. "Well, it looks like the Coast Guard has that situation under control. They are alongside the boat, according to the radar. I'm going to give them a call just to be sure they know we're here." Will reached up and grabbed the mic from the VHF and squawked "Coast Guard, Coast Guard, this is the motor yacht *Carpe Diem* at anchor 300 yards west of your position. Over." Betty mouthed *Carpe Diem* and grinned.

"This is the Coast Guard Cutter Bayberry. We see you. Do you require assistance *Carpe Diem*? Over.

"No thank you. Do we need to move for our safety? We heard gunfire. Over."

"No. It's all over here. We'll be moving on shortly and taking the garbage with us. Enjoy your evening folks. It's a great night on the water. Over."

"Thank you kindly sir. We will. Stay safe and thank you for your service. This is *Carpe Diem*, over and out." Will said in her best southern drawl and giggled after she returned the mic to the cradle.

"Flirt much, sexy?" Betty giggled.

"All the time. It's what I do. It's who I am, but don't be jealous," Will explained, "I only want you. Now, before I pull up the anchor, can I get some of that sweet brown sugar, sugar?"

"Oh Gawd! You're awful, but yes, you don't smell of bourbon and cigarettes, so yes you can. Let's go seize the day!" Betty smiled and offered a playful wink, "But just a quickie. We both have work tomorrow!" and then followed Will down the companionway to explore comforts of the queen bed.

FORTY

Standing on the Manteo dock, Jack and JJ admired the starry night sky. "Boy oh boy, what a beautiful night to be out on the water." JJ commented. "It's moments like this that make me happy I chose to leave Minnesota and move south. This is lovely." She stood and scanned the horizon, looking at the twinkling lights across the water on Bodie Island and the beach communities of Nags Head, Kill Devil Hills, and Kitty Hawk. The radio crackled, and JJ answered by pressing the microphone velcroed to the shoulder of her uniform and leaning her head to that side, "Roger that. 10-4. They are approaching. Said to meet them at the end of the lighthouse. They can make the exchange there." They both took off on a brisk walk to get to that end of town.

Jack turned to JJ and instructed her to peel back and move the car. "I'll meet you at the lighthouse." Jack broke into a jog and when he got to the boardwalk leading out to the lighthouse, JJ was waiting. "Ok, let's get our suspect" Jack said without breathing hard. They watched the Coast Guard Cutter Bayberry slowly ghost up to the dock and several sailors jumped off to secure the ship. Jack turned to JJ and asked, "What's the Captain's name again?"

"That would be me. I'm actually not the captain, I'm Chief Petty Officer Eric Brown, and in charge of this vessel and your prisoner. If you don't mind, we're going to tow the vessel back to our base in Oregon Inlet and quarantine it so your CSI folks can process the evidence. There's a lot of evidence based on a quick look around my second officer had when he arrested your suspect. Everyone that boarded wore gloves, but being a boat, they couldn't wear booties, so their boot prints will be provided to eliminate from the scene."

"That would be great. Thanks." Jack shook hands with the Master Chief, introduced JJ, whom he gave a little extra squeeze to when shaking hands, and then said, "That must be Anatoli Milanovich," as a man in shackles was perp walked down the gang plank by two burly guardsmen.

"Which one of you ordered this piece of crap?" the guard on the right said as they thrust the suspect forward. "He wreaks of cheap cigarettes and bootleg cologne. You'll need to fumigate him, or he'll stink up your jail. I suggest a fire hose, myself."

"Thank you, gentlemen, I think we have it from here." Master Chief Brown commanded. "Sorry about that. Those two had to sit outside the cell with him without much ventilation. Diesel fumes are bad enough, but the stench from this one just threw them over the edge. Makes anyone cranky. Lucky, we had flat water, otherwise there'd be puke all over the place."

"Not a problem. Thanks again. We appreciate the help." Jack smiled, nodded, and shook hands and then grabbed the suspects' elbow. JJ shook Master Chief Brown's hand but wouldn't let him linger this time and she turned and walked the suspect to the waiting car. "Isn't this nice. We're hosting a family reunion! Your sister, Tatiana is waiting for you!" With that, Jack shoved Anatoli into the back seat of the squad car and shut the door.

"He doesn't seem pleased to hear his sister is still alive." JJ noted as the car started violently rocking from Anatoli's kicking and screaming. "They were right about the stench. Roll down the windows before I get in, will ya Jack?"

The short drive to the office was uneventful, if a kicking and screaming prisoner could be considered uneventful. Thankfully, he did all his screaming in his native tongue, which saved Jack and JJ from having to concentrate on what he was saying. The ride was short enough, and the windows were down, so the aroma from the prisoner did not overpower either Deputy. "JJ, I'll send Jeff to help you process the prisoner. Wait here." Jack disappeared around the corner and sought out Jeff. "Ok, Jeff. You're on!" said Jack quietly. "Tim, did you get us sound and picture down there?" Deputy Cudworth grinned and shook his head. "Great. Is Bill Anderson still hear? This was his idea after all."

"Jack! Jack, my boy, wouldn't miss it for the world." DA Anderson said strolling down the hall. "Any trouble bringing the scum in?"

"Nope, the Coast Guard handled everything beautifully. Your call to Captain Baer really paid off." Jack replied while shaking hands with the DA.

"Always pays to start at the top, Jack. Where's the viewing party? Conference room?" Bill Anderson spun around and walked back to the conference room. "You know Jack, while you were gone, I had a chance to chat with the new kids. Angela and Suzie are quite entertaining! Although, to be honest, there seems to be a cat fight in the making, if you know what I mean. Seems there's some tension about a fella. You wouldn't know anything about that, would you Jack?"

"Not a thing Bill. Angie is on loan from her day job at the OBX Insurance Agency, and Suzie is working on a contract, which just started yesterday, but if all goes well, we'll bring her on board. Not sure what has them sideways, but, if it doesn't affect the team, I don't care. Oh, Bill, are these yours?"

"Yes." Bill moved over and gestured, "Jack, meet Dimitri and Sergey. They will be interpreting for us, and this lovely thing is Svetlana, who will be acting as our stenographer. I was pleased at how easy it was to find local folks who speak Croatian. Just a few phone calls and these folks were at our disposal."

"Nice to meet you. I'm Deputy Jack Strong. Svetlana, Sergey, Dimitri." Jack shook everyone's hand. "Well, you have everything you need?"

"Yes, Thank you, we are pleased to help. The Milanovich's have terrorized Croatia for far too long, and the government turns a blind eye because of the bribes they are paid. If we can shut them down, that would be a big win for our country." Svetlana confessed with a thick eastern European accent.

"Whatever we can do to help." Sergey confirmed.

"Tim, make sure our guests have anything they need. Would you like some bottled water?" Jack asked politely.

"Thank you. We already have some. Tim and Tink, is that right? Tink?" Dimitri asked sheepishly "they have been most helpful and very accommodating hosts. Oh, it looks like we need to begin."

The big screen showed the two cells occupied by the Milanovich's. In the holding area the two were separated by the corridor and adjoining cells, which was deliberate so that neither person could whisper and be heard by the other. Both cells were wired for sound and picture. The three interpreters sat at a long table a few feet back from the screen and put on their headsets and court reporter gear. The conversations were being recorded by the DA for transcription and evidence at trial because Tatiana had made a deal and consented to this sting. Bill Anderson was on solid ground. He even ran it past the district presiding Judge, the Honorable Andrew Griffin, who gave his seal of approval on the warrant.

Jeff could be seen walking Anatoli into his cell, now dressed in an orange jumpsuit, his hair wet from a required shower, which really was just a hosing off with powder soap thrown liberally on him and wearing flip flops. Once inside the cell, he was locked in and instructed to turn around so the handcuffs could be removed. For this, JJ stood to the side with her gun trained on Anatoli. Once he was free and secure in his cell, the two deputies left.

It took a few minutes for Anatoli to speak, and as expected, he spoke in his native tongue. Everyone could see him talking, but the sound was only on in the headsets so there was a slight delay getting the interpretation. Dimitri played the part of Anatoli, and Sergey played Tatiana. Svetlana worked the dictation machine like a seasoned court reporter.

"Tatiana, what have you done? You silly cow, you're ruining everything."

"Shut up Anatoli. It is you who have ruined everything with your greed. We had all we ever needed, but you wanted more, and now look. Look what you've done."

"I don't understand you, Tatiana. You were happy to sell yourself to that pig Midgett. You allowed him to treat you like a common whore. Now you are mad because I freed you from that swine. Now you are mad because I eliminated the entire family. Why aren't you grateful? You don't have to share his bed. You don't have to service his needs. You don't have to entertain his friends. Once we are free from American jail, you can live in his mansion and do as you please. You can thank me then."

"Anatoli, you are going to kill me too. I'm one of your loose ends."

"How could you say such a thing, you ungrateful woman! You are my baby sister!"

"Oh, but you had no problem with me whoring for you. I was your baby sister then too. I'm trash to you, and you'd throw me out just like a used carcass. How would you do it? Slit my throat like Carol Lawrence? Drown me like her daughter? Shotgun to the head like the bank manager?"

"Tatiana, you silly child. I didn't do all that. Yes, I killed the Lawrence woman, and her daughter. But the branch manager was killed by the same man who killed Midgett and that whore of a second wife."

"Well, if you didn't kill them, who did, Anatoli? It certainly looked like your handiwork. Remember, I've seen what you did back home. You earned your nickname. The Butcher of Zagreb left a trail of bodies wherever you went."

"Tatiana, sometimes you have to break some heads to get the results we wanted. Kneecaps, arms, fingers, that's so Sicilian. Croatia has a more medieval code. That's what the people understand."

"But this isn't Croatia, Anatoli."

"No, but the government officials can be bought just the same. That's why I am confident we will be released soon. Money is being wired to several important people right now. That idiot Anderson passed on our offer, which surprised me, since backwater DA's usually don't see five million dollars in their lifetime. But that will be one of the last poor decisions he ever makes."

At the mention of his name, all eyes turned to look at the DA. Anderson just nodded. "Yep. I turned the sons of guns down. I've already sent my family to live elsewhere. I know my days are numbered. These guys don't play nice, and they never forget."

Jack mumbled, five million. Damn. You've got some serious cojones, my friend. Serious."

"Anatoli! You're going to kill a district attorney? Are you insane?"

"It's already done! The Judge Griffin too. He turned down ten million. Why do they act so silly? Do principles help when you are dead? Their families are dead. Their parents, brothers and sisters, and their families are dead. Will anyone remember them and their principles once they are all dead?"

"Anatoli, you've become a monster!"

"No, Tatiana, I've always been a monster." Then he sat back on his bed and smiled.

There was a period of silence down in the holding cell and in the conference room. Jack had already raced out of the office to call the judge and order a protection detail on him and his family.

"Anatoli? Who killed my husband?" Tatiana asked quietly with an emotional tremble in her voice.

"Ha ha ha, he laughed heartily. That was the best. All I did is offer that greedy woman, Lawrence, a measly million dollars for herself and a half a million for each of her kids and she said she'd take care of it. Her son arranged the phony robbery as a distraction and then went and killed whore number two and your disgusting husband and shot the bank manager on his way back to Virginia Beach! That was beautiful. So violent. So much rage. He hated his father. All I needed to do was clean up and disappear. Well, I didn't get away, but I will. Two million and I get the bank free and clear. And the cherry on top? We hacked their accounts and got our two million back! Beautiful, bloody beautiful."

Jack came back into the conference room, but it seemed the show was over. A long silence settled in down in the holding cells. Bill Anderson turned to Jack and filled him in on the bits he missed. "We have the Lawrence woman's body and her daughter's body. I wonder if he'll ever find the son's, or did he dispose of it more efficiently. Time will tell. Any idea who else he's bribing, Jack?"

"I have some ideas, but before I get to that, Cora called with a preliminary autopsy. Just like the daughter, he had multiple encounters with her. Seven Times! That's superhuman. He was only there for two hours according to the massage service." Jack stood with a stunned look.

"What happened to the masseuse who was supposed to work the massage? We found him?" Bill asked.

"Yeah. He's alive. Just like the boat Captain, he took the money and lived." Jack responded, and then mumbled "seven times" over and over again.

"I think we have enough to put him away for life, don't you?" Bill asked no one in particular. "I think our work is done here?"

"Yeah, um, No! Bill you aren't going anywhere without two of us." Jack responded forcefully once he came out of his daze. "Tonight, you're at my house with Tim out front. Tomorrow, Tim's place with Jeff out front. We keep rotating every night. Sleep in a different bed so you can't be traced. It's what Bin Laden did to stay alive for so many years. We can do it until that sicko and his whole criminal family are gone. I've already got the Judge and his family out of state and safe."

"Seriously, Jack?"

"Seriously, Bill. After a few days, we'll continue the pretense, but you'll be whisked away with your family and you won't be back until it's all clear. Understood?"

"I don't like it. But I'm grateful you're on my team. Now you said you had some ideas about why he's so confident he's going free?"

"He's working his way up the food chain of the legal system. If you can't bribe the DA and the local Judge, who's next in line? Who can make charges disappear? Who can grant pardon's or clemency? Who can assert Diplomatic Immunity?"

"Shoot Jack, The Governor, The President, The Secretary of State?"

"Yeah. Now do you think the Governor can be bought. You know him Bill."

"He's a snake and as crooked as they come. He can definitely be bought. The President or the Secretary of State, I don't see it."

"Ok, maybe not the current ones, but how about former?" Jack postulated. They both turned white at the thought and their brains went into overdrive trying to think of a solution. They could not let this mass murdering madman buy his way out of this. Jack's cell phone buzzed, and after looking at the screen he said "I gotta take this. Excuse me" and he turned and walked away while connecting the call. "Hello" was all Bill heard as Jack disappeared out the door.

FORTY-ONE

"Anchor up!" Betty called.

"Ok sweetie, get back here so I can get you home." Will made a pouty face, which Betty returned as she worked her way from the bow to the cockpit, careful to use the grabrails along the coach roof while she walked along the narrow gunwales.

"Back safe and sound." Betty rejoiced. "You realize that I've spent more time on this boat then I've spent on all the boats in my life?"

"Enjoying the nautical life? It can be addictive and intoxicating."

"I love it." Betty exclaimed and pulled Wilma in close for a full kiss.

"Alrighty then. Let's put on our hats cause I'm going to open this baby up." Will threw the switch for the running lights and Betty handed her a hat.

"By the way, Will, I like your hair all wind-blown and wild. Very sexy. I know you wear the ponytail for work, but I'm ok with you literally letting your hair down." Then she slid her hand up through the wild mane and gently pulled her head back so she could kiss Will's neck.

With one eye on Betty and one eye on the horizon, Will pushed down on the throttle and *Carpe Diem* took off like a shot. The trim tabs quickly did their job and the boat got to speed and flew across the calm water. Will had the chart plotter on night mode and laid a course back to the condo. It was a quick, smooth ride. They glided back under the Ballast

Point Drive bridge and then took a hard turn to port and then ghosted past the Clubhouse, where Will executed another flawless one eighty and crabbed over to the dock, where Betty, now a seasoned deckhand, jumped off the boat, on to the dock and tied the bow line to the cleat. She then ran back to catch Will's throw of the stern line and tied it to the cleat as well. All secured, Will cut the engine, opened the side door, and invited Betty back on board.

"Will, I gotta get to bed. It's late for me on a work night."

"I know baby. I know. Can I walk you home?" Will pleaded.

"Of course!"

"Ok, well I got you something and I hope you like it."

Betty's eyes lit up and she gasped. "If you got it for me, I will love it."

Will produced a Tiffany's box, complete with ribbons and bow. "Open it. Here, let me put the deck lights on so you can see better." Will reached up to the console and flipped a switch and the entire deck was flooded is soft warm light.

"Will! What did you get me!" Betty screamed in a whisper so as not to disturb the neighbors. She pulled the ribbons and bows off and carefully opened the box and looked at Will with a puzzled expression. "What's this sweetie?"

"That's the garage clicker. The top button opens the outer gate. The bottom button opens door four on the garage. The key opens the basement door to the house, or you can use the keypad and enter the code, which is also the code to the security system."

"What's the code?"

"Keep looking."

"I just see your business card with a lipstick kiss. Oh, on the back you wrote 0515. How did you know that's my birthday?" Betty asked perplexed.

"Are you kidding? That's my birthday!" Will shot back

"Seriously?"

"Yep."

"Well I'll be damned. Too funny." Betty shook her head and they both grinned. "That will be easy to remember. Thank you Will. I love it, and I love our house. Now can you walk me to our condo so this girl can get to sleep?"

"It will always be my pleasure to walk anywhere with you, Ms. Betty Thompson."

They kissed goodnight outside the door, Betty slotted the key into the lock and opened the door. She held up the key and looked up at Wilma and said, "I'll get one of these cut tomorrow for you and drop it off when I come for dinner. Ok?"

"Perfect. Bring whatever you want to leave. You've seen the closet. We have tons of room."

"Night Princess. I had an amazing three days with you. I can't wait to spend the rest of my life with you." Betty cooed with her hand gently stroking Will's cheek.

"See you tomorrow. Sleep tight. Sweet dreams" Will said quietly, and they kissed again, and Betty went inside.

Will felt an emptiness in her gut like she had never felt before. She didn't want to risk it and speak too quickly, but she knew this is what love was. She didn't want to be like her mother and run away and abandon her love. She wanted to run to it and embrace it. She knew she needed to be patient. When the time was right, all will be right.

Betty stood inside the door leaning against the wall, a tear running down her face. The loss was palpable. Betty knew she loved Will, but she was willing to give it time to grow and bloom. She saw the happiness her parents had, and she wanted that 'for all time' love. She could feel that Will did too.

Will walked across the parking lot and clicked the boat key fob. The door opened and she walked to the cockpit and fired up the engine. Then she untied the stern and bow lines and jumped back on, closing the automatic door behind her. As she started away from the dock, she glanced at the condo and saw Betty at the window. Will waved, and Betty blew her a kiss. Shakespeare really got it right. *'Parting is such sweet sorrow that I shall say goodnight till it be morrow.'*

FORTY-TWO

"Hey boss! How was the weekend?" Tim asked cheerfully as he walked across the lobby in a clean shirt and stain free tie.

Betty stopped dead in her tracks inside the front door and watched him walk toward the bullpen with his fresh Styrofoam cup of steaming coffee he'd just picked up from the break room. Shaking her head in disbelief at the rarest of sights, a Tim Cudworth early morning sighting, on a Monday, and in a pleasant mood to boot! 'What in the world happened while I was gone' she thought to herself. "It was good, Tim, very relaxing" she replied as she pulled her buzzing phone from her pocket. 'Can't I get a cup of coffee before the onslaught' she thought as she unlocked the phone to read the new text message.

Good morning lover. I missed you. Our bed was so empty, and I was lost in the shower without you. Have a good day. See you tonight for dinner (can you be dessert?   hehe!).

She felt that melting feeling deep inside her core that she's gotten whenever she thinks about or looks at Will, ever since that first kiss on Friday night. She quickly typed back

I had the sweetest dreams of u all night and was ☹ to wake up without u. Much better now ☐ See you for dinner and dessert!

She paused over the send button, unsure if she should say how she really felt? Not in a text. When the time is right, it will be right. She hit send and walked on to her office.

FLIGHT

As she passed the bullpen, she saw Tim wasn't the only one in early. 'What in the world! Seven thirty on a Monday morning and the bullpen is humming.' Betty thought. 'I guess Jack was the right call to lead Investigations.' She gave herself a mental pat on the back and kept going down the hall to her closed office door. She punched in the code and walked in to find everything exactly as she left it when she bolted out Friday at 5:30 to run home and get ready for Will. Melancholy washed over her, thinking about the excitement she felt having a date with someone she was really attracted to, and then falling in love. Then, frustration descended when her OCD kicked in and she knew she had to clean up the mess on her desk before she could get anything done. She was pleased to see that her work phone had almost no emails or text messages on it, and none from anyone in investigations. Quickly scanning through what she did have, there was nothing urgent. Most were just notices or quick messages to keep her in the loop in traffic, community service, public relations, and politics. There were a few missed calls from numbers she didn't recognize and one voicemail from Chairman Taylor. She hit the button to listen to that. 'Better to rip the bandage off quickly' she thought as the unpleasant man's voice started to play back.

Congratulations Sheriff. Really fantastic work. Solve the murder and bag an international terrorist and head of a crime family. Wow. Get ready for the press. Your 15 minutes of fame is about to kick into high gear.

She immediately picked up her desk phone and punched the ALL OFFICE intercom button "Jack Strong, please report to the Sheriff's office immediately" she said in her best command voice. She cradled the receiver and looked up to see her Deputy sprinting down the hall.

"Yes ma'am? What's wrong?"

"Close the door, Jack." She firmly instructed. "Now", she asked calmly, "Can you please explain this?" and she replayed the voice message from the Commission Chairman. After it finished, she locked eyes with Jack and said "When I left here Friday, we were treading water on this investigation and I come back to this! What are you telling me Jack? What's the subtext? You want me to leave more often? Y'all do better when I'm out of the way? Is that it?"

Jack didn't know what to say. He felt broadsided. He was sure she'd be pleased when he explained the work they'd done. His face slumped and he visibly sagged, which wasn't easy for someone so toned and ripped. His hands on his hips, looking down at his feet, he mumbled "I'm sorry Sheriff."

"Jack!" Betty boomed. "You don't have a god damned thing to be sorry about. You're a rock star. I could not be happier for you and this office. From the looks of the bullpen, you whipped a motley crew into a crack team, in short order no less. That is outstanding work mister!" Jack lifted his eyes off the floor and looked hard into the Sheriff's beautiful face and captivating hazel eyes. "Soldier" she barked. "Attention! Shoulders back! Chest out! Look sharp! You have troops to lead. Get back to it, and when you're ready, give me a full report. Dismissed." Before he left, she stopped him with a sharp, "Jack!"

"Yes ma'am."

She came from behind her desk and walked over to him by the closed office door and extended her hand. "Congratulations! Good work. I'll expect you front and center at any press conferences Barney calls, got it?"

"Yes ma'am." Jack responded as he released her hand from a firm shake.

"And be sure to have the whole team there. They should get the recognition they deserve."

"Yes ma'am. I'll make sure everyone is clean and pressed. And thank you, Sheriff. It was a team effort." Jack opened the door and glided down the hall back to his office at the front of the bullpen.

"I need more coffee" Betty muttered to no one in particular. She saw her mug sitting on her credenza and picked it up. The coffee from Friday was still in it, with unidentified bits floating suspiciously on top. She looked up at the ceiling tile warily and muttered "Ugh. Mondays."

FORTY-THREE

Will stood in her office doorway, sipping a fresh cup of coffee, a nice dark roast with just a touch of sweet cream gave it a nice mocha color and a little sweetness. She decided she liked it this way now. It gave her a warm, happy feeling. She was smiling at her phone after reading the reply she just got from Betty. "Morning Angie! Don't you look nice. Have a fun weekend? Meet anyone interesting?"

Angela looked up from putting her things in her office and said seriously, "Let me get some coffee and I'll join you in your office." She walked down the hall to the break room and Will greeted the other staff members of OBX Insurance as they rolled in to work. She liked doing this every Monday. First in the office. Set the tone. Friendly. Personal. Professional.

"Ok, let's talk" Angie said as she approached the doorway. Will turned into her office and Angela followed, along with Orville and Wilber, who loved the sun streaming through Will's window in the morning. "What's with the mocha coffee? You've always been no cream, no sugar, straight up black."

"Guess it was time for a change. Close the door." Will instructed. "Spill!" she shot over her shoulder as she rounded her desk and plopped into her executive office chair. "You look tired, but oddly invigorated. Did you spend the weekend in bed with some stray you picked up Friday night?"

Angela blushed. "Will, I'm not that bad. Besides, I've got my eyes on someone to take up the slack once the divorce is final."

"Jack?" Will queried.

"Jack…. And yes, I spent the entire weekend with him." Angie beamed, "but we never made it to bed, at least not together."

"Ok. Now, I want the rest of the story."

"Right. Paul Harvey. Here it is…" and Angela recounted the thrill of being a part of the Sheriff's Investigations unit and seeing Jack and the team catch the bad guys. "I gotta tell you, Will, it gave me a whole new appreciation for what our people in service do for us. Not just the cops, but the Coast Guard too. Incredibly professional, poised, and dedicated."

"So, who killed Ralph Midgett?" Will asked while sitting, literally, on the edge of her seat leaning her elbows on her desk, eyes wide with curiosity.

"Steve Midgett." Angela said authoritatively.

"No!"

"Yes."

"His own son! I don't believe it." Will slumped back in her chair in shock.

"Yep. He was paid five hundred grand for it." Angie explained.

"No. A contract killing! Well that brings 'special circumstances' into play for him then. He's in custody, right?"

"Nope."

"Ok, Angie, back the heck up and start over. What did I miss?"

"Steve was asked by his mother to kill Tom Mills and Ralph Midgett. Tom, it was discovered, was Ralph's oldest child, illegitimate. Steve hated his dad so much and saw his other children as a threat to his inheritance, so, when Carol told him her plan for all of them to get his fortune, he didn't think twice. Wife number two just got in the way, so he killed her too."

"Angie, this is incredible."

"But wait, there's more." Angie chuckled with a macabre laugh. "Carol Lawrence didn't realize who she was making a deal with. She got the plan from Tatiana Midgett, but the plan was created and designed by her older brother, Anatoli Milanovich."

"That's a mouthful. Don't tell me. Croatian?"

"Not just Croatian, but the 'Butcher of Zagreb' himself. What he didn't tell Tatiana was that he was coming to Kitty Hawk to personally clean up after the murders. I don't know if he gets 'Frequent Murder Points' or something, or maybe he just hadn't gotten his quota of bodies yet this month, but…" They both laughed at Angie's sick joke. "Anyway, he rolls into town and passes himself off as some hot shot euro trash and picks up Jennifer Lawrence in a bar, wines and dines her at 1587 and then strangles her and dumps her body out past Oregon Inlet. Unfortunately for him, she washed ashore. Then, he bribes the masseuse coming to 'service' Carol in her hotel room, and he goes and has an ungodly amount of sex with her and then slits her throat and leaves. He was escaping on a boat he hired when the Coast Guard stopped him at the mouth of Albemarle Sound. That was pretty cool, watching those guardsmen work. They let us live stream it on the Sheriff's big screen TV."

"Really!" Will thought if she should mention her witnessing the 1587 dinner and the Coast Guard take down. "Wow. And you were there the whole weekend? Did you get to work closely with Jack? I know that's what you wanted."

"Well, not really. Angie said, "I was bangin' away on the computer with Suzie and feeding information to the team to follow up."

"Suzie?"

"Oh, yeah. She's a new contractor for the department. A real wiz on the computer, numbers especially." Angie offered, "When she arrived JJ and I had a come to Jesus meeting with her because she was making serious eyes at Jack and Jeff."

"Jennifer and Jeff, huh? Interesting."

"Oh, careful. Jennifer hasn't told Jeff yet. She's like me. Waiting for the right time."

"Got it" Will nodded. "But don't you think Jack knows, since you spent the night at his house? Come on Angie, he is a cop, and an investigator, and even I could see he was sweet on you when we all hooked up on the beach walking the dogs."

"So, how was your weekend? Do anything fun? Meet any interesting men? Play wild sex games by the pool?" Angie asked with a laugh trying to change the subject, not realizing how close to home she was.

"It was incredibly relaxing." Will admitted "I desperately needed it. I cannot remember the last time I didn't come in here on the weekend. The weather was great, and I enjoyed it thoroughly."

"Cool. Can I ask a favor? I need some time off. I'm not sure when exactly, but I'll need to meet with my attorney and get some personal stuff arranged." Angie asked sheepishly.

"Of course, sweetie. My god you've got weeks of vacation time accumulated. Let me know when you need to leave, and I'll handle it. Now what do we have on this week? Let me fire up my laptop and look at the schedule. Pop on the TV and see if there's any coverage about the big bust on the Banks!"

The TV came on to the local Norfolk station in the middle of the story, with a reporter standing in front of The Outer Banks Bank & Trust with a salacious headline under her "Murder on the Beach." Watching the screen, Will absently clicked on her web browser and it opened to her home page, which was a news outlet. There were multiple stories on the events in Kitty Hawk, including some footage of the Coast Guard capture of the Butcher of Zagreb. Will clicked on it and made it widescreen to watch on her laptop. She almost spit out her coffee when she saw her boat in the frame, faintly recognizable a few hundred yards off the bow of the Coast Guard Cutter.

"You Ok, boss?" Angie asked while Will choked.

"Went down the wrong way." Will coughed and wheezed her reply. Angie, if you could excuse me, I need to make a call."

"Sure" Angie stood and went to the door, where she asked, "Open or closed?"

"Closed sweetie. Thanks" Once Angie had left, Will palmed her phone, and hit the speed dial for Betty. "Hi babe. Call me when you're free. Something we probably need to discuss before interviews and press conferences. Ok, bye." Will breathlessly whispered and then hung up. She looked at her phone and opened the setting to change her screen saver. Now whenever she looked at her phone, that beautiful face with mocha skin, pouty lips, strong jaw, slender neck, and those radiant hazel eyes starred back at her. Will smiled. Then the phone burst to life. Dad? Dad! "Hello pop! How are you doing on this fine Monday morning?"

"I just saw the news. Are you ok? Scary stuff over there. You need me to guard you? I still have my gun, you know."

"I know you do Daddy. How about lunch here today. I can tell you everything I know, and we can catch up. Twelve thirty? Just come to my office, OK?"

"I'll see you then sugar. Bye."

"Bye Daddy. Drive safely." 'Well, that's taking the bull by the horns' Will thought as she punched the phone with her thumb to hang up. Where should I take him to tell him I'm gay? Kill Devil Grill, she typed into her browser. Damn, closed Mondays. The Black Pelican, she typed and hit enter. 'Bingo'. The Pelican it is then. As she was entering her lunch date in her calendar, her phone rang and without looking, picked it up "Will Moore, OBX Insurance. how can we help you?"

A familiar chuckle came down the line. "My aren't you all professional and switched on this morning" Betty's amused voice caused Will to stop and sigh. "You called me, remember?"

"Yep. I did. I was just booking a lunch appointment with my dad. I'm going to have that heart to heart with him today. Listen, why I called. Angie and I had a little coffee conference, we usually do first thing to catch up and get ready for the day ahead, and she told me about y'all's big weekend. Seems Jack caught quite the big fish! Anyway, two things came up that you need to know. They know about the 1587 dinner that we witnessed, and our boat is on the Coast Guard footage of the capture at sea. You can just make out the boat. Can't see either of us. But thought you should know that those things are part of the narrative."

"Oh. O-Kay" Betty drew the two-letter word out to eight or nine while she chewed over this information.

"Listen, if it helps you to mention our date at 1587 or our time out on the water, I have no problem with that. You can reveal as much or as little as you need. I just didn't want you getting caught out. That never ends well."

Betty blew out a breath and admitted "I guess we both will have interesting conversations today. Look forward to comparing notes tonight on the deck with a bottle of wine."

"Red or white? What's your preference my dear? We have plenty of both."

"WE do?"

"Yes, WE do" and Will emphasized the WE.

Betty hummed contentedly and said "WE might have to decide later. Champagne could be in order depending on how our conversations go."

"Oooooh Yes!" Will squealed. "I love bubbles!"

"See you tonight Princess. Gotta go. Bye." Betty rushed off.

"Bye." Will sighed and thought 'I really do love that woman.'

FORTY-FOUR

"Hello! Welcome to the OBX Insurance Agency. How can I help you?" Nicole cheerfully addressed the gentleman as he came through the front door.

"I'm here to have lunch with my little girl" Tom Moore responded.

"Oh…. Ah…. Ok… and who's that?"

"Wilma Ruth! She sits in the big office right there." Tom chuckled.

"Oh. Will. I'll let her know you're here." Nicole replied as she got up. "Wilma Ruth, your daddy's here!" She called from Will's office door.

"Nicole! Do you like your job?" Will shouted.

"Yes ma'am. I love my job." She replied with fear in her voice.

"Well, if you want to keep it, you will never refer to me as Wilma Ruth again. Is that clear?" Will barked at her receptionist.

"Yes ma'am.

"Is that clear, Nicole?"

"Crystal Will. Crystal."

"Good" Will said as she passed her in the doorway. "Hey daddy, can you give me a second?"

"Sure, baby girl."

Will turned and faced Nicole and put her arms around the girl. She knew she wasn't being mean, or fresh, or insolent, so Will whispered to her. "Nicole, sweetie, there are only two people in the whole world who have my permission to call me Wilma Ruth. One is that man right there, and you aren't the other. I'll explain why I'm so touchy about it to you when I get back from lunch. Ok? Now, go wash your face and get a sip of water. I'll be back in a couple of hours."

Tom stood looking out a window at nothing in particular. When Will finished talking, and Nicole walked away sniffling, Tom turned to his daughter "kinda rough on her, weren't you Wilma? She's just a kid, and she didn't mean any harm."

"I get that Dad, but she works for me." Will motioned for them to leave, and Tom held the door. "She's twenty-one, old enough to drink, vote and get her ass chewed. She represents me, and all of us here at the office, so professionalism is essential during the workday." Will pressed the key to the Escalade and got in. "I don't have to tell you" she said looking sideways at her father while starting the engine, "it's the little things that make the difference. Let me ask you, why do you love Chick-Fil-A?" Will pulled out on to the by-pass heading south, but quickly moved to the far-left lane to turn down Kitty Hawk Road.

"Well, the chicken sandwich, I guess." Tom answered with a puzzled look on his face.

"Yeah, sure," Will conceded, "but what's the biggest thing they are known for today. What's the thing that sets them apart from a very crowded restaurant market?"

"Their service." Tom admitted

"Exactly!" Wilma exclaimed, as she turned into the Black Pelican parking lot. "They have a corporate culture that requires all of their employees to be pleasant, courteous, and polite to all customers and fellow employees.' Will threw the car into park and turned off the engine. "That's what people love about them. Excellent, consistent service."

"Hey, aren't we going to Chick-Fil-A?" Tom exclaimed incredulously. "You got me all worked up for a couple of chicken sandwiches and a lemonade!"

"Waffle Fries?"

"Oh, you know it kiddo. Always!" Tom chuckled at how well his daughter knew him, even after so many years of being apart. "Hey, where are you going? The entrance is over here!"

"Follow me Dad. I want to look at the road. The storm took it and the barrier dune." Will said over her shoulder as she walked. "WOW! Would you look at that! NCDOT is really on it. Cleared out all the mess. Replaced the road and rebuilt the dune in less than a week."

"They get a lot of practice, though. Don't they?" Tom grinned. "Between here and Buxton, they have to replace chunks of road almost every year after a monster storm rolls through."

"Yep. Down on Hatteras, just a little south of Salvo they had to put in a temporary floating bridge because the storm opened a new inlet. But, like you said, it's nothing new here. We've been fighting Mother Nature for hundreds of years." Will looked at her dad, threw her arm around his waist and said, "Let me buy you lunch, pop!' They turned and walked back to the entrance of the restaurant.

The Black Pelican restaurant was a local landmark for its fine food and wonderful beachside location, but what make it special, was its history. It was hard to see it today because the building has been added to numerous times over the years, but standing on the road, you could still see the roofline of the Original Kitty Hawk lifesaving station, which is where the Wright brothers notified the world they successfully achieved the first powered, sustained and controlled flight. The telegraph transmitted the simple message

SUCCESS FOUR FLIGHTS THURSDAY MORNING ALL AGAINST TWENTY-ONE-MILE WIND STARTED FROM LEVEL WITH ENGINE POWER ALONE

AVERAGE SPEED THROUGH AIR THIRTY-ONE MILES LONGEST 59 SECONDS INFORM PRESS HOME CHRISTMAS.   ORVILLE WRIGHT.

Will stood waiting for the hostess to seat them while Tom wandered over to look in the gift shop. The Outer Banks was a tourist area. Every place has a gift shop. Wilma leaned over to the hostess and quietly asked if she could put them at a private table since they had important business to discuss, and the hostess gave her a knowing nod and a wink and said, "Follow me sugar."

"Dad! Let's go!" Will called out, and Tom rounded the corner and followed the hostess to their table. Will, as she usually does, stopped to chat with familiar faces along the way. "Hey Frank, what are you doing? Checking out the competition?"

"Hey Will, I can't eat hot dogs every day. I wanted to treat my wife to a nice lunch. Once the season picks up, I don't know how much we'll see each other with her running the ice cream shop and gift store and me in Capt. Franks until the wee hours."

"It does get crazy." Will said and looked at the woman at the table with Frank, "Hi, I'm Will Moore with OBX Insurance." Will extended her hand and they shook and smiled. Will could see the woman had a curious possessive glare in her eyes, and she wanted to ease her anxiety. "Nice to meet you. I need to get over to my table. I'm buying my Dad lunch. Enjoy your lunch. Good to see you both." Will turned and continued through the restaurant. Frank's wife watched her walk away, those long legs on that slender tall frame with that beautiful face and cute blond ponytail and then cut her look to Frank with a 'don't even think about it' stare. He sheepishly looked at his menu and said without thinking "What looks good to you?"

Will slid into her chair across from Tom at a nice two top table in the corner of the "porch", an enclosed area wrapped with windows. They had a view across to the beach and down the beach road to watch the world go by. "Did the hostess get a drink order?" Will asked as she picked up her menu and opened to review the specials. "I really wanted to thank you for putting Angie and me and the dogs and cats up on such short notice last week. We all really appreciated it. I hope we didn't leave you with too much of a mess."

Tom looked over the top of his menu, pulled down his reading glasses, looked straight into Will's blue eyes and said, "Ok, cut the pleasantries. I appreciate the lunch, and the song and dance, but you didn't invite me here for a father daughter campfire meeting. What's up?"

"Jesus dad, can't a girl be nice to her daddy?"

"Wilma Ruth, you are always nice to your daddy. That's how I raised you. So, what's on your mind." Tom was blunt, but he always came at issues head on, and that's how he taught Will. Straight up, no chaser.

The waitress came for their orders, and they each ordered a beer, and more time to discuss the menu. Wilma took a deep inhale, played with her silverware, and looked up at her dad. His face was etched with concern and his eyes, tired from a lifetime of worry, and work, were moist. She didn't want to break his heart. She didn't want to lose his respect. She didn't want to lose his approval, but she knew she had to be honest, to him, to herself. "Dad, I'm gay." Will sat still, letting her statement sink in, watching for the most minute changes in Tom's expression.

"Ok." Tom said with the hint of relief. He hadn't realized that he was holding his breath, and he slowly exhaled through his nose. "That's it? That's why you wanted to have lunch with me? Thank you, Jesus, I thought you were sick or in trouble financially, or caught up with something dangerous. I knew it was serious, I can still read people ya know, so my radar was in hyperdrive."

"So... you're ok with it?"

"Honey, of course! I mean, I've always suspected. Remember in high school, I had you enrolled in that Christian school. They called me for a meeting and expressed their concern that you seemed more interested in the girls than the boys, and they didn't approve of homosexuality."

"Really?"

"Yep," Tom said. "That's why you changed schools. I know I told you about changing for better coaching and stronger athletic programs, competition and potential, but it was their attitude."

"I had no idea!" Will sat stunned with her mouth open and her eyes flashing hot and moist. "Daddy..." and the emotion flowed from her eyes, her throat tightened. Will couldn't speak.

Tom wanted to hold his little girl, but she wasn't a little girl anymore. "You are drop dead gorgeous, and I'm not saying that because I'm your father. I see the way people look at you. I remember the way the guys at the office used to drop everything to come to my office when you were there, and I heard their lusty comments around the coffee station when you'd left." Will blushed, blew her nose, and wiped the tears from her cheeks. "All that attention, and you just ignored all the men. I always thought you were driven to succeed and didn't want romance to sidetrack you."

"Well, there was that." Will sheepishly admitted. "I kinda got thrown into the deep end of the pool when Bart died. I was only 27 when I was handed the insurance agency, and I still felt like the new kid around here. I had to focus just to keep my head above water."

Tom nodded "and I was immensely proud of you accepting that challenge and making it work beyond my wildest dreams. Look at the life you've built for yourself! That house, your cars, boat, jewelry, clothes, club memberships ... and you're only 35!"

"Thank you, daddy. I'm proud too."

"So, have you and Angie hooked up? Is that why you wanted to tell me? I saw how comfortable you two are together."

"Oh, no, not Angie. She's definitely not gay." Will grinned. "She's not even bi. She is all in on men. She and I are very good friends. She's my work wife, my girl Friday, my right hand."

"Ok. So, who is it?" Tom leaned forward and propped his elbows on the table and rested his head on his folded hands.

Will took out her phone and opened the home screen, flipped it around and said "her."

"Wilma Ruth! Oh My God, she's as gorgeous as you are! Wow, those eyes. Man, you don't mess around."

"Dad! You look like the men in your office used to look!" Will laughed out loud as she put the phone away. The waitress came with the beers and asked if they were ready to order. Tom ordered the shrimp and grits, and Will ordered the Greek salmon. Tom picked up his beer and offered a salute. Will picked her beer up and they clicked bottles.

"Congratulations. So, tell me how you two met."

"We've known each other for a while, just casually at business functions, Chamber events, fundraising socials. We'd say 'hi', but we'd never really talked. You know, I was working the room, she was glad handing. Just never talked. Then, last Tuesday when the bodies were found, I got involved because of the policies we have for Ralph Midgett. I called the Sheriff's office Wednesday and asked to have lunch with her."

"Wait. That woman is the Sheriff? Here? Damn. Where did I go wrong? All those years with crabby men when I could have had that for a partner!"

"Dad. Really! Calm down big fella." Will chuckled. "So, lunch. I just wanted lunch to discuss Ralph Midgett's death and offer to assist. That's where Angie came in. She had already been pulling information on Ralph for our investigation of the claims we knew would be coming.

Betty, that's the Sheriff's name, responded exactly the way you responded to a civilian offering help. But we had a nice lunch, shared some about our personal lives and our history, and by the end, she agreed to have Angie come over to their office and talk. That blew me away."

"You are some salesman, Wilma."

"Well, thank you daddy. After she left, I sat for a bit and realized I liked her. Obviously, there was a physical attraction, but more than that, she's a good person, and a kind soul. I didn't know how she'd take it if I asked her out on a date, but you know me. 'You only really fail, if...'"

"'... if you don't try.' I used to preach that to you in kindergarten! You still remember that?" Tom asked with some moisture gathering in the corners of his eyes.

"I say that to myself almost every day." Wilma replied, reaching across the table to squeeze her father's hand. "So, anyway, I called her Friday afternoon and asked her out for dinner Saturday night."

"So, where did you take her?" Tom asked eagerly.

"Wait!" Will commanded. "I'm getting there. She counter offered that we catch a beer and have a casual evening discussing our options for Saturday night. So, I agreed, and came to pick her up at 7:30. I'll spare you the details, but we spent the entire weekend together. I dropped her back last night about 10pm. I gave her access to my place, and she's having a key cut to her place. I think we're a thing now. Are you happy for me?"

"Oh, baby girl, I am over the moon thrilled for you" Tom crowed. "When do I get to meet her?"

"Well, soon, I think. She's really busy wrapping up this murder and being sheriff, but we'll definitely make the time." Will gushed, "Oh, and you two can swap war stories. She worked for the FBI for a couple of years after Georgetown Law, and then got recruited to the Secret Service for 4 years. And her Dad's a former DC police detective who runs a private security company now, so y'all will definitely have stories to share."

The lunch arrived and another round of beers were ordered. Will wasn't worried about being able to focus this afternoon. She'd already gotten her 'win' for the day.

FORTY-FIVE

Jack Strong and Bill Anderson walked down the hall to the Sheriff's office, both carrying the files for the prosecution of Anatoli Milanovich. They were coming to brief her prior to the press conference. It was going to be quite a show. All the cable news networks, and the broadcast networks had all sent crews. Media had flown in from all over the world. Sky News 9 from Australia was the farthest so far. Newspapers from London, Washington, NY, and LA had reporters in town, and of course Michelle Wagner and Mark Jerkowitz from the Coastal Times.

"Sheriff?" Jack knocked on the open door. "Can we come in?"

"Take a seat Gentlemen. I've been reading your report Jack. Like I told you earlier. Outstanding team leadership. Outstanding teamwork." Betty said as she looked up from her laptop. "Bill? Did we have to give the store away with Tatiana Midgett? Seems she was in up to her neck. We're going to let her skate?"

"Betty, you know how the game is played. If you want the big fish to fry, you have to let some little fish live." DA Anderson waxed philosophically.

"I'd prefer she lived behind bars." The Sheriff retorted with a smirk. "When does she go into WitSec?"

"I don't know that. That is a federal thing and they are very tight lipped about it, for obvious reasons." Bill replied dryly.

"Is there anything I need to know before we do the dog and pony show. Arrangements all made for this presser?" Betty scoffed. "I hate that lingo."

"Yes ma'am. The folks at the airport have been super on short notice. They moved a few planes out and have lined up chairs. Camera crews were already setting up. Using a hanger was brilliant because the news crews could pull their vans right in. I hear they even had a portable stage brought in."

"Ok. What time is showtime?" Bill asked.

"We're set for 2pm. Sheriff, you do introductions and an opening statement, turn it over to the Coast Guard, and they will pass it off to the Feds. You can bet that they will hog most of the time after that." Jack informed them both.

"Right, Jack. One modification though. I will introduce the attendees, but then pass it off to you for a statement and introduction of your team. You can pass to the Coast Guard. Like I told you, I want the whole team recognized."

"Well, Sheriff, the Chairman nixed that. He said he only wants you, Bill and himself up on stage representing the County." Jack said without making eye contact with Betty.

"Did he now! Jack? You're a good soldier, but I'm your commanding officer, and frankly, I don't give damn what His Excellency wants. This was a team win, and I'm going to make sure the team, the whole team is recognized. Am I clear?" the Sheriff commanded.

"Yes ma'am. Crystal." Both Jack and Bill snapped together.

"Good. Now there's something I need to discuss with you two. I need your feedback. We've all seen the video from the Coast Guard, and my guess is they will play it today for the press to show their impressive skills."

"Probably." Everyone agreed.

"Well, anyone notice that boat sitting a few hundred yards ahead of the cutter?" Jack and Bill both nodded. "I was on that boat. Had a front row seat to the whole thing. We had no idea what was going on, so it all scared the crap out of us." Betty confidently revealed. "I doubt anyone will be able to learn I was there, but you need to know, in case some journo corners you with a scoop."

"Ok, but I don't think it will ever come up." Bill offered reassuringly. "It was a beautiful night for a party on the water. Hope you enjoyed yourself." A wry smile crept up the corners of his mouth.

"It was and I did." Betty shot back with a grin. "But there's more. I ate dinner at 1587 Saturday night. I observed the person I came to know as Anatoli having dinner with the woman, I came to learn was Jennifer Lawrence. I noticed him acting suspiciously, but assumed it was first date jitters. Now, I didn't pay, and there are no cameras in the restaurant, so it would be a stretch for anyone to put me there, but it could be done. Thoughts?"

Bill was the first to speak "Betty, it was a Saturday night. You'd taken a few days off and left things with your lead investigator. You'd had no contact with the office, I assume, so you had no idea about the breaks in the case or the direction the investigation was going. You went out and ate dinner, just like the rest of the world did Saturday night. I don't think I can see anything to worry about. As you said, you learned of the significance when you read Jack's report."

"Yes. That's true. I just don't want anything to rock the boat." The Sheriff worried.

"I think we're good Sheriff. Now that we know, we can handle it. Won't be a surprise if it ever comes up." Jack seconded.

"All right then. Are we riding together to the airport? I'll drive" Bill offered.

"Great. One o'clock in the lobby? Oh, and Jack, call Angela Peterson and make sure she's on that stage. She was the one who connected the dots." Betty called as the two men headed for the door.

"Roger that." Came Jack's reply.

FORTY-SIX

Tatiana Milanovich Midgett was being transferred into witness protection this morning when a gunman shot her, once in the chest and once in the face. The gunman was killed by federal agent at the scene. Mrs. Midgett was rushed to the Outer Banks Hospital, where she was pronounced dead. More on this story at five, six and eleven.

"Boss, we have a situation." Tim announced as he entered Sheriff Thompson's office.

"No fooling, Tim!" as Betty looked up from her computer screen. Our key witness has been assassinated. Any ID on the gunman?"

"Nothing on her. Cora Mae will run her prints and dental records, but that will take a bit. Right now, she was a ghost." Deputy Cudworth reported.

"She?" the Sheriff responded with shock.

"Yep. Not something the Marshall Service is releasing to the public just yet." Tim went on, "She was dressed as a delivery worker and pulled the gun right out of the package she was carrying. It was clearly a hit, and we assume it was carried out on orders from Anatoli Milanovich, or his crime family. We'll wait to see how that plays out."

"But Boss, the 'situation' I was referring to was the notice the DA just received from the State Department." Tim spoke with a heightened sense of alarm. "Apparently, pressure has been applied to the Croatian Government by an influential American family, to declare Anatoli

Milanovich a special emissary, and therefore, entitled to diplomatic immunity. He's being released today! The son of a gun is going to get away with murder!"

"Holy Christ. Where's Bill Anderson?" Betty asked urgently. "Get me Jack, Pronto!"

"We don't know where Jack is. After Tatiana was killed, he left. Said something about taking out some trash. No clue. Bill Anderson is in his office calling everyone he knows to see if he can reverse this travesty."

Standing behind Tim was the shadowy figure of Anatoli Milanovich. "It appears I am a free man. Isn't America wonderful! Everything is for sale, even your soul. I just wanted to stop by and wish you good luck and a long-life Sheriff." Milanovich said with a grin as Sheriff Thompson rose from her chair. "I also want to congratulate your team. Your office is the first to catch me red handed. Fortunately, I know many people who lack the scruples or morality to punish a criminal such as myself. They saw my arrest as an opportunity to extort my family. My freedom for a donation to their family foundation.

"Tragic, what happened to your sister. We're so sorry for your loss." Betty offered without an ounce of sincerity.

"Yes. Gun violence in America. It is a Pandemic. She wanted to disappear. Now she did. Very sad indeed." Anatoli said without emotion. He then reached into his pocket, causing Betty and Tim to both draw their weapons. "Please, I'm just getting my cigarettes and lighter."

"There's no smoking in this building, just like the restaurant Saturday night." Betty quickly spoke, and for the first time saw an honest reaction from the Butcher of Zagreb. His eyes went wide, and his jaw went slack.

"You were there? 1587?"

"Yes. I saw you with Jennifer Lawrence."

"Lovely restaurant, but I wasn't very hungry. I had a lot on my mind. Did you enjoy the food? Oh, look at the time, my ride should be outside now. I need to leave. Miles to go before I sleep. Sheriff, you have a lovely community here, but I don't think I'll be coming back. Perhaps if you visit Croatia, I could show you our coast? We have fabulous resorts on the Adriatic. You'd love it. They are to die for..." and with that, he turned and walked out of the office, laughing as he went. Both Tim and Betty stood in shock and watched him leave the building. A black limousine sat at the curb, but when he approached it to get in, the car sped off, leaving Anatoli cursing at the sky. His anger was short lived, as a sniper's bullet ripped through his right eye and blew out the back of his skull. Anatoli was dead.

FORTY-SEVEN

"I was told by a sommelier friend of mine that this is one of the finest bottles of champagne in the world. I think tonight calls for it." Will popped the cork carefully so as not to spill a drop and gave the opened bottle a sniff. "Beautiful, could you bring me those two glasses on the counter? This needs to be sipped."

"These are interesting. I always thought champagne glasses were long flutes." Betty questioned as she strolled out on the deck.

"Modern ones are, but these were the champagne glasses my parents used at their wedding." Will explained "It's more of a 1940's style. My folks aren't that old, but their style is."

"Well, I like them. Makes it easier for the bubbles to tickle my nose." Betty said as she and Will grinned and took a sip. "Oh, wow. That is wonderful. Dry. Light. Refreshing. No bitterness or aftertaste. A complex aroma of fruits, pear, and ginger. Excellent depth layered on the palate" Betty offered, barely able to conceal a full toothed grin.

"Ok, did you read the reviews?" Will asked suspiciously.

"Angie isn't the only one who can do research." Betty laughed.

"Speaking of Angie, did you know she has a major hard on for Jack?" Will asked.

"Good God woman, I'm not blind. The janitor has to follow her around to clean up the drool. She's head over heels for him. But here's a truth bomb. Jack feels the same way about her. As soon as her divorce is final, he will be all over that girl, but he won't do anything before then. Jack is a great guy, and he will be a rock for Angie."

"I also heard that Jennifer and Jeff could be a thing." Will confided, and then took another sip of the fine wine.

"Well, you're behind there. They have been a thing for a few weeks now. He's practically living at her place in Colington Harbor. I have to admit, that girl has almost as big a smile on her face when she struts into work in the morning as I do after a night with you. As long as one doesn't supervise the other, the County is Ok with dating. We've already had that talk."

"So, What would you think of having a party here Saturday? Since your team didn't get their moment in the media spotlight, I'd like to have everyone out for a BBQ and pool party at our house. I'd invite the folks from my office too so that we can have a nice crowd. Nothing fancy, just casual. If your parents are down here, they are invited too. I was going to see if my Dad can come as well. What do you think beautiful?"

"I think that would be perfect", replied Betty slipped her arm around Wilma's waist and pulled her in for a kiss.

"Good. I'll make all the arrangements." Will exclaimed, as she went into party planner mode. "I'll send you access to an evite so you can email everyone on the team. Now, it's Monday night so maybe you should call your Mom and see if they can make it. I've got a caterer I use that makes killer ribs, pulled pork and a super low country boil, so food should be ok, and they do all the set up and throw away. You won't know we've had a party when they leave. Thought we'd just serve beer and wine, and if anyone drinks too much, we have 6 bedrooms upstairs for passing out."

"Hey, Wilma. Chill girl. We got this."

AUTHOR'S NOTE

Thank you for reading my book. It has been a lifelong ambition to combine my enjoyment of spinning a yarn, playing with words, and telling others about the area I love. I hope you enjoyed reading it as much as I enjoyed writing it.

I grew up vacationing in Kitty Hawk. My first experience there, I was an infant. The next year I experienced the beach fully as a toddler, and it became the only place my parents ever wanted to vacation. Early on, the trips from my home in DC to the beach were an eight-hour one-way ordeal, but with the completion of the Interstate System, travel was eventually shortened to four hours. I used to joke to friends, when I would talk about the natural wonder and beauty of the OBX, and the history, lots of history, that I could be a tour guide I know it so well. Now, through these books, I guess I am.

Follow me on Facebook, Instagram, and Twitter to get updates on new releases in the series, special offers, and insight into the characters and the OBX.

    Facebook: @jolyn.duffyshields
    Instagram: @jolynduffyshields
    Twitter: @lyn_shields

Reviews are critical to the success of any author. Please feel free to add them on Amazon and any of the platforms above.

THE OUTER BANKS COZY MYSTERY SERIES – BOOK 1

ACKNOWLEDGEMENTS

I'd like to thank the following people who assisted in the research, writing and editing of this book. Their help, patience and guidance has been invaluable.

Mary Duffy, author of **Nicole's Cozy Clairvoyant Mysteries**

Florence Walsh, Author of **Lizzie's Delicious Cozy Culinary Capers**

RJ O'Neill, author of **Jack Strong: Hitman For Hire Series**

Desiree A. DeMond, author of **The OBX Adult Romantic Thriller Series**

For more information about the Outer Banks, I would encourage you to read some of the following:

- *Outer Banks of North Carolina 1584 – 1958* by David Stick
- *NC 12: Gateway to the Outer Banks* by Dawson Carr
- *Vintage Outer Banks: Shifting Sands & Bygone Beaches* by Sarah Downing
- *Outer Banks Mysteries and Seaside Stories* by Charles Harry Whedbee
- *The Bishop's Boys: A Life Of Orville and Wilber Wright* by Tom D Crouch
- *The Wright Brothers* by David McCullough

THANK YOU FOR READING!

I hope you enjoyed your visit to the Outer Banks!

Reviews are more important than ever, so show your support for the series by rating and reviewing the book on Amazon! Reviews are **CRUCIAL** for the longevity of any series, and they are the best way to let authors know you want more! They help us reach more people! I appreciate any feedback, no matter how long or short. It is a great way of letting other readers know what you thought of the book.

Being an independent author means this is my livelihood, and every review really does make a **huge** difference. Reviews are the best way to support me so I can continue to do what I love, which is to bring you more mystery, thrillers, and romance.

<u>DO NOT FORGET TO RATE AND REVIEW ON AMAZON</u>

Made in the USA
Middletown, DE
30 November 2021